M000119687

About the Author

Mike Oppenheim has been interested in entertainment since he was a child, but became serious about it in 1999 when he began a career in music and film that eventually led to a focus on writing. In 2006, he started his weekly essay series, The Casual Casuist, which continues to be featured online and in various print forms.

In 2011, he earned an MFA from Mills College in Creative Fiction with his first novel, *Dysfunction*. Two years later, he published his second novel, *Baby Doll: The Book*, followed by *Too True to be Good* in 2017, and *The Apology* in 2021. That same year, Mike and his wife began their podcast "Coffin Talk" a weekly show that explores "The Meaning of Death."

In his spare time, Mike eats avocados, facilitates writing workshops, and hangs with his family. For more please visit http://mikeyopp.com

This is a work of fiction. Names, characters, businesses, places, events and incidents are either the products of the author's imagination or used in a fictitious manner. Any resemblance to actual persons, living or dead, or actual events is purely coincidental.

Ardor

Mike Oppenheim

Ardor

Vanguard Press

VANGUARD PAPERBACK

© Copyright 2023
Mike Oppenheim

The right of Mike Oppenheim to be identified as author of
this work has been asserted by him in accordance with the
Copyright, Designs and Patents Act 1988.

All Rights Reserved

No reproduction, copy or transmission of this publication
may be made without written permission.
No paragraph of this publication may be reproduced,
copied or transmitted save with the written permission of the
publisher, or in accordance with the provisions
of the Copyright Act 1956 (as amended).

Any person who commits any unauthorised act in relation to
this publication may be liable to criminal
prosecution and civil claims for damages.

A CIP catalogue record for this title is
available from the British Library.

ISBN 978 1 80016 497 0

Vanguard Press is an imprint of
Pegasus Elliot Mackenzie Publishers Ltd.
www.pegasuspublishers.com

First Published in 2023

Vanguard Press
Sheraton House Castle Park
Cambridge England

Printed & Bound in Great Britain

This book is dedicated to my son, Tyler. Thank you for teaching me time and patience, but most of all, love. No words can describe the affinity and love this father has for his son.

Acknowledgments

Ardor would not be possible without so much help, from so many people, but I'd like to specifically acknowledge my alpha readers Erika Gerhart and Nichol Daniels; my beta crowd at the Red Sands Writing Group (in particular, Justin Tate, Gail Chambers, Rachel Feeck, and Robin Wayland); Olivia Nicholls for immense moral *and* editing support; my parents, brother, wife, and family; Ann "Mom A" Cone-Sevi; Pablo and Blinky; and most of all my son, Tyler, who made this impossibly possible.

1
Granny

I spent most of my childhood with my grandmother while she ate buttered popcorn and trained my psychic abilities. I remember little about her, except that she wore plain clothes, tied her gray hair back so her scalp looked stretched, and she got a peculiar wrinkle on her cheek when she smirked. She seemed to get a joke no one else heard.

She was a chronic knuckle-cracker and loved to make popcorn for me and my older sister Alba while she babysat, which was often since my parents were drunks.

I'd be in the TV room, playing with my wood trains, while Granny sat behind me and asked questions like, "What color am I thinking of?" "What number is Granny considering?" "What person am I thinking of?" "Do you know what I dreamed about last night?"

With no hesitation, I'd answer. "Blue." "Thirty-three." "Your friend Ross." "You were driving a car very fast on a highway, going the wrong way, and you crashed and killed a lot of innocent people."

When I messed up, which wasn't often, she'd crack her knuckles then tap her fingernails on the sofa's wooden armrest before correcting me. "Close, Ardor. But the driver was your father, and your dad killed those innocent people in that dream. Let's try a different one. What did Granny eat last night?"

One day I asked her, "Why won't you be coming here any more?"

"You know?"

"When you came over, I heard this was the last time to say goodbye."

She stroked my small hand. "You *heard*?"

"Um, yeah. I mean, I just sort of *knew*."

"That's Source, Ardor. Source is your friend. When Source tells you something, you listen. OK?" She started to cry.

"Why are you crying, and why are you going away?"

She wiped her tears and tried to smile. "I'm sorry honey, but I have to go to the other side." She smirked. "But you knew that, didn't you, Ardor? Thanks to Source, you know a lot of things."

That evening I overheard my parents arguing about burial costs, and a few days later Alba and I were at something called a funeral, where everyone was talking about their favorite memories of Granny.

***

When I got a little older, I still didn't think of myself as psychic, but I always knew weird things I wasn't supposed to know, which impressed the kids at school.

Nothing really came of this, but I do remember going to a friend's house for a birthday sleepover and telling his mom to get a mammogram, which wasn't even a word I knew.

Two months later the doorbell rang on a school day afternoon. My mom was already drunk, as usual, so Alba and I hid in the hallway behind the door to see what would happen when she had to talk to someone else.

Mom was a functional drinker. She dressed in nice clothes, wore makeup, and held herself together well enough to shop and cook for our family. She always finished her errands by noon, in time for her first drink. But she still tried to avoid social interactions.

She opened the door a crack and I recognized the mom from the sleepover.

She smiled and said, "Good evening, Gretchen. I know this sounds weird, but I wanted to stop by and thank your son."

"Ardor?"

"Yes. He — he somehow *knew* I had breast cancer. He saved my life!"

Mom looked at the floor and said, "Ardor has the most peculiar mind."

"No. I don't think you understand. This was… this was truly amazing. He came up to me and—"

"I have to get back to cooking. I'm glad you think… I'm glad you like my son. Thank you." Mom closed the door and returned to the kitchen and her crossword.

Alba turned to me and whispered, "What did you do?"

I was about to tell her when the thing Granny called Source told me not to.

"Nothing."

She rolled her eyes. "I can tell you're lying. You should be more careful. If you upset Mom and Dad, it makes them drink more."

I nodded. Even though I was young, I understood how our childhood was tougher for her. She was two years older, so after Granny died, she became responsible for keeping order in a house of drunks.

My parents meant well. They never intentionally hurt us, but it was hard to grow up with parents who passed out during the evening news.

Dad was off to work by six every weekday, but I always saw him at five fifteen when he'd drunk-park his car, lumber his swollen frame up the driveway, then head straight to the bar to make *another* drink. He worked in insurance, and it was common for his team to start drinking at lunch. When he died a few years later, I realized I'd barely known him.

I don't remember much else of interest from my childhood, but after the breast cancer incident, I purposely hid my powers from my family, my peers, and even myself. That was until my high school girlfriend Veronica forced my hand.

12

2
Veronica

I remember feeling lucky in school because I could *remember* answers for tests that I didn't or shouldn't have known since I never studied. But I had no self-awareness of what I was doing. I just thought I had some cool ability to listen even if I wasn't paying attention.

Teachers noticed. They wrote the same thing on all my report cards: "Ardor, please try harder. I know this seems easy now, but you must develop your potential instead of handing in the bare requirements to pass."

I should have recognized my ability, but no one in the suburbs of Phoenix, Arizona talked about psychics, so I didn't think about it until my senior year of high school. I was fooling around in my bedroom with my first girlfriend, Veronica, when *Source* delivered a stunning message: *She does this with others*.

I lost my breath. I thought I was in love, and that Veronica and I had a special bond. I was even planning our marriage. In my head, I replied to Source, *You must be mistaken*.

It replied, *Ask her.*

I stopped kissing and pulled my head back to look at Veronica. There was no way this lovely girl was seeing other boys behind my back.

I tilted my head. "Vee, I have to ask you something, but I don't know how."

She smiled. "Ask away."

I swallowed then said, "I heard a rumor that you cheated. It's a lie, right?"

Her soft hazel eyes became fierce. "What are you talking about?"

I felt like I'd been punched in the stomach. With a sense of dread, I asked, "So you didn't?"

She stood and put her hands on her hips. "How could you ask me that?" She turned around and fumbled with her purse.

"Well, did you?" My heart raced.

She continued to ignore me.

"OK. Answer this, then. Who is Mark Krowles?" Source had given me the name.

Her mouth gaped.

"Who is Mr. Golden?" I continued. "Is he a *college professor*?"

She turned around. "Where the... how did you...?"

"Tommy Bilbow from the baseball team? Mike Ganook from Chemistry? Keith Swanson, the *backup* quarterback? How could you do this? You're a terrible person!"

She came back to the bed, punched me in the face, then grabbed her bag and walked to the door.

14

I pinched my nose to blunt the pain and yelled in a nasal voice, "It's nob my fauld that you are who you are! Don't shoot the messenger!"

She slammed the door as she left.

I eventually went to check my face in the bathroom. My nose was still swelling, and I knew it would upset Alba when she came home from her community college class.

Sure enough, the second she saw me she said, "What on earth did you do?"

"Nothing," I lied.

Her eyes softened. She led me to the couch and motioned for me to sit.

I silently obeyed.

Her thin black eyebrows formed a V. "Who did this to you?"

I felt bad for her. She wasn't even twenty-one and she was basically a single mother, only she was caring for her brother and her dysfunctional mom. Meanwhile, between that and school, she didn't have time to date, which disappointed men everywhere. She was so attractive we couldn't even stop for gas without some guy flirting with her.

"Who did this to you?" she repeated as she took my hand.

"Veronica," I said to a spot on the wall.

"That bitch!" She covered her mouth and blushed.

"You knew?" I asked with wide eyes.

She looked away.

"No need to lie," I said in a shaky voice. "What did you know?"

"I mean, they were just rumors, until now I guess." She squeezed my hand.

"Were they about the college professor?"

"A *what*?"

"Keep it down!" Mom called from upstairs. We were ruining quiet time, which had recently been extended to all day, every day. Quiet time had started two years before, after the police came by to report our father's death.

We called it 'our father's death', but the news had called it "One of the most reprehensible alcohol-related car accidents in local history." Dad had driven onto the highway, going the wrong way, and when he saw headlights coming his way, the forensic experts say he'd increased his speed. He was one of nine deaths and twelve injuries, many featuring permanent paralysis, from the eight-car pile-up he caused.

His insurance had covered the damages and medical bills of his victims, but nothing could stop our mom's collapse. She tried to work a few jobs, but her drinking always got her fired, so we made ends meet with welfare and a small, monthly life insurance payout.

This had inspired Alba to seek a career in health care where she felt like she might be able to pay off Dad's karma as a nurse. She enrolled at the local community college, and stayed home to save money, but also to look after my mother and me.

16

"She told you she was seeing a college professor?" Alba whispered.

I cracked my knuckles, smelling phantom popcorn.

"Answer me."

"No. I just… I just *knew*," I said.

"What do you mean you *just knew*?"

"Remember Granny?"

She laughed. "She was *our* grandmother, silly."

"No, I mean did Granny ever play, um, games with you?"

Her brows furrowed. "What?"

I crossed my legs and uncrossed them. "She used to, um, quiz me, and ask me weird questions. About dreams and stuff. They were like, secret psychic quizzes."

She sighed and started to stand.

"I'm not lying!" I leaped to my feet.

"Shut up!" Mom shrieked from above.

"What are you getting at?" Alba asked in a hushed voice.

"Think of a number," I said.

"What?"

"Just do it. Think of a number. Any number."

"Fine." She rolled her eyes. "Thirty-four."

I retorted with my own eye-roll. "I said think of it, don't tell me."

She grinned. "Sorry. I forgot I was at a carnival." She squinted and made a funny face.

"Thirty-five," I said. "How boring, Alba."

She flinched then scowled. "What is your point, Ardor?"

"I think… I think I'm psychic," I said, for the first time ever.

Her eyes grew wide. "Did you tell anyone about this?"

I scoffed. "No. They'd think I was crazy."

"Yes, yes, they would. I mean, even I think that. You should pretend this didn't happen, and let's never talk about it again."

"Really?" I asked. "Aren't you curious? You *were* thinking thirty-five, right?"

"Really." She sighed. "Between Mom, the bills, and school, I don't have time to indulge in your fantasies, and neither do you. You need to focus on graduating high school. Are we clear?"

I was a little disappointed, but I saw her point. "OK. It's a deal."

3
My First Job

It was 1999. I shared a two-bedroom apartment in Phoenix with Brian, my only friend from high school. We were both acned and eighteen. We'd been there for two months, but I was jobless, so Brian was floating my rent.

Things were tight, so we let this guy, Rinco, move in after he promised to pay a large share of the rent. He was overweight, over twenty-one, and overwhelmingly psychotic, but Brian wanted booze, and Rinco was able to get it for him. Thanks to my parents, I didn't drink, but I loved paying less for rent, so I didn't care what Brian did.

Meanwhile, Alba was in nursing school and living at home with our dementia-ridden mom. I was finally on my own, doing my best to find freedom while avoiding family.

The first week with Rinco was pretty mild, but in the second week, my life changed forever.

It was early on a Monday. I was sleeping in my room on what I called 'my nest,' a pile of clothes on the floor with a blanket wrapped around them. Rinco was conked out on the two-seat part of our L-shaped couch in the front room, and Brian, the only name on the lease, slept like a king on his full-sized bed in his bedroom.

I was thrust awake by the sound of a fist hammering the front door. I eyed my watch. It was seven a.m. We'd gone to bed three hours earlier.

"Who the hell is that?" Rinco yelled.

"Someone *please* get the door!" Brian groaned.

I rolled over, hoping the situation would resolve itself, but the banging continued. I got out of bed, pulled on my boxers, and threw a shirt over my noodle-shaped torso. I would've checked my beloved Armenian form in the mirror, but it didn't sound like a woman was knocking.

I got to the door and noticed no one had latched the chain. I'd never lived in a bad neighborhood until now, but in one week I'd been scared enough by tweakers and gangbangers hanging out at the nearby gas station to worry about it. I made a note to scold Brian later.

I opened the door a crack, hoping the person outside wouldn't notice the unchained latch.

A stout man with a bad toupee wearing a collared shirt looked up at me with a sneer.

"Mr. McDonald?"

"No," I blinked at the intimidating sun as summer heat smacked me in the face. He was looking for Brian. "He's not here," I lied, about to close the door.

"Who's there?" Brian asked from behind.

I turned in time to see him pulling a T-shirt over his chubby upper body as he approached us.

"Brian McDonald?" Toupee asked. He was trying to push past me to get a better look of our apartment, so I kept the door where it was to block him from doing so.

"Yeah, that's me." Brian shoved into me. "Ardor, let me through!"

I moved and cringed at a wave of dank air as it whistled into Toupee's face.

He coughed then frowned. "Who is *that*?" He pointed at the 250-pound mostly covered mound of Rinco. "I thought I was clear. All overnight guests *must* be reported!" He drew a handkerchief from his pocket and patted his forehead. His armpits were soaked.

"Mr. Carlson," Brian said, "Let me explain—"

A wave of specific knowledge came to my mind, just like that time with Veronica. I somehow *knew* something I didn't actually know.

"There is *nothing* to explain." Toupee sneered. "You're also late on rent. I've had it. I'm evicting you, post-haste."

"Please, sir," Brian fumbled. "I'm sorry! I can get rent and clear this up."

I pushed him aside and cleared my throat. "If you insist on evicting us, I feel a moral obligation to call your wife, Deborah, to discuss room 212 at the Motel Six near Tucson."

Toupee's face developed a temporary sunburn.

I squinted. "Or, if you prefer, we can negotiate…?"

"I, well, I am certainly *not*…" He sneered then said, "I don't know what little detective work you did, but you could have spent that money on rent, and besides there's nothing to what you're saying."

I shrugged. "I could also call the IRS and have them look into your filings? Do you think those deductions will hold up in an audit?"

He lost his haughty look for a moment then recovered his scowl. "This is silly. I'm here because you're in violation of your rental terms!"

Rinco hollered, "Shut up! I can't sleep!"

I pushed Brian into the walkway of our second-floor unit, and shut the door behind us.

I pointed a finger at my head. "Look, I know what you're thinking, 'How could he know?' But what you fear is the truth: I can read your mind, and I can go deeper. You want me to get into any other memories?"

He covered his heart with a hand and took a step back. He shook his head. "No. Thank you. I've seen enough."

An awkward silence enveloped the three of us until Toupee finally looked at Brian, whose expression defined disbelief, and said, "Mr. McDonald, I want that guest on the couch off the premises by tomorrow. I told you no permanent guests!" He glanced at me. "But I do want to be fair about things. So you can get me that rent in installments."

I moved into his line of sight. "We'll get you the rent. Don't worry. We aren't the cheating type. You can trust *us*."

He looked down and shook his head as he walked away.

I waited until the top of his toupee left my field of vision as he descended the stairs, then turned to Brian, expecting a high five. Instead, he grabbed me and shoved me against the door.

"What the hell, Ardor?" he screamed. "Why are you getting up in *my* business?" He was shaking.

I intuited another message from Source and understood Brian's tension. He was preoccupied with his recent weight gain and full of self-loathing. I lost my sense of joy, calmly removed his hands from my chest, and put them at his side. "It'll be OK."

He flinched and stared at his feet.

I opened the door and motioned for him to follow me. Inside, I glanced at Rinco then whispered, "I'm sorry, but that *had* to happen."

"Had to? What the hell do you mean?" he shouted. "That was some... I mean... that was some really weird stuff, dude!"

Brian had been my best friend since sixth grade, but I'd never dared to tell him how I knew about Veronica's infidelity, or anything else about my 'psychic Source', but now it was time to set things straight.

"Bri, you know how I said I was gonna apply to that psychic store at the mall?"

"Uh, yeah...?" He cocked his head to the side.

"Well, it's not just for laughs. I'm... uh... I'm actually psychic."

He tried to giggle, but it wasn't convincing.

"What an imagination," Rinco said from the couch. "There's no such thing as a psychic."

"I'm not lying!" I said, turning to face him.

"Really?" he asked, sitting up and lighting a cigarette.

"Yeah!" I said.

"OK. Where does my hookup live?"

He was referring to his pot dealer. This was going to be easy. I asked Source then blurted with pride, "1522 West Hazelwood."

He coughed and choked a little.

My stomach turned. He didn't want me to know that answer, psychic or not.

He stood up. "Did you follow me?"

"No, no way! I knew it! Just like I know you're thinking right now about—" I cut myself off, just in time. I didn't want to say the next part.

"You wanna finish that thought?" His face turned red as he glared at me.

I couldn't tell if he was daring me to shut up, or say what I'd learned, so I stayed quiet.

He walked towards me with a menacing look.

I read his mind again. He was sure I was working with the police.

"Rinco, I'm not a snitch. And I didn't follow you! I swear! I just know things," I pleaded.

He was now a foot away with curled fists.

As a last resort, I tapped into his mind to find something to show him some compassion with. I got what I was looking for and said, "I'm sorry your older brother did that to you! I'm sorry and if I could—"

He leaped toward me and next thing I knew his full weight was on top of me and the back of my head hit the floor. I was dizzy, but still conscious, which wasn't great since that left me fully aware of his savage beat down.

He pummeled me, and no matter how many times Brian jumped on his back or tried to intervene, nothing worked. I felt blood oozing down my face and one of my eyes was swelling shut, but all I could think was, *Please don't knock out my teeth!*

He finally stopped, and I swallowed a thick glop of blood before checking my teeth with my tongue. One was chipped, but nothing was dangerously loose.

I could only open one eye, but I held it open long enough to see him lean over me and say, "You ever come anywhere near me or my hook up, and I promise — don't even try me."

He ignored Brian's babbling apology as he grabbed his only possession, a trash bag with clothes, and left the apartment, slamming the door.

I was petrified of the idea of him returning for further retaliation, but Source told me I had nothing to fear. He was going to forget all about this in a day or two, and he'd get murdered in a drug deal in two years.

I felt something soft land on my shoulder. It was a roll of toilet paper. I mumbled, "Thank you," and wiped my face with it. I still couldn't open one eye, but I cleaned out my 'good one' then sat up and looked at Brian, who was sitting on the couch smoking a cigarette.

I crawled his way and extended my hand. He passed me the cigarette and I felt and heard a crackling in my ribs as I inhaled.

We finished it in silence, then Brian said, "Ardor, you should get that job at the mall. But this other stuff, this *psychic* thing? Keep it to yourself. You can stay here, but only if you never bring it up again. It scares me, and I don't want to get in trouble with it, like you just did. OK?"

I didn't seek Source's opinion. "You got it," I said. "And I'll go and apply today."

4
Esmeralda

I eventually limped my way to the bathroom to evaluate my face. It looked like an eggplant.

I took a shower, trying to ignore the sting of water on my bruised face, then put on my Sunday's finest, a fading blue T-shirt over jeans with only one hole. I walked in the blistering Phoenix sun to the bus stop.

Fifteen minutes later I was struck with nausea as I met the stale odors of air-conditioning and human filth when the bus doors opened. I dragged my sweaty, yet somehow dry body, a Phoenix phenomenon, onto the bus and found a vacant seat.

The ride was only four minutes, but walking was not an option in that heat. I arrived at 9:20 and was surprised to discover that The Psychic Shoppe didn't open until ten.

I opted to wait at the indoor play center where I sprawled out on one of the cushioned benches surrounding the playpen. The kids were shrieking and having a blast, but all the parents looked worried and stressed. I wondered if I'd ever have kids.

Of course. Source answered me.

I laughed. Me, married with kids? Yeah, right.

I never said anything about marriage.

I shook off a sense of alarm and checked my watch. It was five after ten. I returned to The Psychic Shoppe, but the door was shut, and it looked like no one had been there yet. I jiggled the handles just in case and the glass doors moaned and rattled louder than I expected.

"Just my luck," I muttered, turning around.

I bumped into an attractive woman who looked about five years older than me. She was wearing a tight mini-skirt and a revealing top.

She scowled and said, "No one has patience here!" in a thick Russian accent.

"I'm sorry!" I blushed. "I was just—"

"Americans are so strict." She sighed. "Open zee shop at exact time. Satisfy customer no matter what. What insanity!" In one graceful motion, she unlocked and pushed the doors open, pinned them in place, and walked inside.

I waited, watching her flick on lights and adjust furniture with dignity and poise.

Until that morning's interaction with Toupee, I'd never identified as a psychic, but this woman made me want to be one.

I shut my eyes and thought, *Hey, um, Source, Do you think I can get a job here?*

Sadly, it is certain.

I didn't like the wording, but didn't follow up. I was too busy fantasizing about spending time with this intriguing woman.

She eventually came my way to flip the open sign, after which she smiled and said, "Come in, dear!" She turned and took a seat in a gigantic chair behind a large, sturdy desk.

I followed her and took the seat that faced her. She stared at me with hypnotic eyes, and I found it hard not to flinch. I'd never seen orange eyes. I figured she wore special contacts.

She batted her long eyelashes. "Vant to know what fortune avaits you?"

"Your accent is fake." I covered my mouth. I needed to develop a filter for Source.

Without an accent, she said. "Interesting. You have real powers, but I also see that your face looks like an eggplant. So, why should I hire you?"

"I never said I wanted a job..." My face felt hot.

She rolled her eyes. "You want to play games or get on with this?"

Source said, *Be careful. She's powerful. Do not let her fool you! Keep your guard.*

"I've never met another psychic!" I said with glee.

She seemed deep in thought and her face became ugly, somehow. It was brief, but frightening.

Source said, *She is not honest and never will be. She will not come around.*

Come around? What does that mean? I replied.

Take the job, but don't get involved with her.

I shook my head and smiled. "You're right. No games. I want to work here, ma'am."

She cackled. "Ma'am? Please! Call me Esmeralda." She nodded and pursed her lips. "OK. I *will* hire you. But this job is not easy." She leaned in and her forearm brushed against mine. "And it's not *fun*."

I took a deep breath and exhaled. "When do I start?"

"Now." She smiled and pointed at the back wall. "Go find an outfit."

I looked at the cheesy merchandise, full of fake-looking movie props for every psychic cliché one could imagine. I laughed. "Are you for real?"

Her face again briefly contorted with anger.

In a flash, I *knew* this was what Source had tried to warn me about. I realized it wasn't too late, and I could go find another job, but I didn't want to. I pictured my granny and felt a sense of family pride as I decided to stay the course and learn more about my powers. "Sorry I laughed. I didn't mean to insult you."

She frowned. "I don't care about intentions after I'm insulted."

An unpleasant stillness came between us until I asked, "Can I make it up to you?"

She threw her head back and laughed like a Disney villain. "You're as stupid as you look, but your access to *Source* is off the charts. You're a psychic clown."

"*Source*? What's that?"

"Don't play dumb." She narrowed her eyes. "Your granny told you. If you lie one more time, you're fired." She reached across the table and stroked my wrist.

I felt an electric sensation, like nothing I'd experienced, and it came with a strong sense of arousal. It wasn't too much to handle, but it was very distracting.

Just the job, Ardor. Just take the job, Source warned again.

Buzz off, I thought. I nodded solemnly at Esmeralda. "OK. Sorry. No more lies."

"Yes. And stop using Source in my presence, please. It's cheating."

I felt like this was unfair, but Source was sort of putting a wedge between us, so I nodded again.

She touched my hand again, only this time it sent a wave of pain into my temples.

"Ow!" I yelled.

She laughed at my pain, and I realized two things: I didn't trust this woman, but I liked her attention and I wanted to control my own decisions. Like it or not, I was going to play by her rules, at least for now.

She rested her palm on my hand and spoke slowly, "Yes. No more kid stuff. You must work hard to cultivate your energy, and I will help you."

I tried to ask Source what to say next, but her physical contact was somehow cutting me off.

"I said *do not* use Source!"

I frowned. "Are you somehow *blocking* me?"

She removed her hand, folded her thin arms, and rested them in her lap. "It takes very little skill to contact Source, but to control it? That requires mastery."

Source said, *Ardor, you are in way over your head. Please trust me, you have to —*

She leaned forward and squinted, and Source stopped speaking. "That is what mastery looks like. Do not disobey me again, or I will have to resort to other forms of reprimand."

I lowered my head. "I'm sorry."

"Instead of being sorry, you should not make so many mistakes. No one respects a person who is *sorry* after careless actions. But… I will give you one more chance."

I looked up. "So, I'm not fired?"

"Don't ask silly questions, and stop thinking about my body."

"I wasn't thinking about—"

"Don't lie, Ardor."

Even though she'd more than proven herself, I was surprised that she knew my name.

She smiled seductively. "Follow all my rules, and we're going to be fine." She rose from her seat and headed to a blue door at the back of the shop. She opened it just enough to slip inside then left the door open just a crack.

I waited, figuring she was getting an application.

After a minute, I wanted to summon Source, but I remembered my promise and didn't.

I waited another three minutes, then gave up and tried to contact Source, but I instead heard Esmeralda's voice in my mind!

My God you are so bad at this! You don't know how to ping?

"Ping?" I asked aloud.

Use your mind, you idiot! It's called pinging. It's how we send and receive messages.

I 'thought' back to her. *Like this?*

Yes. Good. Now come back here for your next lesson.

I stood and made my way to the blue door. When I got there, she pinged, *Come inside but leave the lights off. And close the door behind you.*

I did as instructed. Thanks to a sliver of light from under the closed door, I was able to see the outline of her body standing against a couch along the opposite wall.

"Come here," she whispered. I walked over and she took my hand. "You took forever." She sounded annoyed.

She placed my hands on her shoulders and pulled me towards her into what is normally called a hug, but this felt different. I got sensual and intense feelings from it. But at no point did it get romantic. I didn't feel like I was being used, but I also felt out of control.

After five minutes of this, she leaned in and gave me a close-mouthed kiss, but when I leaned forward for a second one, she pushed me back.

"I'm not easy. And this milk isn't free." She broke our physical contact. "You may leave now."

I was starting to feel like Source was right, but I was hooked on whatever it was that she kept sending me when she touched me. "When can I see you next?"

"Tomorrow, at ten a.m."

"What? That's sort of early for a date?"

She laughed. "It's not a date. It's for work. Your first day. Goodbye."

I sighed and did my best to ignore the budding panic in my stomach as I left the store.

5
Work Wife Life

It had been two months since I'd met Esmeralda, but it hadn't taken more than a week to get sick of her attitude. She was strict and treated me differently from the other employees she'd hired. Her excuse was that they were frauds, so they weren't worth her time, but that didn't matter to me: I didn't like being yelled at, especially in front of customers.

She would stalk up to me in the middle of a reading and say in her phony accent, "Do not talk to client like zis!" Then she'd take over, but make me stay and watch.

My crime? Telling the truth. Esmeralda's main rule was to never tell a customer demoralizing news, which was often the only thing that lay in their future. Plus, wasn't that the point of a reading? To know the future so you could best prepare for it?

I would argue my case, but she would just bite her lip, squint, and repeat the same phrase: "Never, ever tell a client anything they don't want to hear."

I should have considered all of these obvious red flags and walked away, but I was addicted to her attention. I never thought we were in love, but I'd had very few friends growing up, and besides my year or so with Veronica, I'd never received any female attention, unless you counted Alba's sisterly nagging. Besides, lots of people were in my situation, working for an abusive boss or dating a controlling partner.

My favorite part of the job was the mornings since I was alone and got to open the shop by myself. I would arrive around 9:50 a.m., with the key Esmeralda had given me after admitting I was better than her at one thing: punctuality. I would then hit the lights and zombie-walk through the uncomplicated order of operations for opening a mall psychic store. I sprayed the dank shop with Febreze, I made sure the various display decks of cards weren't too even or too straight since "Clients enjoy a state of slight disarray when visiting a psychic. It's part of the stereotype they are paying for."

I then donned a stupid feathered hat Esmeralda had bought at a costume store. My co-worker Steve (whose name tag said Svengali) got to wear the much cooler 'Rasputin' hat, and Diana, our only other co-worker, had to wear a Cleopatra costume that accentuated her cleavage. Esmeralda ran a circus, not a psychic shop.

And *she* didn't wear a costume. She dressed the same way on and off the clock, preferring tight clothes that made men *and* women give her a second look.

Even off the clock, she was always fishing for prospective clients. While her accent was fake, her heritage was not. She was of Romanian descent, and her

36

mother had come to America from some place she called "The Baltic" which reminded me of Monopoly. Her accent was her mother's real accent. This also explained her jet-black hair and long Roman nose with a bump.

On a normal day, I'd be bored by quarter past eleven, because we never had any early customers. I never understood why we opened so early. We got foot traffic at eleven thirty at the earliest, which was when Esmeralda was supposed to arrive, yet she insisted we open at ten.

So there I was one day, missing my bed but afraid to think about it, since Esmeralda would soon arrive, ping me, then give me shit for having lazy thoughts.

Predictably, she arrived late, at quarter to twelve, but to my surprise, she arrived in loose blue sweat pants and a baggy gray hooded sweatshirt, with no makeup.

Not only was her appearance unprofessional, but it was also especially strange for a Thursday, our second busiest day. She wasn't going to attract any window shoppers.

Before I could ask her what was going on, she held up her palm and said, "Under *no* circumstances will you open the door to the office." She then stalked to her office and shut the door, hard, just short of a slam.

Screw you, I thought.

"I perceived that!" she shouted through the wall.

Good! I pinged back.

I felt a cold chill run down my left arm, and it became difficult to breathe. I felt a sharp, gut-pulsing paranoia. Then a violent orange hue clouded my vision. The more it tried to overtake me, the more frightened I became, and the more I gave in to it. The orange hue felt distinctly evil. Amidst all these physical symptoms I then inexplicably thought the same thing, no matter how hard I tried to ignore it: "This is permanent. You will always feel this terror. This is inescapable."

I was about to shriek from the overwhelming dread when Source stepped in.

Instead of focusing on your fear, try merging into the terror.

I moved my sense of awareness *into* the fear I was feeling, seeking it, instead of running away, and it shrank. I did it some more and it vanished.

The office door burst open, and Esmeralda emerged with a raw look of disgust that was new to me.

She strode up to me and slapped me in the face, four times. The fourth time she curled her hand into a fist and the blow knocked me out of my chair. She did this right in front of the windows.

Grabbing my horrified face with a hand on each of my cheeks, she cackled and said, "I will show you fear, you ungrateful, privileged baby. I will not suffer your mutinous ways. You will *never* disrespect me like that again. You will obey me!"

38

"What the hell?" I shouted back, hoping people in the mall were watching and could hear me. "Screw you! I don't have to obey you! I quit!"

She laughed. "You want to quit? You cannot *quit*, silly boy. You cannot *quit* what we have started."

"Yes, I can!" I pulled myself up from the floor. "I'm not your *slave*!"

She laughed insincerely and glared at me. The orange hue returned, and my face went numb. I chased after the hue, like Source had instructed, but this time it didn't work, and my vision faded to black.

***

I came to and opened my eyes, to find myself immersed in pitch-blackness. Terror seized me as I tried to make sense of things. I was lying on a couch, I was cold, and I had no memory of how I'd gotten here. The last thing I remembered was getting on the bus for work that morning, but I felt like that had been a long time ago. I'd never lost my memory or time before, so I wasn't sure what to do. I tried to hug myself to warm up and realized I didn't have a shirt on. I reached down to my thighs and learned that I was completely naked.

"Hello?" I shouted. "Where am I?"

"Shut up!" Esmeralda's voice commanded in a loud whisper.

I obeyed.

"You fainted."

"What? Where? When? Where am I?"

I felt her long, thin fingers stroke my stomach. "You came to work, dear, but then you were bad, so I had to teach you a lesson. You were behaving like a naughty child. You don't deserve me, but you are lucky, I am a good, strong partner."

"I don't understand?" I asked, still panicking from my lack of memory.

She exhaled a growling, rumbling sigh and pinged, *You are a child who needs to grow up, so I'm helping you with that.*

"What?" I asked aloud.

Don't speak. Ping me. It's good practice.

She moved her hand to graze my upper arm then ran it lightly down to my hand, took my hand in hers and squeezed it. I empathed her lust, and resented it.

I tried to sit up, but she gently pressed me back into place. She then squeezed my hand again, and her lust grew. I hated being an empath. Her feelings were gross.

"I hate you," I said, trying again to sit up.

This time she let me sit up, but then grabbed my face and bent down and kissed me. I wanted to break away, but I was aroused.

We started making out and she pinged, *Now you are growing up* then climbed off me and the couch.

The moment she let go of me, I recalled every moment of that morning. I was able to process *exactly* what had happened, and it dawned on me: I was in big trouble. She clearly had powers beyond anything I had imagined or even believed in. I felt hopeless.

Good, she pinged. *You understand our situation better now. You have psychic powers, but I know how to run energy. I can run it out…*

I felt a wave of peace from a release of all stress in my body.

Or I can run it in!

My body trembled with pain as that same orange-hued paranoia returned.

"Please stop!" I begged.

Ping it! she replied.

Please stop! Please? I begged.

The pain went away.

She laughed. *What did you learn today, Ardor?*

What did I learn? I don't… What do you want me to say?

She laughed again. *You cannot deceive me, Ardor. Do you understand?*

I heard her place her hand on the door knob at the other end of the room.

Now thank me, she pinged.

How could I be grateful? Go Away!

She opened the door then shut it behind her.

The orange hue resumed, and my body felt hot, but the pain was manageable. It felt like I had a body-wide sunburn. I stood up and felt a pile of clothes at my feet. I blindly sifted through them: they were mine. I put them on in the darkness, saying "Ow, ow, ow, ow!" over and over again while clenching my teeth. I recalled Rinco's beating and realized that this pain was somehow different and worse. It was mentally painful.

I walked to the door and was about to open it when Esmeralda pinged me.

Just remember, I am not an unfair woman. Your suffering will lessen with obedience and increase with mutiny. It's your choice. You have free will, you know.

6
Ping Me Once, Shame on You

After Esmeralda's psychic bullying, my instinct for survival kicked in. I don't know what she was thinking, giving a teenager an ultimatum about suffering and choice, but that's her fault. Obedience? How about mutiny, piss, and vinegar instead?

Esmeralda was wicked and smart, but she had an obvious flaw: her ego. She knew I was psychic, but she was too self-absorbed to realistically consider or fear my potential for greater abilities, and thanks to Source, I *knew* this was possible:

If you pay attention and make virtuous decisions, you can do great things.

I needed to hone my psychic abilities, but I didn't know how. I mean, there wasn't a local class like Psychic 101 or Introduction to Clairvoyance, and the Internet was still in its early stages in those days, meaning it was mostly porn.

My real issue was also that I didn't want to predict things, I wanted to be able to protect myself from Esmeralda's energy and coercion.

I needed to *develop* my skills, so I relaxed and asked Source, *What can I do?*

Pay attention and make virtuous decisions. We went over this.

I know, I know, I replied, *But I want to stop Esmeralda. Can you help me?*

Increase your vibrational energy and dispel all selfish intent. To practice, raise the vibrational energy of the mind. Only at the highest vibration will you succeed.

I understood the individual words in this message, but I didn't actually understand what to do, so I decided I would figure it out on my own. This would be the first of many such mistakes I would make, but I was stubborn and immature.

***

"I don't care, Ez." I sighed and pulled my shirt over my head then walked into the kitchen. I still lived with Brian, but I'd spent every night at Esmeralda's place since about two weeks after she'd hired me. Her place was much nicer, and she knew how to cook, and regardless of our bickering, we had regular, psychically enhanced sex.

By this point, Esmeralda had fired the other employees and I was now working more than full-time, on what she called "salary," which was not legal or fair. She gave me enough cash every month to send to Brian to cover my cost of rent and utilities, plus a little extra to buy food at the mall on my shifts, but I was not getting enough to save any money, so I was mostly beholden to her for food and other basic stuff I needed.

My situation appeared envious, but was not. Sure, I was dating an intelligent, attractive, and confident woman. But my situation wasn't cool or ethical. She was manipulating my lack of life experience and controlling my every move.

The worst was how much she used my youthful lust to get what she wanted. She paraded around her apartment in lingerie, and anytime I argued with her about getting more money or time off, she'd seduce me, so I'd drop the subject.

But I wasn't entirely dumb. I was also letting her think she was getting away with this while secretly training with Source.

Since Esmeralda could read my mind, I only did this at night, when she was asleep. I'd wait until I heard her snoring, then I'd check in with Source and read her mind. She was commonly dreaming of dark things, and the thoughts didn't make sense, but I knew she was actually afraid of me, on some weird level. I would often catch her thinking things like, *That will not happen! You will not succeed! The prophecy can be changed. I will get what I want, and you will never win.*

One day I got so comfortable with reading her mind that I tried doing it when she was awake, but she could tell I was doing it, because she was a control freak and would never let me know what she was thinking. Ultimately, it didn't really matter since her waking thoughts weren't usually of any use to me. But her dreams were usually about me, and they involved some prophecy about me and her, and she was *seriously* afraid of that.

***

The next two years of my life were more of the same. I never slept at Brian's but still paid rent, spending nearly every waking moment at work, at Esmeralda's place, or alone running her errands while she worked or slept.

My one saving grace was an occasional meal with Alba at a diner in our hometown. She was in the final year of her nursing program at Arizona State and still living at home, only now she lived alone. Our mother's drinking had led to full-blown dementia, so she was now living at a state ward for people with dementia.

It was a week before my twenty-first birthday. I stopped at Brian's to drop off rent and check the mail when the phone rang. I wasn't going to pick it up, but I noticed a note, in thick black sharpie ink, in Brian's sloppy script: "Call your sister back!"

Source said, *Pick up the phone.*

"Hello?" I asked.

"Ardor! It's you!" Alba's warm voice responded.

"Hi, Alba," I said, feeling like crying. I really missed her.

"How's the job?" she asked.

"Um, it's OK, I guess." I lied.

"You can go to school, Ardor. You don't have to be a janitor — I mean custodian."

I cringed. Ever since the time in high school when Alba told me not to tell people about my abilities, I'd stopped telling her anything about that side of my life. I therefore never mentioned my run-ins with Toupee, Rinco, or even my job at the mall. Instead, I'd lied to her, saying I was a custodian at a local elementary school.

"I love my job!"

She sighed into the phone, so I pinged her — a first. She was thinking, *Why is he so tense?*

I took a deep breath. "Sorry, Alba. I'm just tired from working so much."

"So much? It's only five days a week, right?"

"It is," I lied. "I just… I'm just, you know… I don't know."

I knew it was a violation of privacy, but I didn't care, so I continued to ping her. Now she was thinking, *He's such a terrible liar. I hope he's not on drugs.*

"I'm not on drugs!" I snapped.

"What?"

I pinged her again. *Is he reading my mind?*

I wasn't sure how, but I felt like she knew I was pinging her. I shook off the thought and cleared my throat. "Anyway, what's up? I'm, uh, I'm kind of busy."

"Wow. OK. You know we haven't talked in forever. It's been five weeks! And your birthday is on Saturday, so I was hoping to make plans."

I pinged her. *I can't wait to surprise you with concert tickets!*

I blushed. What a nice sister. "You're too kind!"

Too kind? All I said was let's hang out. He is definitely reading my mind.

It occurred to me that maybe she was also a psychic, so I decided to block my pings from her. It couldn't hurt to be careful.

She continued, "Anyway, I was hoping to meet you at the usual diner then take you to a movie after?"

A week earlier, Esmeralda had called me into her office and said, "I am scheduling you to work on Saturday, for your birthday. It will teach you to be a man and to not be selfish. Only stupid, spoiled American brats celebrate birthdays."

I sighed. "Alba, I'm sorry, but I can't."

"What?" Her disappointment was palpable.

"I… I have to work."

"Work? It's Saturday! Schools are closed."

I pinged while blocking her from scanning my mind. *He's lying. He doesn't want to see me because he's hiding something. I hope it's not drugs. Oh God, Ardor… what is happening to you?*

I felt so bad for her. She was seriously worried about me, but for all the wrong reasons. I held back tears and said, "I can't go with you because I have plans with

48

friends, uh, from work. We're going to a bar since I'm turning twenty-one!"

"You're going to drink?" Her tone insinuated dreadful shared memories of our parents' alcoholism.

"C'mon, just 'cause Mom and Dad—"

"I know *you* never had to wipe Mom's butt and that *you've* never even visited her at the clinic, but you really want to drink? You want to risk—"

I pictured Esmeralda punishing me with more restrictions and psychic attacks and stayed the course. I relied on her for food, transportation, and work, so now I was lying to my own sister. I wondered if I was even making my own decisions or if she was so powerful that she was somehow guiding me.

Source, what am I doing?

Making lots of mistakes, despite good advice not to. Just be honest and do good.

I didn't like that answer, so I did what most adolescents do in an ethical dilemma: I doubled down and tried to burn a bridge.

"I'm going drinking, Alba, and if you have a problem with that, then maybe you have a problem with *me*." I was on the phone, but I still puffed out my chest.

I pinged thick sadness as she thought, *What did I do to fail him? How did I mess up?*

She started crying and trying to hold the phone away so I couldn't hear the sobs, and it made me cry and try to do the same. We didn't talk for a minute.

Finally, she broke the silence. "Ardor, I'm sorry. I didn't mean to pressure you. I just... I love you, and I wanted to see you, and wish you a happy birthday."

I thought of my love for her and felt a wholesome energy in my heart that gave me support and courage. So *this* was what Source called higher energy.

"Alba, I've been lying to you, for years."

I pinged her. *I knew it!*

"I've been working at, and for, a local psychic. Her name is Esmeralda."

"What?" She asked with a far more serious tone than I'd expected.

"Let me finish. It gets worse. I have also sort of been living with her, and dating her, and, um, I dunno, I just, um, I feel really, I feel out of control. But anyway, that's why I'm busy. I have to work this Saturday, for her, at the store."

"I can't believe this. *Esmeralda*?"

The way she said the name was weird, like she'd heard it before. I tried to ping her, but I suddenly couldn't. Was she blocking me?

"Wow, Ardor. This is a lot to digest. Well, can I at least visit you at the store?"

I didn't answer her. I was terrified at the thought of Esmeralda and her meeting.

In a chipper voice, she said, "Where's the store? I'll bring your gift there!"

I pictured Esmeralda inflicting psychic pain on my sister and flinched. "I don't think that's a good idea. I want to be professional, and besides, Esmeralda, she's — she's very shy."

Alba didn't reply. I tried to ping her, but couldn't.

"I know this sounds like bullshit, but..." I trailed off. I was out of lies.

She remained silent. This was Alba at her finest, giving me enough rope to hang myself.

I finally caved. "OK. Fine. It's called The Psychic Shoppe. It's at the Paradise Valley Mall. But I seriously don't want to make a scene, and I don't know if Esmeralda will be there, but if you want, you can—"

"I can't wait! I'll be there. Oh, and I swear I won't embarrass you."

"Great," I said with fake enthusiasm. I was now terrified of my own birthday.

"Cool. I'll see you at the store. On your birthday!"

"Uh-huh. Awesome. Great," I lied.

"You still don't know how to get off the phone." She laughed. "It's easy. You say bye and hang up. Try it with me!" She waited a second, said, "Bye!" and hung up.

7
All Tomorrow's Parties

After we hung up, I stood alone in my apartment thinking. I wanted to see Alba, but when I pictured her coming into the shop, I felt sick to my stomach. I also didn't trust my ability to hide this news from Esmeralda, as I was sure she would not approve.

I walked to the couch and took a seat, thinking about my life and the decisions I'd made that got me here. Enough was enough. I had to break things off from Esmeralda and move back in with Brian, with no delay.

I quieted my mind and asked Source for help, but nothing happened.

"C'mon!" I shouted.

"Can you shut up already?" a voice shouted from behind the closed door of my bedroom. I didn't recognize it. I stood up and looked at the door.

Source said, *Don't open the door. Leave now.*

My first instinct was to ignore this message, but then I remembered my decision to turn over a new leaf. Source had told me not to date Esmeralda and warned me about many other decisions that had culminated in disaster.

Lesson learned.

My heart raced as I opened the front door and stepped outside. I was about to lock it when Source said, *Hurry! Leave now!*

I ran down the stairs and kept running when I got on the street. I felt dumb, but I was committed to following Source, with no exceptions.

A few blocks later, I was huffing and puffing, but Source said, *Keep running,* so I choked down my skepticism and kept at it. Four blocks later, my lungs were searing, and my shirt was soaked.

Source commanded, *Keep running, you fool*!

I had enough adrenaline to keep going, but something was off.

I stopped at a bus stop to catch my breath and think. Source had never insulted me. Its messages had always been neutral and boring, like a teacher's instructions.

Keep running! it repeated.

I shook my head and remained in place, but instead of feeling better, my vision became groggy. I figured it was from running so much.

I tried to take deeper breaths, but my vision weakened, and I felt on the verge of passing out. I thought, "I could die," which opened a floodgate of paranoia.

A woman at the bus stop asked, "Are you OK?"

I wanted to answer, but I was sure that if I nodded or shook my head, I was going to pass out and crush my head on the pavement.

"Help! Someone help!" The same voice shouted.

I felt several hands reach under my armpits to give me support.

"OK, buddy," a man's voice said. "It'll be OK. What's your name?"

Before I could answer, an orange hue clouded my vision, and I passed out.

***

When I came to, I was at the same bus stop, lying down on its bench with five people standing over me.

A woman yelled, "He's OK! He's waking up."

"What's your name?" a wrinkled man's face asked.

Source said, *Ask for Brian.*

"Brian… is Brian here?" I asked.

"Who?" the man replied. Even his wrinkles looked relieved.

"Brian. My roommate. He lives, um, we live close to here," I said.

He smiled. "Thank God you lived, 'cuz you have no ID and you passed out, and we were about to call an ambulance, and, hey — you want us to call one?

I shook my head, relieved that I no longer felt sick. I sat up and pulled my legs off the bench to face the street. The people around me gave me some space.

An older woman said, "Boy did you scare us!"

I cringed with embarrassment. "Um, thanks. Thank you, everyone. I'm really glad you helped me. But" — I stood up, surprised by how normal I felt—"I have to go."

"What?" The old man standing in front of me asked.

I walked around him, and he looked like he was debating whether or not to stop me, but I didn't give him time to decide.

I took off running towards my apartment, and when I arrived, I ran up the stairs to the front door then paused. The voice I'd heard from my bedroom had told me to shut up after I yelled at Source, but it had been quiet the whole time I'd been on the phone. Why hadn't it yelled at me then?

This had to be more of Esmeralda's vengeance. Stifling my fear, I pushed the door open, bracing for a monster from hell, but nothing inside had changed since I'd left.

I crept to my bedroom door. It was still closed. I squeezed my eyes shut, turned the handle and pushed it open, yelling *"Gotcha!"* with squinted eyes.

There was no one inside.

Just to be sure, I looked in the room's tiny closet: Nothing, no one.

Closing the door behind me, I knocked on Brian's door. I waited, knocked again, and after a minute of silence, I opened his door and scanned his room. It was dirty and smelled like unwashed gym clothes, but empty.

I walked back to the main room, threw my hands in the air, and screamed, *"Screw you, Ez!"* My body shivered, and I felt a dull nausea in my stomach.

Please stop, Ez! I pinged.

The nausea faded. "Thanks," I muttered. I sat on the couch to stew. I'd gotten the message, pun intended. Esmeralda had impersonated Source and told me to run. And I'd fallen for it until I saw her patented orange hue at the bus stop.

I'd been duped, yet again. I closed my eyes and tried to think of a way to combat Esmeralda's attacks, but nothing came to mind. I eventually fell asleep.

At eight o'clock, I woke to the sound of keys in the door and laughter. The door burst open, and it was Brian with Veronica of all people! I didn't need ESP to know what was going on, but I wasn't offended. I actually felt sorry for Brian.

Veronica made a sour face when she saw me, but I could also empath some fear. Brian's face dripped with guilt. He probably thought I would consider this betrayal.

"Ardor, dude..." he said while looking down at the floor.

Veronica hung behind him, wearing a loose sweater that fell low enough to reveal part of a bright-pink bra. She had skin-tight jeans on and as much as I didn't want to admit it, she was still attractive.

I rose from the couch with my hand out like a cop. "Don't worry, guys," I sighed. "I just came to check the mail and call Alba back, but then I got distracted."

Veronica stepped forward with squinted eyes and crossed arms. "By what?"

Source said, *She's defensive and scared. Be gentle. She thinks you're angry.*

"Sorry," I said. "Life hasn't been so great recently, and I wanted a quiet spot to think."

Brian stepped forward with wide eyes. "Dude, are you OK?" He looked at Veronica and took a half step away from her.

"What the hell?" she said with a scowl, punching him in his shoulder.

I walked closer to them. "Guys! It's OK. I'm happy for you two. Don't mind me. I just have to…" I trailed off and started towards the front door to leave.

"Wait…" Brian said.

"It's OK," I said. I went outside and shut the door behind me.

Source said, *He does not understand how to improve his life. Help him.*

I remembered how much Brian had done for me three years earlier by letting me live with him rent-free for a month so I could escape life with my drunk mom.

Source said, *Brian is unhappy. He hates his body. He doesn't know how to meet women. He knows Veronica is using him, but he is desperate for some form of intimacy.*

I sighed. So this was being psychic? Helping others when you want to mind your own business? Maybe this gig was going to be tougher than I thought.

Source confirmed, *Help others if you want to stop Esmeralda from hurting you.*

I nodded with confidence. I intuited that this moment was critical and felt goose bumps from the thrill of courage. This was my path.

I turned around and opened the door. Veronica was facing Brian, her back to the door. Brian was looking at the floor. Veronica was mid-sentence, speaking *at* Brian in the same tone she had used with me when she wanted to hurt my feelings.

"You're disgusting. You're lazy and fat. You keep gaining weight. And your job is a joke. When are you going to get a better job so you can treat me to nice things?"

"Brian!" I said in a cheerful tone.

He looked up and grinned.

Veronica spun around. "What are *you* doing back here?"

"I live here, and pay rent. Oh, and I'm Brian's best friend." I smiled at him.

He gave a small nod.

"Veronica, I think it would be best if you left now, before you say or do something you'll be forced to regret." My voice was calm and even.

She opened her mouth, but nothing came out.

"Uh, huh. Just like that," I said, bubbling with confidence.

She pretended to scrutinize various spots on the floor as she walked to the counter to grab her purse then left.

I was thrilled! Without using psychic tricks, like Esmeralda, I'd held her accountable for her behavior. I'd used firm, civil words, and they worked.

Brian thanked me, and we ended up talking late into the night.

He related how Veronica had roped him into their bad relationship, which I compared to my awful relationship with Esmeralda. Then I told him everything I'd learned as a psychic including how to try to defend against Esmeralda's orange attacks.

At one point, I was speaking so freely that my words surprised me. I hadn't realized how many thoughts I'd been holding inside.

"It's hard," I said. "I feel like I'm in a situation I can't get out of. Esmeralda is smarter than me, and every time I think I'm in control, she does something that catches me off guard, and makes me feel... like a loser."

"So why don't you just leave?"

I looked down at the floor. "Low self-esteem, I guess?" I was afraid to look up. I felt stupid admitting that I was insecure. "I'm afraid no one out there will want to be with me. I'm tall and awkward, I don't know how to relate well, and I'm... I'm scared of being alone."

"Gosh. I thought it was just me."

I looked up. Brian's face was as grim as I'd ever seen it. I felt a rush of love in my heart. "Wow. Here we are, two old friends, but I feel like we're really only getting to know each other now. I feel much better."

He made a weird face that didn't seem to exactly agree with me, and I felt a pang of regret. "You don't feel better?" I asked.

He put up a hand and shook his head. "Look, it's not that I can't relate. We do have a lot in common. And for what it's worth, I trust you and admire what you're doing. But I can't lie. This conversation makes me really nervous. Especially Ezmeroosha." He paused. "Just thinking about her scares me, dude."

"Yeah. I understand." I saw the issue. Whereas Veronica was manipulative and somewhat controlling, I was with a seriously powerful psychic who seemed to be on some sort of mission that required using me.

I nodded then shrugged. "I see what you're getting at. Our situations do have a certain point of departure. But I think this conversation helped. You gave me the courage to do the right thing. I'm going to break up with her tomorrow and move back in. I can't thank you enough for staying up with me and helping me figure this out."

He gave me a weak smile. "Hey, it's getting late, but I do have to tell you something."

I read his mind and my heart grew heavy, but I let him tell me in his own words.

"So, well, I've wanted to get out of Phoenix for over a year now. And now that I'm done with Veronica, well, I have a cousin in Boston who told me a month ago that she can get me a job there if I want one, and I'm going to take her up on it."

I winced. He was doing the right thing, but I couldn't afford his place on my own.

"But I know this is short notice, so since we're paid up through this month, and I have to give thirty days' notice, I'll give notice and pay the final rent tomorrow. But even if I leave sooner than that, you can stay here until the lease is up." He grimaced. "But after that, you're on your own. I just can't stay here."

I wished I had a cousin in Boston. "I understand. You're doing the right thing. You should definitely go."

We called it a night and when I got up the next day, he was already at work. I looked around at the apartment and felt an odd sense of nostalgia, which didn't make sense, since I was still going to live there another month.

Why do I feel this way? I asked Source.

Because this is the last time you'll ever see this apartment and Brian.

8

Happy Birthday to You

I was tired that day from lack of sleep owed to my anticipation about seeing Alba. I was terrified of having Esmeralda meet her, but I was lucky. What was once an act of punishment, Esmeralda scheduling me to work alone for ten hours on my birthday, was now a relief. They would not meet.

My only concern as I got up that morning for work was how Esmeralda was going to react to my disappearance the night before. Had I been a good boyfriend, I would have called her from the apartment to explain that I was spending the night at my own place. A no call, no show was nearly a declaration of relationship war.

However, she wasn't a good girlfriend, so I didn't care about being a good boyfriend. I'd had it. I wanted out, from the relationship, her apartment, and my job.

I didn't have anything to do at my own apartment, so after I showered and dressed, I was bored and decided to leave early for work. The buses were quicker on Saturdays, so I got to the mall forty-five minutes early.

I was whistling some pop song as I unlocked the store door, when I felt a sense of nausea along with Esmeralda's patented orange hue clouding my vision.

"What now?" I yelled at the ceiling, wincing from the pain.

I want you to come here, into my office. Esmeralda pinged.

The hue vanished. I shook my head, trudged to the shut door, and realized that I wasn't afraid, for once. After my success with Veronica, I didn't think I was bulletproof, but I wanted to show Esmeralda that I wasn't afraid of her.

I swung the office door open, ready to rant, scream, and plead my case for not calling or coming home, but the sight of Esmeralda knocked me out of my staged bravado: She was lying on the couch in loose sweatpants and a hoodie, sobbing and cradling herself in folded arms.

"Esmeralda?" I asked, rushing to the bed.

She shook her head and avoided eye contact.

I reached down to pat her hands. When I touched her, I felt a cold, static electricity. I took my hands off and backed up a step. "What's wrong?"

She turned to the wall and didn't answer, still sobbing.

"Ez, I uh—"

"Leave me! Fine! Leave me, like every man does. Leave when you don't need me anymore," she sobbed.

I knew I was being duped on some level, but I couldn't ignore what I was empathing: genuine sadness.

I was also surprised because I did not sense any rage, which was what Esmeralda usually connoted to me.

My compassion was real, but after two years of her bullshit, I couldn't buy that one night away had hurt her this much. I sighed. "What do you want from me?"

"Leave me! Go away! Go! Now!" she screamed, still facing the wall.

"Ez, *you* pinged *me*. I didn't even know you were back here."

"See! You don't care. Not at all."

I'd grown up with an alcoholic mom. I was plenty used to manipulative hysterics. "Fine," I said. "I'll set up the store," and I left.

After I had prepared the store for the open, I glanced at my wristwatch and realized I still had time to kill, so I went back to the office door and knocked on it.

Esmeralda pinged; *I knew you would do this to me. Every man does this to me, but I thought you might be different, since you have the calling. I know sometimes I push hard, but to go away, without even an explanation, or a call…?*

I spoke through the closed door. "I didn't see it that way. I just needed some time to think." I *knew* she was full of shit, but I was still empathing genuine sadness.

Source, I asked. *Is she faking this?*

No. She is really sad, and you are an expert empath.

Is she an empath?

No. Not at all. And she doesn't really understand how it works.

64

"Esmeralda, can I come in, so we can talk, face to face?"

She didn't answer.

I pinged her, *I'm sure this is a misunderstanding. I just needed time to think.*

All the sadness I was empathing evaporated and was replaced by her usual fury and rage.

You liar. I'm psychic. You don't think I know the truth?

In a flash, I knew what she knew: Alba's call, my talk with Brian, and worst of all, my exit strategy. She knew it all. How could I have been so dumb? Just like I could read others' minds, she could read mine. I needed to learn how to block her.

Esmeralda, I'm sorry. I don't know what to do. I feel trapped.

You feel trapped? You? You live like a king at my apartment. You eat my food, you sleep in my bed, you enter my body! How could you possibly feel trapped?

I was about to reply when the door flew open. I had to jump back to avoid it.

Esmeralda's face was blank. "Leave," she said through clenched teeth.

"What?"

"You're fired is what. Get out. I will mail your last paycheck."

"Esmeralda, please…"

"You're sick, Ardor. Just plain sick," she said.

An orange hue crept into my vision. I chased it and it dissipated. I felt proud.

"What are you talking about? What's sick?" I asked, trying to hide a smirk.

She sneered and said, "Your love for *Alba*," she intoned Alba's name how most say Hitler. "It borders on incest. You can only hide this from yourself."

I cringed, but not because it was true. The notion was sick. "What on earth?"

She pushed me out of her way and stalked to the door as she said, "Happy Birthday, you ungrateful boy. Enjoy your present, you bratty child."

"Present?" I asked.

She opened the door, and without a glance said, "I'm pregnant," then left.

***

I stood alone for what felt like eternity, obsessing over her words. I came out of my daze when a plump man in a suit coughed loudly near the door.

I was still standing in the back by the office door. I hadn't noticed him when he entered. I blinked and stared like an idiot before walking over to him.

"Are you open?" He smiled, a bead of sweat on his forehead. He was in the process of going bald, but his eyes had a youthful energy.

"Yes, sir!" I said in my best attempt at customer service tone.

He smiled and looked around. "Um, so…"

"Right here!" I said, pointing to my desk. "Sit here, and I'll be right with you." I watched him take a seat and pinged him.

He was thinking, *There's no way this kid is the real deal. Sam is full of shit.*

"Sam is right," I said, taking a seat across from him.

His eyes grew wide.

"I know," I laughed, forgetting all about Esmeralda and fatherhood. "It scared me too; the first time I knew I could do it. But yeah, I'm the real deal. Sam, who incidentally is a married woman you're in love with and work with—"

"Whoa! Slow down kid," The man put his hand out.

I felt my face scrunch in confusion.

"I didn't ask you anything... That's very..." he blushed. "personal."

I felt bad. I still hadn't learned not to tell people things they weren't ready to hear, but he had aroused my excitement when Source told me his name was Bill Hacker and he was going to offer to be my first agent.

I blushed. "Sorry, sir. That was rude."

"Call me Bill," he said, not offering his hand to shake.

"Forty-seven," I said, yawning. "And do the second thing before the first thing, but wait until March to start both. When a man named Neil offers to help, be careful and polite in declining him, which you must. And eat less salt, for God's sake."

He blushed. "Holy shit you really are—"

"Psychic?" I smiled.

He then did what everyone does after they believe me: he tried to hide his own thoughts in a spiral of fear of vulnerability. Once someone believes you can read their mind, they will never be the same around you.

As Bill was busy trying to shield his mind from me, I was busy trying to pick out which thoughts were worth noticing from his insane mental spin:

Does he know about Sarah and Janice? What if I really did hurt that man? Does he know what happened? Would he turn me in?

I didn't know what he was talking about, but I didn't want to know. On a moral level, I now worried about all sorts of things I'd never thought about. If I heard someone admit to a crime, was I obligated to report it? Not legally, but ethically? It got worse:

But I don't know what happened. And I know it's not nice to want to hurt someone, but it's a fetish, and... I'm not guilty. I pay those women. I don't know. I read the newspapers. Every day. For a whole week! There was nothing in them. Nothing happened.

I wished I could shut off his mind, like a television, but I couldn't, and the next part forced me to empath a bit of his anger, which was another 'side effect' I'd never asked for:

Shut up, Bill! Stop thinking. Just work the deal. Do your job. Get him interested, get him to believe in himself, then turn on the charm. You can do this. You know what to do. It's all about self-efficacy, remember?

He'd hit a dog with his car. It wasn't a human, which was all he cared about since he was afraid of going to jail for hit and run. He didn't care that he'd hurt someone, or possibly killed them. Just about self-preservation. Meanwhile, I knew the dog had survived.

I intuited that he didn't want to think I could read his thoughts, so I didn't tell him it was a dog. Instead, I asked, "What do you want to know from me?"

He coughed into his fist, and I pinged him once more: *I want to make money off you. Damn. Don't think that. That's rude.* He then asked, "What can you do?"

"Well," I said slowly, actually thinking about my answer, "I can do… I don't know. I haven't tested all that I can do. I just sort of…" I paused and thought about it. I didn't know what I could do, but everything I'd ever tried to do had been possible, so shrugged and said, "I can do anything, I guess."

Source cut into my prideful moment with bad news, *Ardor, I wish you weren't so easily distracted. You should have checked in when Esmeralda left, instead of stewing in self-pity. She is on her way to intercept Alba and it's too late to stop her.*

I must have shown my panic on my face because Bill's body language tensed and I empathed apprehension.

"You OK?" he asked, leaning towards me.

"Bill, I'm sorry, but I have to stop. Now." I took off my dumb hat and put it on the desk. "Um, no cost, and please come back." I stood up and pointed to the door.

"Wait!" He reached into his pocket.

"Yes. Yes, we can work together, but I need you to leave now." I had no concern for how he would perceive my haste. Nothing I could say or do would get in the way of his greed and how much he needed me to accomplish his goals.

He bit his lip and slapped a business card on my desk. I didn't need to look. It said he represented the Heavenly Talent Agency in Los Angeles, California.

9
Cheers!

When Source said it was too late to do anything, I thought maybe it was too late to stop Alba and Esmeralda from meeting, but not too late to interrupt them. I didn't know where Alba would be, but I knew Esmeralda hated leaving our apartment, so I figured she'd tricked Alba to coming to her place.

I kicked Bill out of the store, locked up, and was at the bus stop in less than two minutes, which got me to Esmeralda's stop in under twenty minutes. I was huffing and puffing by the time I jogged the half-mile from there to her place, where I slammed my fists into her thin red apartment door. She had never given me a key, another nuance of her efforts to control me. She would lend me her key when I went home from work early and make me wait for her there to let her in, and at all other times, I had to knock so she could permit me to enter.

I banged and screamed, "Let me in!" until a neighbor came out, staring me down with hard eyes and asking me if he needed to call the cops.

The neighbor and I recognized each other, and I had always sensed that he didn't like Esmeralda's vibe, but now I was in full panic mode, so my rage didn't care about my reputation. His tone was angry, however, so just in case I read his mind: he thought I was an addict hooking up with Esmeralda, my dealer, and he was dying to call the cops on both of us to get us evicted.

I backed away from the door. "Sorry, man. I'm out of here."

There was no point in staying anyway, I couldn't feel any human energy in the apartment.

Source, where is she?

You shouldn't be doing this. You should have stayed at the store.

What? You told me Esmeralda had intercepted Alba!

I also said you couldn't do anything about it, yet you're trying to control things.

Source was a prick. I gave up and figured my best bet was that Esmeralda had gone to visit Alba at home, the house we'd grown up in, so I ran back to the bus stop to catch the first of three buses to my house in the suburbs.

When I got to the stop by my house, it had been two hours since Source had told me about Esmeralda's plan back at the store. So much time had passed! What was I doing? Was I going insane?

I shook off my doubt and this time, I didn't have to bang on the door. I had a key. I thrust the door open, stepped inside, and yelled, "Alba?" But the house was still. I turned around in a circle, hoping to see her hiding in a corner or something. But it was obvious that no one was home. I gave in to defeat and threw my keys as hard as I could against the white wall next to the door. They made a dent in the wall and white paint floated across sunlight and onto the floor.

I smelled spaghetti and meatballs. It made me miss Alba's cooking, even though her meals had always been one of five generic meals made from a box purchased with food stamps. I went into the kitchen and saw a pot on the stove. The stove was off, but I could see steam rising from the pot. This wasn't normal. Alba was a neat freak. She would never have left food out if she were leaving the house. I ran into the garage. It smelled of faint exhaust. It seemed like she'd left in a rush.

Where is she? I demanded.

Meeting Esmeralda.

Where?

You won't find them, and you're not supposed to be doing this. Please listen?

I returned to the entryway to find my keys. I crouched down, picked them up, and muttered, "Happy Birthday to me." I stayed in a crouched position and started to cry. I backed up into the wall, sat against it, and thrust the back of my head into it, to add pain to my woe. I made heaving noises that sounded and felt foreign.

Memories of previous birthdays floated in and out of my mind, featuring clips of self-pitying stories of my parents trying to stay sober long enough to make me happy. I recalled more than one party when my dad said something offensive to another parent, or when my mom fell asleep in a lawn chair during Pin the Tail on the Donkey. These memories somehow felt new and for the first time I cried for my parents, not just me.

In all those years, Alba had been the one staple in my life. I cringed at the memory of our earlier phone call, when I'd read her mind and found out she thought I was avoiding her. I cried even harder.

I *was* avoiding Alba, but it was for exactly the reason I was now slumped against a wall, terrified and utterly helpless: I didn't want her to meet Esmeralda. Esmeralda had a knack for hurting people. Or was it an affinity? Or both?

Crying, with my head in my hands, I didn't keep track of time, but when I ran out of tears and looked at my watch: it had been a full hour since I'd arrived.

I steadied myself and asked Source for advice, but nothing came, not even a finger wag or scolding comment.

"Fine! Screw you, Source!" I yelled, pointing a shaky finger at the ceiling.

I heard laughter in my head. Was God laughing at me?

A nasty orange hue appeared in my vision along with a budding headache, but then a green hue developed in the bottom and top of my vision and the pain lessened. It felt like two energies were fighting each other in my body!

The laughing grew louder, and the orange hue and pain increased.

The green energy did not subside, and I rubbed my temples while they fought one another. After a minute of squeezing my temples — hard — everything vanished: the laughter and the orange and green hues.

Esmeralda pinged, *Come home, Ardor. Time to kiss and make up.*

I felt a pulse of anger, but Source interrupted me. *Be nice, Ardor. You aren't ready to fight. Just go home and play it cool.*

It was lovely advice, but I didn't care to follow it. I wanted some payback.

Coming, Ez, I pinged. I smiled. Revenge was going to be fun.

***

In the time it took to take the three buses back to Esmeralda's place, I never once wavered from a Zen-like state of focused hatred, hell-bent on slow, careful, revenge.

I didn't know what Esmeralda had tried to do, or had done with Alba, but I knew she was evil, and it wasn't enough for me to leave her. Things had gotten too messy. I had to make sure that she was going to leave my sister and me alone.

I reviewed my plan on the way, which was to practice a cultivation of false thoughts for her to read. I had already theorized this plan months ago, but I had been too tired or afraid, or both to try it out. But things had changed. I used all that time on those buses to pretend that I was on my way home from a long day of work, and I let it hover in my mind, like a real thought, so when Esmeralda read my mind, which I knew she'd do, she'd be reading my lies and the truth of my day would be concealed. I felt like I was in the next level of some psychic video game.

I eventually got to the apartment, still pretending to be annoyed by a long, uneventful day at work, and knocked on the door.

She pinged, *Enter*.

I went in, my monologue still playing, and tried not to laugh at Esmeralda's expression as I came in. She was on the couch, eying me suspiciously as I thought: *What a day. I can't believe she made me work on my birthday. What kind of girlfriend does that? And she's pregnant? I guess we have to reconcile. Start over. Damn.*

As she read my mind, I noticed that she was no longer dressed in sweats. She'd showered and put on a sexy outfit and makeup.

I didn't dare read her mind, since she could tell when I did and it pissed her off, but I could also tell when she was reading mine, so it was hard not to laugh at how well I was pulling off my new trick. She had no idea about my real day.

She was lying on the couch, legs curled up, with her cold eyes trying to pierce my confidence, but I didn't let her do that. I just continued to pretend that I was mad, but ready to 'kiss and make up,' just like she'd pinged me earlier.

She stopped reading my mind, stood up, and sashayed her way past me and into the kitchen. In a barely audible voice, she said, "I've met your sister, finally."

Without any hesitation, I thought, *You will pay.*

She turned around, giggling. "For what?" She grabbed a large green bowl of popcorn and walked back to the couch, motioning with her chin to join her as she sat down, placing the bowl on the coffee table.

She grabbed a few pieces from the bowl and used her tongue to suction a piece from her hand. I'd seen her do this with male customers in the store before. She thought it was sexy. At first it made me jealous, but only before I hated her.

She rolled her eyes. "Alba didn't like me. Women never do." She made a pouty face then released a patented ice-queen cackle. "Women are such fickle cats."

Through clenched teeth, my face shaking, my body hot and vibrating, I said, "Esmeralda, you are pushing me over the edge and the only reason I'm civil right now is because you told me you are pregnant, but—"

"Oh," she looked at the floor, then back at me with a serious expression on her face. "Is that hard for you to consider? Such responsibility for a boy?"

"What the hell, Ez. Can't you just be direct?"

She patted the love seat. "Sit down."

I obeyed and she put her hand on my thigh, just under my crotch. I resented the maneuver, but I nevertheless felt a sense of arousal. I needed more control.

She squeezed my thigh and exclaimed, "Oh! Happy Birthday, Ardor!" She rolled the r in my name. She next leaped up from the couch and ran to the fridge.

"What are we going to do?" I asked, thinking about our child.

"Silly! Stop worrying. I got us something to celebrate!" She slammed the fridge shut and revealed a big green bottle with an orange label.

I squinted. "I don't know what that is?"

"Such a little boy, you are!" She laughed.

I heard gunfire, and my heart jolted as a projectile came barreling at me. I ducked and it nailed a spot behind me on the wall. I looked behind me: it was a cork, from a Champagne bottle. I'd really thought it was a gun.

"It's bubbles, silly!" She put the bottle on the counter and reached high above her to grab two Champagne flutes, but she couldn't reach. She then jumped to grab them, nearly knocking the bottle over with her chest. "Champagne, to celebrate the birth of Ardor Agopian!" She turned around, holding both glasses. "Ta da!"

She licked her lips and poured some Champagne into the flutes, then walked over to me with both of them. "Let's celebrate, baby!" She handed me a glass.

I laughed. "You're crazy. You know I don't drink."

"You do tonight, Ardor!"

She clinked my glass and swallowed all of hers in one gulp. I held mine up to my nose and smelled it. It smelled like medicine. I'd never once tried alcohol.

"Are you a man, or a boy?" She glared at me, with a twinkle in her eye.

Her challenge made me indignant. I swallowed the whole glass in one gulp. It burned, but also tasted good. It brought a mouth-touch feel I'd never experienced.

She grabbed my hand and thrust it to my side. I dropped the flute and it smashed into pieces. She laughed and shoved her tongue in my mouth. We fumbled around, making out, and in minutes were lying on the couch, her underwear around her ankles, high heels still on. When we were finished, she lay on my chest, as our breathing slowed down in unison, and I could feel her heart beat under the palm of my hand.

"I'm glad you can understand and forgive me," she smiled.

"I am too," I said, truly proud of myself.

I couldn't have been happier. My plan had worked perfectly. Especially the part where I got angry. Esmeralda wasn't as sharp as I'd feared. I'd rehearsed all of this, every part of it, and it worked. She'd believed all of it. Who was dumb now?

10
Sunday at the Mall

I woke the next morning in bed next to Esmeralda. She was sleeping with her mouth open, facing me. Her breath was wafting an ugly post-drinking vinegar scent my way. I turned to face the wall. She wrapped an arm around me and tried to pull me back towards her, like a happy lover.

This was a total turn. In two years of what I suppose normal people call 'dating', she'd never sought my affection, let alone cuddled with me. Perhaps it was the dawn of a new era, but I wasn't into it. I pulled away and scooted myself towards the edge of the bed so I could exit without further physical contact.

"Don't leave me," she cooed, half asleep, fluttering her long, fake eyelashes. She feebly stroked my groin, which featured a solid pole of morning wood.

"I gotta piss!" I said with a tinge of disgust.

She bolted into a sitting position, pulling the covers over her breasts. "You can't be an asshole, just because you've trapped me."

I felt a headache coming on. "Get over yourself, Ez. I gotta pee."

You are not in control, she pinged.

You're a relentless bitch, I retorted.

Big talk for a little boy.

I slammed the bathroom door behind me and glanced in the mirror. My eyes were puffy, and I looked tired. I took a lengthy piss, marveling at the wonders of my first hangover. My urine was dark yellow with lots of sudsy white bubbles. My breath tasted bad, which was strange, not because it usually tasted good, it was that I'd never tasted my own breath. My headache was also new. It wasn't a pulse in my eyes or temples. It was a universal pain that clenched my entire skull.

I wanted to think about the next step of my plan, but I was starting to get better at telling when Esmeralda was in my head, and I could tell she was, so I instead concentrated on the wonders of my hangover and took my sweet time brushing my teeth and washing my face, hoping my casualness would irritate her.

When I returned, she was lying face down with a pillow over her head. She said, "The worst part of a hangover is that even Source cannot help." She tried to laugh but it was more of a raspy cough. "Well, at least I don't work today."

It was Sunday, our busiest day at the store. This was a flagship shift that Esmeralda never missed and preferred to work alone.

"I hate to break this to you, *boss*, but it's Sunday!" I said with intentional glee.

I hate to break this to you, but I'm your boss, I'm pregnant with your child, and I'm not going anywhere. Hit the showers and get to work, Ardor.

I had been avoiding this pregnancy talk for too long. I asked Source, *Is it true?*

Yes. It is a boy.

I felt so many feelings that I wasn't able to pick even one to indulge in. On top of that, my first ever hangover was growing even more painful by the minute, so I concentrated on that, instead of the news, sort of grateful for that and the excuse of work to keep my mind off such a big, looming life-changing event. I'd just turned twenty-one.

I showered and was grabbing the keys to Esmeralda's car when she pinged: *I need the car, silly. Take the bus.*

I knew better than to argue, so I shelved my anger and walked to the bus stop. Sunday bus schedules are a mess, and I rarely worked this shift, so by the time the bus lolled into view, I looked at my watch and realized I was going to be late.

I got to the mall ten minutes late and as I left the sunshine for the dark, tinted windowed, air-conditioned mall, my heart pounded. With every step, I felt more of what is called mass cognition. I was reading the energy of a crowd, somewhere close, and it was overwhelming for my psychic senses.

After I passed the first row of shops, I sensed a crowd in a line at my store!

Sure enough, after I rounded the corner to my store's strip, I saw a giant line and swarms of inconsistent thoughts smacked my mind:

Is that him?

He's scrawny.

I need a soul mate.

Can he help me?

Why is he late?

I tried to pretend I wasn't aware of their thoughts, but it was hard not to blush at the meaner comments people were making about my body, my age, and my style. When I got to the store's entrance, I saw Bill, the customer from the day before, standing at the head of the line.

When he saw me, he beamed with pride and stuck out his hand and clasped me on the back like we were old business partners.

"Ardor! So good to see you! Can you believe it?" He motioned to the crowd.

I didn't buy his glee and pinged him. His actual thoughts were, *Learn to be on time, kid. You're not big enough to be a diva, at least yet. What a pain.*

"What's going on?" I asked, trying to ignore his insulting thoughts.

Some psychic, he thought.

"I *am* psychic. I'm just not — Look, I'm tired, Bill. What is going on?"

He leaned in and whispered with hot breath, "I told you I'd make you a star!"

I recoiled. "Actually, you didn't." I frowned and reached in my pocket for my keys and fumbled with them before finally unlocking the door. Then, in the loudest voice I could muster, I said, "Hi, everyone. I'll start taking clients in a minute. I'm sorry for the delay. If you want to blame someone, blame the Phoenix bus system."

I pinged the crowd and got mixed results:

That's not funny.

He's funny.

I hate the bus.

What kind of amazing psychic can't afford a car?

I'm going to ask for money back if he doesn't know about my grandma!

I sighed and went about opening the store. Two hours later, I was exhausted, as the line never ended, and the whole time the clients in line fought and argued about how long the line was taking to move.

Normally, I was flexible with time. We offered ten, fifteen, and thirty-minute readings, but I'd always go a little over for all of them, just to make sure the client left happy, plus, it was good for tips. But today was different, clients were not tipping, and they weren't like the regular ones. These were desperate, hopeless people who wanted clairvoyance, but didn't actually want to believe in it. I normally saw wide-eyed, open-minded teenagers or bored parents waiting for kids.

My track record had never been amazing, but only because Esmeralda had forbidden me from revealing anything life-changing or actually helpful to a client. She said nothing was worse than sycophants and suckers. Her business model was aimed at keeping those people out. I'd thought she was full of it when she warned that my energy would suffer if I took on real problems and formed relationships with clients, but she more than proved her point that day.

The work was exhausting, and I ended up skipping my lunch, thanks to Bill, who handed me a hundred-dollar bill and said, "Just keep doing your thing!"

"OK," I replied, "But I don't want my boss to see you standing near me, OK?"

He laughed and said, "Don't worry, kid. I could buy your boss' business with my expense account alone. If she gives us any flak, I'll take care of it."

I pinged him — he wasn't lying he was loaded. Besides, even if Esmeralda did come by, he was helping me. His presence made the people in line feel like there was an authority monitoring and keeping things moving along.

I'd been there for six hours and was just about out of gas when I looked up to see Alba, of all people, waiting at the head of the line.

She wasn't smiling. She approached my desk and said, "Gosh, Ardor. I can't believe how much you've lied to me. When Esmeralda told me that—"

"You can't believe her!" I shouted. "She's not to be trusted!"

Her eyes grew sad. "So you're not expecting?"

I blushed. "Well, no, that part is true."

"And what about being psychic?" She pointed at the line. "These people, they're all suckers?"

"Hey!" Bill scowled at us, eyeing the line. "Save that kind of talk for later."

I fought an urge to cry. "Look, I'm just like... did you know that Grandma—"

"Grandma told me it was a curse, not a gift, Ardor."

I pinged her. *It's why Dad drank, and Mom drank when Dad drank. You idiot.*

"No one ever told me any of that!" I screamed.

"Told you what?" Alba sneered. "I didn't *say* anything."

"Fine!" I shouted again. "I can read minds. I guess it runs in the family!"

Alba shook her head and didn't blink. "I thought you were smarter than this."

Bill walked up to us. "You two need to stop shouting." He pointed at Alba. "Do you need me to ask this woman to leave?"

Alba shot him an annoyed look. "I'm his sister. Go away."

He looked at me with a quizzical stare.

I nodded.

He left, shaking his head and thinking, *Great. He's also got family issues?*

Alba continued, "Just because no one warned you, doesn't mean you shouldn't be careful about it. Besides, I told you when we were kids to stay away from all this,

86

remember?" She sighed. "I just don't understand, Ardor. Why have you kept me out of your life? Are you ashamed of me?"

I looked down. "No."

"And worst of all, you hid your lover from me. Is it because she's older?"

I pushed myself back from the table. *My lover?*

I pinged her, not patient enough to wait to get the story via conversation: Turns out Esmeralda had called Alba and told her she couldn't wait any longer for me to tell her "our wonderful news." That's why Alba had left the house in such a hurry that day — it was to meet Esmeralda, who'd promised to explain my erratic behavior. When they met at some café, she'd told Alba I was embarrassed to be in a relationship with an older woman, but now that we were with child, she wasn't going to let me hide her from my family. She'd insisted that Alba had a right to know about her own nephew. She'd also bragged about my psychic abilities.

"Alba, I am so mad right now. So mad."

"Why? What did I do?"

"Because you're not my mother! I'll talk how I want to." I took a breath and refocused my hatred on a deserving target: Esmeralda. "Alba, Esmeralda is *not* my lover. Actually, I hate her. She's… I mean, I know this sounds dramatic, but she's evil. She's scary and evil. And yes, she is pregnant, but that's my problem, not yours."

She started crying. "*Problem*? Ardor, what do you mean?

I sensed she was hiding something from me. I pinged her and got, *I still need to tell him about Croatia…*

"Crow ate she-uh?" I asked. "What does that mean?"

She folded her arms and blushed. "First of all, stop reading my mind! It's rude." She unfolded her arms. "But, to be fair, I guess I've also been a bit secretive." She sighed. "Croatia is a country. Have you ever read a newspaper? It's been all over the news. There's a civil war in that area, and I have a chance to help."

I pinged her, *International Red Cross. Dream come true. Don't hold me back!*

"I can't believe you're leaving me…"

"I'm not leaving *you*." She was the maddest I'd ever seen her. "How can you be so selfish? I'm twenty-four years old and I've never done one damn thing for myself. After Dad died, I took care of you and Mom, working and going to school the whole time. I even had to wait two extra years to get my degree because I kept having to miss classes for Mom while she was dying. And you didn't help, not once! I even had to pay for her hospice and burial fees. So here I am now, in debt, and when I finally find a program to pay it off, you say *I'm leaving you*?" She stood. "You can't ruin this for me. I'm taking this opportunity. I'm leaving. In a week!"

She turned towards the door, and I stood to meet her at eye level, but I became overwhelmed by the crowd.

It's about time.

This is taking so long!

Jesus! What did he tell her? She's crying! Maybe I should leave…

He must be damn good!

I held up a hand. "Alba, Wait!"

She stopped in her tracks, eyes cast at the floor.

I walked around the desk and hugged her. When I let her go, she was crying more than before, but they were cleansing tears.

She nodded. "Thank you, Ardor. Thank you so much. I promise I'll write."

I started to smile, but Source interrupted me and ruined my good vibe. *Listen carefully. Tell her you are scared about your son, and you need her on your side.*

She is on my side! I argued.

Not fully. You need to be more honest. She thinks you are OK with Esmeralda.

No offense, Source, but that's between me and Ez. I don't need to burden her!

Ardor, please. You don't understand anything! Esmeralda is very clever.

I know, and that's why I'm going to leave Alba out of all this!

Ardor, this is important. Just tell her all about Esmeralda. This is urgent.

She looked frightened. "Ardor… Ardor, are you there?"

I shook my head and donned a fake grin. "Huh?"

89

"You looked distant. Is everything OK?"

I tried to give her a happy look, but it was hard to ignore Source's warning. I had a bad feeling that I was making a mistake, but I also didn't want her to worry about me. What if I told her about Esmeralda and she didn't go to Croatia? I'd be in the way of her dreams.

She grabbed my wrist. "Ardor? Hello? You OK?"

"Huh? Yeah, it's nothing. Sorry. I'm fine!" I pointed at the line. "I'm just a little overwhelmed. Are you OK?"

She looked annoyed. "Are you sure?"

I nodded. "Trust me, Sis. I swear I'm OK. Just keep in touch, and come back soon to meet your... um..."

"Nephew?" she smiled.

When she said nephew, my heart leaped. Maybe I was ready for this.

Someone in line whined, "Isn't her time up?"

I glanced at Bill, and he told the person to wait.

I returned my gaze to Alba. "I love you. So please be careful, OK?"

She smirked. "Me? You're the one with a pregnant girlfriend."

I pinged her: She was worried, but I'd said enough to clear her conscience.

"Ha. Good point." I smiled. "So, uh, write me?"

She laughed. "What's your email?"

I smirked. "Why? Who cares about the Internet."

"Ardor. You're a Neanderthal. Just get an email account before I leave. It's hard to trust the postal system in a country in the middle of a crisis."

"Fine, I'll sign up for the Internet," I said.

"You mean email?"

"Whatever. Yeah, don't worry." I wanted this to end. I was afraid I was going to cry in front of her and I wanted to pretend I wasn't desperate for her to stay.

"Don't forget," she said. She took out a pen and notepad from her purse and scribbled some weird thing on it with a funny @ symbol and told me to email her. Then she gave me a hug and left.

11
Los Diablos

Alba left and the line stayed pretty busy but eventually waned in time to shut down the shop on time. As I closed up, Bill told me he'd seen enough 'talent' to report back to his bosses. He said to expect good news within a week.

I didn't think any of this was good news. I boarded the bus feeling empty inside. My sister was leaving the country, my manipulative, angry girlfriend was pregnant, and trying to help so many desperate people had left me feeling drained of enthusiasm and joy. Their problems had been mostly the result of years of living a life that wasn't aligned with their heart or inner child.

It wasn't that I was angry with any of them, but it wasn't fun to give people advice and know within a second that they weren't going to follow it. All these people wanted was a quick 'psychic fix' for their woes. They wanted to hear that their cancer would cure itself, that they'd win the lottery and suddenly fall in love, or that they could continue to eat four meals a day but somehow lose weight.

I spent the bus ride hoping we'd careen off the road, but alas, I was dropped off safely at my stop, with nothing to do except walk the plank to Esmeralda's.

I hoped that she somehow wouldn't be there, but I opened the door and saw her on the couch with closed eyes.

When the door shut, she kept her eyes closed but said, "We're moving to Los Angeles." She looked calm.

"What?" I asked.

She opened her eyes and shook her head. "My God, you twerp! Check into Source and stop clowning around. You're going to be a father and you were gifted with phenomenal clairvoyance, yet you ask me 'What?' all the time!"

I checked in. Sure enough, Source said I was going to be famous. Real famous. Tuesday's newspaper would carry a small feature in the entertainment section about the line at my store, and *USA Today* was going to run that same story in their 'local state' section under Arizona. Then a TV station in Los Angeles was going to request an interview, but Bill was going to approach me in time to sign me and tell them to take a hike so he could groom me for success.

I was upset by all of this. I didn't like Bill, I didn't like attention, and I especially didn't like the idea of traveling to Los Angeles. It sounded big and scary.

I pictured people lining up to ask me for advice and gave into hopeless anxiety.

"What are you frowning about?" Esmeralda asked.

"I don't like any of this." I snapped.

"You don't like groupies?" She smirked.

I pictured attractive women in those same advice lines, and my anxiety was replaced with adolescent fantasies. I'd never thought about *groupies*.

"Calm yourself!" she said with a sneer. "Remember at all times that you are *mine*, and you're soon to be a father, so you can forget about a bunch of sluts feeding you grapes at the Playboy Mansion." She cackled with mirth. "Or else!"

A flicker of orange-hued terror toyed with my vision. I shoved it aside and asked Source, *What's next*?

Ask her about the boy, it replied.

I sighed. The last thing in the world that I wanted was to talk about that. I was twenty-one years and one day old. I'd never thought about having kids in any realistic sense. But now that I was imagining it, I pictured many sad moments from my childhood, like my dad parking the car on the lawn, my mom's consistently bruised face from clumsy falls, and most of all, I pictured myself as a child, feeling lonely, every day of my life. I'd spent most of my life living in my own head, and I wasn't sure if I was ready to be the sort of parent that didn't make my kid feel the same way. I tried to think without so many emotions, but I couldn't.

I told Source that I didn't want to ask Esmeralda about the boy. I wasn't ready to imagine the responsibilities and attachments that were attached to a child. I tried to shove these thoughts away and instead gave into the fatigue of the hardest day of work in my life and started towards the bedroom to take a nap.

Don't even think about it! she pinged.

I'm tired, Ez. What now?

Mama needs some love. Come here.

***

Two weeks later I was in a spacious office in a high rise in downtown Los Angeles, my first-time leaving Phoenix, with Esmeralda at my side, looking at the top page of a fifty-six-page contract I hadn't read because every other word was an SAT word I'd never learned. The contract was to allow the Heavenly Talent Agency, specifically Bill, to manage me.

Prior to this, *USA Today* had indeed picked up the story, but the next day, when the CBS affiliate called the store, Bill had arrived in person just in time to stop me from committing to them. Since Source had told me this was inevitable, I'd let him tell them no, and now I was about to sign a contract.

At first, Bill had asked if he could sign Esmeralda and me, as a 'psychic package', but Esmeralda said she'd never make a public appearance.

When he asked if we were married, she laughed and said, "I'm not property," and when I was about to mention our kid, she pinged, *Do not mention the child.*

In our previous encounters in Phoenix, Bill had worn jeans and a collared shirt, but now he was dressed to the nines in an immaculate three-piece suit with shiny cufflinks and wearing too much cologne. I called this "LA Bill."

I was staring at the top page, trying to ignore everyone and everything when Esmeralda nudged a pen into my hand and said, "Just sign it, silly."

I checked in. Source told me if it wasn't this contract, it would be another. Ultimately, it didn't matter who I selected for management: they were all going to rip me off, but I also wasn't going to care. Source said I was destined for fame one way or another, that my life work was to help humans understand how Psi energy worked, which was sort of funny since I didn't even understand how it worked myself.

I eyed the pen in my hand and asked Source what lay ahead of me if I did choose to shun all contracts and fame. The answer was *Even more Esmeralda*, so I signed the document on every page with some weird highlight colored sticker with an arrow. This took more than ten minutes, and when I thought I was done, Bill had to sign it, then some notary, then Bill's boss even had to come in and sign it, and the notary still had to sign something else after that.

That boss was a real piece of work. He was intimidated by the prospect of my powers, yet so into his ego that he nevertheless hit on Esmeralda right in front of me. I tried to ignore his thoughts, but his mental chatter was relentlessly offensive, so it was hard to block him. It would be like closing the door on a room of people talking about you behind your back. The funny part was that every time he thought about stealing Esmeralda from me, I wanted to say, "You'd be doing me a favor."

**

A week after that, I was sitting in a prep room at a network studio, still in LA, with an attractive young woman putting powder and blush on my face (she called it rouge) and other products I'd always considered feminine. I thought I looked like a clown, but Bill came by and said, "Looking great, kid!"

"I look like a clown," I replied.

He laughed and thought, *A clown that's going to make us so goddamn rich...*

"Is money really all you think about?" I asked.

He blushed and adopted a plastic smile. "Save that stuff for the show, kid!"

The makeup girl shot me a weird look as he left to talk to some executive.

I read her mind: *If you're really a psychic, then you'd know that I'm thinking you are pretty cute, and if you were a little older...*

I smiled at her. "I'm twenty-one. How old are you, Katrina?"

Her smile evaporated. She thought, *What the hell? I never said my name...?*

I pinged her memories, a new technique I'd been mastering. She was twenty-five, shared a one-bedroom apartment with an aspiring actress, and had grown up in Hollywood with an alcoholic mom and no dad, but with an older sister who had helped her stay on a decent enough path to make it this far. We had a lot in common. I looked at her through the mirror in front of us and smiled warmly. "You should give me a shot!"

Before she could reply, Esmeralda entered the mirror's field of vision. She looked at Katrina and said, "He doesn't date children. Please just do your job."

Katrina hung her head and walked to her makeup kit to pretend she was looking for something. *She's so beautiful*, she thought, looking at Esmeralda.

She was wearing a new dress; one of six she'd bought on Rodeo Drive that week with a significant portion of the monetary forward from the agency.

Bill returned, thinking, *This Esmeralda is something else. The poor kid is in way over his head. Oh well. He'll learn one way or another.*

Esmeralda gave Bill a spiteful glance and he rubbed his temples. He covered his mouth and burped. "Excuse me!" He ran toward the bathroom.

Katrina looked at Esmeralda with concern. Esmeralda raised an eyebrow and Katrina looked away, trying to mask her obvious fear.

Esmeralda eyed me and patted her stomach. This was her not-so-subtle way of reminding me of our commitment when we were in public.

I pinged her, *Why can't we tell anyone about him? You told Alba!*

You concentrate on what you have to do, and I'll do my part. If you start worrying about the boy, your abilities will wane, and we can't afford that.

I looked at her pearl necklace and said, "We?"

She smiled as she ran her thin fingers along it. "I look lovely, don't I?"

"You do!" a man said, approaching from behind. I didn't need clairvoyance to know it was the same man from the contract day, the President of Heavenly Talent.

"Everyone on the set in five!" A voice yelled from the studio's PA system.

I stood up, trying to ignore my anger with Esmeralda. She was somehow more in control than before, even though I was the one supporting us now. I didn't understand how advances worked, but I was concerned with her spending habits.

"I guess I'm going on stage." I eyed Esmeralda. "Try not to buy anything before the gig ends, OK?"

She stuck her tongue out and flipped her hair.

The President mimicked a cat's meow.

"You guys want some time alone?" I asked, squinting at him.

He smirked. "I just wanted to wish you luck!" But he thought, *Maybe later, kid.*

"Do all you LA hacks throw the word *kid* around like that?" I asked.

99

He looked startled, but Esmeralda shot him a look that calmed him down. She then placed a hand on my chest and said, "Boys, boys. This is nonsense."

The President released a shallow laugh and looked me in the eye. "Ha! For a second there I *actually* thought you could read my mind!"

Bill returned. His hair was wet, he was sweating, and his face was flushed. He'd tried to mask it, but I could smell a trace of vomit on his breath. He coughed and looked embarrassed when he saw the President. "Mark! I didn't know you'd be here!" he said.

I felt sorry for Bill. Like me, he was in over his head and following orders, but at least I had Source to guide me when I was in doubt.

Mark gave Bill a condescending smile, put his hand on the small of Esmeralda's back, and nodded at the sound booth behind us.

"Mademoiselle," he said in a bad French accent, "you can watch from the executive suite, with me." He looked at Bill and me. "Bill, you stay with Mr...." he paused and smiled. "No. He's Ardor. Just Ardor." He winked at Esmeralda. "Now we're ready for success."

Esmeralda giggled and patted his shoulder. "I think it's perfect."

She pecked me on the cheek and left with Mark, pinging, *It's all for the show. You do your part, I'll do mine. You know I'm all yours. So don't screw this up.*

I saw a tinge of orange but before I could fight it off, it receded on its own.

A man with a headset and clipboard came up to me and wordlessly led me to a chair on a stage that faced another chair. There was a blue screen behind the two chairs, and a fake potted plant in between the two seats. "Sit," he said.

He left me alone to fidget until the most plastic-looking human I'd ever seen came onto the stage and sat down, facing me. This doughy mannequin with piercing unintelligent blue eyes kept touching an ear piece and looking annoyed.

I pinged him: *How many more dog-and-pony shows before I get my break? A psychic? Are you kidding? This is more low-rent than that talking stick guy.*

The PA boomed: "In Five... four.... three..." Bright lights flashed two times.

The man's expression completely changed, and he said with a cheery smile, "Good evening, and welcome to another edition of *Prove It*! America's show for skeptics! I'm your host, Stephen Mahogany, and tonight, we have a young man who is a self-proclaimed *psychic*." He used air quotes to coat this already sarcastic claim just in case anyone watching thought he was on my side. "As a matter of fact, *Ardor* here—" he used air quotes again, even though it was my real name.

I'd had enough. "Is this thing on?" I interrupted.

He looked at me like I was a fly, buzzing too close, "It is. But—"

"I don't think you're being fair." I looked at one of the three cameras, the one that seemed to be focused on me, and, alternating my eye contact between it and Stephen, I said, "I *am* psychic, and my real name *is* Ardor, unlike you, '*Stephen Mahogany.*' What's wrong with Michael Montzcowski anyway? Too Polish?"

He winced, but I didn't care. I'd given him an easy choice: concede that he was treating me like a phony, and stop, or continue to lampoon my existence, but he did not choose wisely.

"I have no idea what you are talking about," he said. "And I would ask that you please respect protocol. You'll get more than enough time to—"

"What name do you use when you hire prostitutes in bar bathrooms on Hollywood Boulevard, and how much do you pay these men for—"

The lights cut. Stephen didn't look at me as he left his chair and ran off set.

12
Vacation

The fallout from the television appearance wasn't bad: It was television gold. The networks had been unable to stop the live broadcast in time, and even though you couldn't see the part where the host left the set, the tabloids were all over it, and me.

The paparazzi in Los Angeles were so fierce that Bill took it upon himself to hire me a security guard, some guy named Robin.

"Don't worry, kid, I'll take care of it," he said, all the while thinking *but it's coming out of your pocket, not mine*.

But that was the least of my problems. At this point, Esmeralda was my biggest issue. She was mean to me every moment we were together, but also when we weren't, thanks to her ability to ping me at all times. I wanted out, but I didn't know how to leave. I was scared of her energy, but I was also afraid of being alone. Every time I thought about leaving her, I imagined living alone, without Alba in the country, and with Brian on the East Coast, and my brain told me to stay. I knew it wasn't logical, but I couldn't overcome those fears. I felt stuck.

We'd been in Los Angeles for over a month now and I was regularly appearing at all sorts of gigs, from live TV to concert-hall lectures. My work routine was doing these gigs in between sitting with Bill and his talent management team who would prep me and make me attend boring think-tank meetings where guys in suits threw darts of ideas at a target of money. Esmeralda was rarely in attendance at these events, thanks to her morning sickness, which somehow got me excited about having a son, which was the reason I was hell-bent on putting up with her shit.

It seemed like an eternity ago that I'd been hugging Alba as she left for Croatia and making minimum wage at a mall psychic shop. I was now getting steady checks from the gigs Bill set up, and for the first time in my life, I didn't feel poor.

I was still a punch line on lots of TV shows (one late-night host had a good one about how I could somehow predict a divorce, but not any other storm, like a recent hurricane that had devastated Florida), but all press was good press, and people were flying to LA to attend my speaking events, which were total cash cows.

Even though most of the events I attended used me like a circus animal, I was ultimately able to give plenty of strangers good advice from my forecast for the trajectory of their soul and mind's unified (or divided) goals, which satiated a part of me. It seemed to confirm what Source had told me, that this was the point of my life.

Because Esmeralda spent all day alone in the hotel, when I got home, she was usually loaded with blame for "The boy who trapped her with a gestating animal."

I would wake up in the morning to the sound of her shrill complaints about how I'd "made her" bloated, tired, and cranky, then she'd wait until I was on my way out the door to "remember" another errand she needed from me before I could leave. I would fulfill her tasks, often making me late to work, but it was never enough.

And the busier I got, the more she pinged me, especially when she knew I was performing at a live gig, which was distracting and hazardous to my career.

Things came to a head when I was at a live appearance with a bikini model. The cameras were running, and I'd just blown the model's mind with an honest report on what her soul wanted her to accomplish in this lifetime. I called these "life readings" and they were always a big hit with what Bill called the 'under-thirty demo'.

The model, with tears running down her chipmunk cheeks, said, "Wow, Ardor! I can't believe you don't actually know me." She was wearing a skimpy bikini and we were standing in front of a pool. It looked staged, just like all TV in the late '90s. I was so gangly, pale, and awkward that Bill had me wearing loose pants and a big T-shirt instead of a swimsuit. The outfit landed somewhere between Gothic and kid who brings a gun to school.

In spite of my low self-esteem, I was happy with how this shoot was turning out. The model had a truly gentle, good soul, so I was happy to be exposed to her energy. I wanted so badly to feel connected to someone, anyone, even if it was just for a quick TV spot. I couldn't take much more of Esmeralda's enmity.

"Can I hug you?" the model asked, looking down and thinking, *I wish I could meet a nice man like him.*

I wanted to keep my feelings for the model from Esmeralda, but there was no way I could read the model's mind, remember to look at the camera instead of the model's gorgeous body, and block Esmeralda from pinging me. No one could.

So Esmeralda read my thoughts and decided to make me pay. As I leaned in to return the model's offer of a hug, a nasty orange hue raced into my field of vision. I let go of the model and ran my fingers through my scalp, wincing with pain.

"Um... Ardor?" the model asked in a worried tone.

I crouched down and pushed at my temples, hearing, *I warned you, Ardor!"*

"Just. Give me a second." I pushed my focus into the space of Esmeralda's energy, but this required tremendous concentration and made me look constipated.

"Um, should we like cut?" The model asked the director.

He whispered back, "We are live," thinking, *What is wrong with this idiot?*

I couldn't focus on the energy and lost my battle. The next thing I knew, with no self-control, I heard myself say to the model, "By the way, your career is basically over. You're so boring that even with your looks you make people yawn."

She stepped back and crossed her arms. "Excuse me?"

The orange hue attacked harder, and I doubled over. I pinged Esmeralda, *What do you want? I'm trying to work! This could ruin me! You have to stop!*

Good.

Good? We need this money! C'mon! We have a child on the way and —

We? We have nothing, you ungrateful little two-timing brat!

Ez, please! I'm just performing. I would never cheat on you. Please stop?

The hue began to fade. The model looked terrified, but I assuaged her by saying, "Sorry about that. Sometimes I have these headaches. They're just all part of my, uh, gift." I paused and got a positive message to relay to her. "Guess what?"

She didn't smile, but I could tell she was still on my side. "What is it?"

"I have good news! I can see that the next man in your life will be the right man, a good man. He might even remind you of your beloved grandfather," I smiled, proud to have steered the show back on course.

She looked horrified then bawled with no restraint.

My smile faded. "What's wrong?"

"I can't believe you would say that. It's so inappropriate!"

"What do you mean?" I took a step back.

"My grandfather is in prison. He's awful. Everyone knows that! He abused me and my siblings. I can't believe you!" She thrust a finger in my face. "There's no way you're psychic!" She stalked off the set.

The director shouted, "Cut!" then furiously whispered something to Bill, who didn't look defensive. He looked mad.

Esmeralda pinged, *Serves you right, swine. That'll show you why you shouldn't talk to sluts!*

Ez, I can't believe you did that!

There's a lot you won't believe if you continue to anger me.

Oh, screw you! I'm so tired of your bullshit. I can't believe you just did that!

Don't push me.

You crossed a line. Consider yourself pushed.

She didn't reply, and I was glad. I was shaking with rage and feeling a violent temper I'd never experienced.

I pinged Bill, *What a child,* he thought. *I should never have trusted him. All that time wasted. We're done. We're ruined.*

I walked to him and the director. They looked like they wanted to spit in my face. "Bill, uh, can we talk?"

He exhaled loudly then said, "You screwed up."

I wanted to argue, but I couldn't. He was right. I was a failure. My life was doomed. I suddenly felt lucky to have Esmeralda. This thought made me cry.

"How pathetic," the director said before turning and walking away.

"Wait!" Bill called after him.

The director gave us the finger without a glance.

I cannot believe this, Bill thought. "What the hell just happened?" he asked.

I looked at these kids with backstage passes standing near us. They were kind of watching us, but I could tell they didn't really care.

"I don't know," I lied.

Bill said, "I'll tell you what happened. You blew it. You blew the whole thing. More than a month of appearances, and all this work to sell you like you are not only an adult, but a goddamn psychic, and you pick the most important event of all, a live one that's going to hit the demo we need the most, and have the least of, and you blow it! The whole world is going to *know* you're a fraud." He was spitting from excitement.

I wiped stray saliva from my face. "*Know* I'm a fraud? Are you serious?"

"Yes, Ardor. A fraud. Just like Esmeralda and every other charlatan like you. Jesus, kid! Do you see how mad I am? You did this! You and that awful bitch. I knew it was all a scam. Even when you—" He stopped talking. Terror seized his face and he groaned, burped, and wobbled.

I caught him as he lost balance, but he pushed me away, saying, "Go away!" I let go, and he bent over and puked. It splashed all over both of us.

The kids yelled, "No way!" and one of them took out his camera and took a picture of the two of us, me crying and Bill soaked in vomit. It would be on the cover of most newspapers shortly thereafter with the headline, "Ardor is a fraud!"

Bill remained crouched, rubbing his temples for another minute. Eventually he shook his head and stood up. He squinted and said, "I don't want to see your pathetic, scrawny face again. *Ever!*" He walked away.

Since I'd paid for Robin's security services, he gave me a ride home. He was quiet, at all times, so he didn't talk to me, and I spent the ride obsessing over how everyone in the world was going to hate me. Even though this was all Esmeralda's fault, I was lonely, so I pinged her, but I didn't get an answer the whole ride.

We parked and as we entered the hotel, Source told me, *She's not here.*

I was despondent and defeated, so the last thing I expected to discover upon learning that Esmeralda wasn't waiting for me was to feel even more sadness along with a feeling of betrayal. I wondered if I was experiencing Stockholm Syndrome.

With a lowered head, I walked to the elevators, and we rode to the penthouse.

When we got to the door of my room, Robin looked sad. I pinged him. *Please don't make this awkward.*

110

I nodded at him. "Thanks for your service." He dipped his head once and I entered the unit.

The normally messy room was sterile. The usual clutter was gone. Moreover, nothing of Esmeralda's was there. One of the mirrors on the wall let me glimpse into the bathroom. Her cosmetics were gone.

I stopped in my tracks and stared at the empty room with disbelief.

Source said, *Check the bed.*

I walked to it and found a note, written on the hotel pad, which it was still attached to. It said, "I'm leaving you. Don't try to find me. Have a good life."

13
Source in the Mud

A note. A note! A note? I became engulfed in a fit of rage. To say I was indignant would insult every word in the dictionary. I'd been trying to ping Esmeralda from the moment I got in the limo, with no success, so now I was frantically wracking my brain to think of any other way to figure out where she had gone.

I grabbed the lamp from the bedside table and threw it to the ground. It exploded, but my body still felt hot and out of control.

I rose from the bed and began to pace as I recalled all the nasty shit Esmeralda had done to me. I was crawling into a cave of despair when I realized that thanks to my rage, I hadn't even thought to ask Source for advice.

I looked at the bed and blushed when I noticed that in my tantrum, I'd crumpled the notepad into a ball. I shook my head and asked Source, *Where is she?*

You cannot resolve this situation.

I pounded my fist into my other hand and again asked, *Where is she?*

No answer came.

My eyes watered. I pleaded, *What can I do? Please help me!*

No answer again.

I started crying. Alba was gone. Esmeralda had fled. I'd lost my job. I was going to be the laughing stock of America's weekly press cycle. *Please, Source, give me something!* I begged.

Source said, *You keep ignoring your gift when it really counts.*

What? I asked.

You have a gift. Using it correctly is what is important.

I felt a shiver of recognition. I was receiving information that resonated on a deep level. It was like my DNA understood a truth that I had yet to realize.

Fine. I give in. Where do I go next? I asked.

Home.

I didn't like the answer, but I gave in and started to pack. I had the backpack I'd brought to the hotel, and a ton of new clothes hanging in the hotel closet. I didn't want anything I'd bought in LA, so I only put stuff I'd brought from Phoenix into my backpack and walked out the door.

I checked out of the hotel and walked to the bank I'd opened my first ever account in. It was four thirty p.m. and the line looked long. It would only be open for thirty more minutes. I asked Source, *How long will this take?*

Twenty-four minutes. The elderly man ahead of you will leave the line soon.

113

I rolled my eyes. *How come you answer some questions, but not others?*

Only your selfish and indulgent queries will receive no reply.

I didn't like the answer, but I didn't make the rules, so I shrugged and stayed in line. Sure enough, the man ahead of me soon turned around, put a hand over his heart while keeping his other on a cane, and sighed. "I'm pooped. I'll come back tomorrow."

I feigned surprise, and watched him plod away. I waited patiently until I got to the teller and asked her liquidate my account. She told me I had to ask a desk agent to close it and called an assistant to help me.

Exactly twenty-four minutes from when I entered, I left with $18,000 in cash.

What now? I asked Source.

Take the seven-p.m. flight from LAX to Phoenix and return to Esmeralda's.

***

I stepped into Esmeralda's apartment at twenty past ten p.m. after a quick flight but a long bus ride. I realized after a thirty-minute wait at the airport for the bus that I had enough money for a cab, but I wasn't used to having money, so I took the bus anyway.

When I arrived, I saw that her car was missing from its assigned parking space and the apartment was ransacked. Her bedroom closet was empty, there was no

114

note for me, and no attempt to disguise the hasty departure.

What the hell? Why did you tell me to come back here? Where is she?

She's gone. She was four gates away from where you deplaned.

Why didn't you tell me when I was there?

Because you aren't supposed to find her. She's a distraction from what matters.

What are you talking about? She ran off with our unborn child!

Your life purpose is what matters.

I held in a scream and said, *Fine. So what the hell is my life purpose?*

To balance our Universe.

This was too much for me to handle. I disconnected from Source and sat on the couch, looking around. Without Esmeralda, I realized I didn't hate the place. It was cozy, the furniture was nice, and I knew where everything was. I thought back to the apartment with Brian, its sparse furniture, and how I'd had my face punched in, and thought, *I might not have had it so bad.*

As soon as I thought that, I felt guilty at the notion of not trying to be a father to my son. I asked Source, *I understand my life purpose, but what about my son?*

Source replied, *Follow your life purpose, and it will all work out in the end.*

I didn't like that answer, so I stayed on the couch and like a lunatic, I asked Source some variation of that

115

same question all night, and Source continued to reiterate its same reply each and every time.

I didn't really sleep that night and by morning I decided I needed to talk to Alba, but I realized that I'd never set up an email account, and worst of all, I realized that in the time that had passed I'd lost the slip of paper she'd given me at the mall.

I slammed my fist on the table. If I couldn't find Esmeralda, then come hell or high water, I was going to find Alba. I left for the library to use the Internet to search for Red Cross agencies in Croatia.

I got there, and tried my best to search for her, but I wasn't good at the Internet, and couldn't get anything even close to a lead. Finally, I gave up and tried a different approach. I punched in the latest website to advertise cheap airfare, and looked up round trip flights to the capital of Croatia. The cheapest one that left that day was $10,000 but there were a few the next day for "only" $5,000. I had a fear of poverty, but it was nothing compared to my burning passion for action in this time of despair. I tried to book a ticket, but I had to set up a travel visa, so I wrote down the number for a travel agent and returned to the apartment to call them.

When I picked up the phone there was no dial tone. I hung up and thought about asking the neighbor if their line was also out, but he was the guy who hated me, so I instead sighed and asked Source, *What happened?*

Esmeralda hasn't paid the bill for months. It's disconnected.

For months? Why did she do that?

She's also psychic, but unlike you, she checks in with Source and can plan ahead.

What do you mean, unlike me?

Ardor, you only check in when you're desperate, or when you need something. If you want to master your skills and fulfill your destiny, you need to start checking in with Source regularly, to make sure you're always acting in your own, and others' highest interests.

I knew Source was right, but this felt like a lecture, and I wasn't in the mood for one. I stormed out of the apartment and went to the nearest gas station and waited in line behind some meth heads to buy a phone card. When I paid for it with a one-hundred-dollar bill, the middle-aged clerk looked surprised and nodded at the junkies lighting up cigarettes outside the doors. In a protective tone he said, "You be careful, son."

He had a point, but I was lucky. I was still wearing those stupid clothes from the gig with the model, and I hadn't showered since before that. The tweakers weren't going to jump someone who looked more disheveled than them.

I walked around the corner to use the payphone, but someone had ripped the receiver off. I looked across the street and saw an ad for mobile phones. I went in and soon I had my first cell phone with a prepaid contract.

The airline was my first call, made on the walk home. I asked if they sold tickets for cash purchase. They did, so I hung up, called a cab, and an hour later I was forking over $5,634, the price after taxes, all cash, to an agent at the airport.

My flight was the next day, so I took a cab back to the library and went online to research Croatia. It turned out that it was a somewhat dangerous place. Even worse, it was cold there. I'd never seen a winter. Alba was in the anti-Phoenix. I shivered at the thought of it.

As I left the library, I could smell my own body odor, so I went back to Esmeralda's, showered, then took another cab to the mall, where I went on a shopping spree, culminating in the purchase of a parka, a hard task in Phoenix.

The next day as I boarded the plane, I still had more than $11,000 dollars. I'd brought my backpack and a new carry-on suitcase, which I'd put most of the cash in, and stowed above me on the flight.

How do you like me now? I asked Source.

Please Ardor. This is a huge mistake. You are about to alter a crucial time continuum, but it's not too late. Just get off the plane and there will be minimal harm.

Minimal harm? I laughed aloud, and a few passengers stared at me.

Yes, Ardor. It's not too late. Please listen!

I think I've listened enough. I have nothing to live for. I'm finding Alba, dammit.

Please reconsider.

I shook my head and put my seat back, but then felt stupid as I realized I hadn't thought to bring a book or any other distraction for the flight. Luckily, I was used to this feeling. I'd spent my formative years quietly sitting and thinking, in order not to anger my passed-out mom, who hated the noise of television or music.

My situation was sadly familiar. I was depressed and with little hope. I felt a tug in my heart and didn't understand how to talk myself out of this sadness. I just felt like feeling sorry for myself, and when I realized that, the cold, dead, empty, bad feeling in my chest grew and made me think there was no hope for anything good to ever happen to me. Before take off, the attendant came by to tell me to put my seat in its upright position, and I asked him how much longer the flight would be.

"Eight more hours, buddy," he said with no smile.

14
A Night to Remember
(if You're an Accountant)

The first of two flights to Croatia wasn't boring like I'd thought it would be, because I learned that the world is your oyster when you have clairvoyance!

I was in the middle seat, so I started with the man to my left, Bernard, who spent most of his time imagining potential meals at the steakhouse he was going to in Frankfurt where I would transfer flights.

Tuning in and out of him was a riot. I'd never understood the pathology of a glutton, and since that was only one part of his personality, I invented a game. Each time I checked in, I'd guess ahead of time which of his three obsessions he would be thinking about, food, how much he resented his wife, or his fantasies about the woman next to me, a thirty-something blonde from Switzerland.

The blonde, Emma, was on her way home from a two-week business trip to America where she'd had another affair with a man she didn't even like, but who gave her something to do while she was bored on the lonely weekends. Her husband was a wealthy pretty-boy who she'd married at nineteen. She didn't resent him, but he didn't care about her, so she flew around the world throwing herself into the unexciting world of international insurance.

She didn't think about Bernard once. All she thought was, "Life is boring."

Bored by her boredom, I checked her future: She would fail to overdose on pills in the next five years, and instead drink so much she would die from cirrhosis. I felt really bad about this, but I was a psychic, not a healer. There wasn't anything I could do to help her.

I got lost in my thoughts again until the flight attendant flirted with the businessman in the aisle seat next to Emma. Bored and curious, I pinged his mind and discovered that he was afraid his small penis would disappoint her.

To compensate, he planned to impress the attendant with his expense account, and the good news for him was that she was into this. Good news all around!

The man seated behind me was grumpy because he'd wanted a better breakfast at the airport and the price of airport food was too expensive.

The young French woman next to him, Claire, thought I looked "dirty" and assumed I was a gypsy. She couldn't figure out how I afforded the flight, but she hoped "people like me" would stay out of Europe.

The pilot was mad at a recent amendment to the International Flight Code's rule for service hours. He'd decided to protest by drinking instead of sleeping for four of the six mandatory hours of leave he'd taken the night before. Fortunately, he wasn't going to crash the plane. He was actually about to meet the woman of his dreams on a flight instructor continuing development course who would encourage him to seek anger counseling which would curb his drinking issues.

There were sixty-seven passengers on the plane, and I checked into each and every one of them. It was exhausting, but the time flew by. By the time I deplaned and transferred to my three-hour flight to Zagreb, I was dead tired, so I ended up sleeping for that whole flight.

***

I didn't understand exchange rates or anything else about money, so I forked over five thousand dollars in cash at the airport in Zagreb and converted it to local Kuna which looked hilarious to my young, American eyes.

Flush with cash and optimism, I asked Source, *Where is Alba*?

We told you not to take this trip.

Still flush with cash but now resentful of Source's attitude, I ignored its reprimand and pinged the mind of the most attractive woman in the taxi line. Her name was Chiara, and she was from Venice, just across the Adriatic Sea. She was headed to Hotel Esplanade to wait for her boyfriend, Nicola, to arrive that night.

Now that I knew her boyfriend's identity, I decided to try something new. I tried to ping him, and I could! I learned that he was a wealthy, older man from Milan, and sadly, he was going to tell her in two hours that he couldn't arrive in time because of work. But he was lying. He was staying an extra night in Slovenia with a woman he'd been seeing for months. His plan was to arrive Saturday to wine and dine Chiara before leaving again to meet a third girl in Malta. What a creep!

Chiara was far ahead of me in line, so I waited my turn before cabbing to Hotel Esplanade where I arrived just in time to see her entering the elevator with a bellboy and enough bags for two weeks, even though she was on a weekend trip.

She was going to grab a drink at the hotel bar in three hours after a girlfriend would tell her to get drunk since "Nicola is obviously too busy to care." Even though Chiara was somewhat high-maintenance, she had a good heart, and like most Europeans, she spoke decent English, so I figured I'd come down in three hours to flirt, or at the very least make conversation. I didn't know what I wanted, but I was lonely, and I was enjoying my reckless fun with Psi powers.

At check in, the hotel receptionist thought I looked ugly, poor, and unable to afford their rates, but he donned a smile and greeted me with, *"Zdravo,"* which I could only assume was "hello" in Croatian.

I didn't know how to respond, so I asked Source, *Can I use you to translate and speak foreign languages?*

Da, možete, Ardor.

I heard those words and somehow knew they meant "Of course."

Kako je to lako? Hvala vam! I replied. Thanks to Source, I was fluent. I'd just thought, *Wow! How easy. Thanks!*

I proceeded to have the following conversation in impeccable Croatian.

"Hi, I'd like the best room you have. Spare no expense!" I was tired of being stereotyped as a gypsy, thanks to my lanky frame and dark features.

"How many nights?" the clerk asked.

How many nights until I find Alba? I asked Source.

You're not finding her

"At least a week," I replied with no emotion.

"We need a credit card."

"I don't have one. Can I pay in cash?"

The clerk looked more surprised than I thought was warranted, even if I did look like what he was thinking, "Gypsy trash." What a jerk. I pinged and saw that nothing I did was going to change his bigotry. This was a popular sentiment here.

"I'll pay for tonight in cash and figure out the rest tomorrow. OK?"

He booked the penthouse, and I tipped him a 1000 kuna note, $150 US.

As I walked to the elevator, he thought, *I wonder how he made so much money. Probably stole it or killed someone. Maybe I should contact INTERPOL.*

I went up to my room and took a shower. As I stepped out and toweled off, I realized that I didn't have nice clothes to wear when I went down to the bar.

Where can I find some nice clothes? I asked Source.

Have them delivered. But really, you should go home. This is a huge mistake.

Thanks, but no thanks. Either help me find Alba, or go away.

Ardor, persistence has no effect on Source.

OK. Fine. Tell me something good then. I'm tired of your dire warnings.

OK. This is the last time you will ever have to worry about money.

This made no sense. I wasn't worried about money. I had a ton and was having a blast spending it on room, board, and soon, clothes. Source was dumb.

I called the front desk and booked a personal shopper to come to my room.

The personal shopper, Greta, was a woefully unattractive older Croatian woman, but man did she know what she was doing! She even brought clippers to tidy my hair. She made me look three years older and like I had the greatest sense of fashion in the world. She also made me look rich. Was being rich always this fun?

By the time Chiara was heading to the bar, I looked so nice I barely recognized myself. I was even starting to relax and forget about how much I hated Esmeralda. I was sure my plan to use Psi skills to flirt with Chiara would succeed.

I'd already ordered some *rakija*, a disgusting local drink, when Chiara took a stool two down from mine. I took a sip and fought back tears as it burned my throat and made me want to run to the bathroom to hurl. This was my second attempt at alcohol, and I'd been excited for it, but it was terrible.

I forced a smile and asked Chiara, in English, "Are you on vacation here?" knowing already why she was there and a whole lot more about her.

She thought, *Oh great. This guy wants to hit on me. What was I thinking? I just want Nicola.* Despite those thoughts, she gave me a slight smile, sensing that I wasn't a bad guy, but also to make sure I wouldn't take it the wrong way. She said, "My, er, boyfriend he is, er, not able to make it at this time to see me."

"I am very sorry," I said.

Source, I need help!

She is attracted to humor, but this is just a distraction. You need to go home!

I grinned. "I'd like to buy you a drink, but only if you promise me that no matter what, you won't flirt with me or take the offer as anything more than pity!"

She grinned, her shoulders relaxed, and she nodded.

I motioned to the bartender. He came by and she ordered a Negroni, which I would end up also trying, as my second drink. After that, we would have three more, and when she was buzzed and I was as drunk as I'd ever been, she asked me to come back to her room under the pretense of lending me a book for my stay in Croatia.

After she gave me the book and our hands touched longer than necessary, she thought, *Nicola is cheating on me. He is. It would be fair to do the same.*

We kissed, and I thought of how different it was to kiss her than it was with Esmeralda. Just as we were starting to move towards the bed, a wave of guilt struck me in a way I'd never felt before. I tried to ignore the feeling, but it worsened until I had to stop kissing her and allow Source to speak to me. What a nag!

Under no circumstances will you do this. You must not manipulate others.

I didn't even bother to argue. Like it or not, I was the one who felt guilty. Source had nothing to do with it. I pulled back from our embrace and told Chiara how appreciative I was of her company, but that I didn't want *her* to cheat. I said it in a rush, looking at the floor. When I finished, I looked up to see her blush, nod, then look down.

I went back to my room and passed out on the bed and awoke the next morning with a much worse hangover than after my twenty-first birthday. Rubbing my eyes, I walked to my suitcase to grab more cash to pay for another night, but the money wasn't there. I emptied the whole suitcase and went through every pocket numerous times, but I knew the money had been stolen. I'd never felt so scorned.

What happened? I asked Source.

You were robbed. We tried to warn you about coming here, but you didn't care.

15
Josip

Hangovers suck, but not as much as the sucker punch of being robbed. I was furious with my situation, but I also knew that I had no one to blame but myself. However, this wasn't my only problem. I was now broke, and thousands of miles from home in an expensive hotel room I could no longer afford. Normal people in my situation call the police, but I had Source, which I figured could do more than the police.

Source, who took my money?

Irrelevant. It's gone. Stop abusing your powers and start listening to me.

Abusing powers? Are you kidding?

Meeting girls in bars, staying in the penthouse? This is not the high road.

Fine. I give up. What's next then?

A walk.

A walk?

Yes.

Where? With who? Can you be a little more specific?

A walk alone. Take a walk and see the city.

I sat back and tried to relax, but even with Source, I felt so lonely. And now I was supposed to go sightseeing, alone, without any money? I was learning a hard lesson. You can give someone clairvoyance and all the psychic and intuitive powers one can imagine, but that doesn't deliver human connection, support, or love. I missed Alba. I needed someone to talk to.

I caved into self-pity and went beyond sadness. Sadness is a feeling, but where I existed, I had no feeling. I was numb. Even suicide sounded like a hassle.

I shuffled into the shower and robotically washed my oily hair, which reinvigorated my hangover. I slathered penthouse Croatian soap on my body before rinsing and toweling off with no enthusiasm or joy.

I felt like a puppet. After dressing, I found myself sitting on the bed, staring at the television, which was off. I looked at the warped reflection of my lanky body on the bed and a feeling struck me, seething hatred.

This was all Esmeralda's fault. She had used me for her amusement. She had wanted to screw then screw over a fellow psychic. I was just some toy for her.

I summoned the energy to pull myself from the bed and put on my shoes. I grabbed the big winter parka I had bought, slung it over the roller suitcase, put my backpack on, and headed down to the lobby.

I used Source to talk to the same concierge from the day before. I told him I changed my mind and would find lodging somewhere else. I asked him to store my luggage while I ran errands, and he seemed delighted.

130

I pinged him and learned that I'd softened his heart with my tip the day before. I embraced this good news (it was all I had) and walked outside into the crisp morning.

The air felt clean, and when I breathed, I felt a sense of restoration that I didn't feel in the Phoenix desert. I thought, *Maybe I kind of like the cold!*

I felt this wonderful, restorative energy for four more breaths until it was replaced with a biting pain in my ears, nose, and hands. I realized then why the cold sucks, and always will. Unlike heat, a stagnant oppression, cold is a ferocious Chihuahua, perennially nipping at your nerves with piercing fangs.

Where do I go now? I asked Source.

It's dangerous here. You need to be careful.

OK, that's good to know, but can you be more specific? Can you tell me what to do?

I got no reply, which I assumed meant "Free will time." So I forced myself to think about what a smart, careful person would do, and I got a weird idea. *Gypsies!* I decided I would try to meet some of these people everyone was stereotyping me as. Maybe it would lead me somewhere.

Two large steeples loomed high in the distance. Those were a sign of God, I figured, and gypsies, according to bigoted minds I'd read, were godless.

I turned around so the steeples were behind me and walked with confidence as Source told me which streets to take. I didn't pay attention to my path and started to enjoy myself. This city was beautiful.

I left the busier confines and entered a cozy neighborhood that looked safe by American standards, but Source told me to use caution.

Stuffing my hands in my pockets, I did my best to puff out my chest, hoping to look big and tough, but I wasn't fooling anyone with my skeleton shaped body.

I don't remember what happened next, but I woke up lying flat on the ground, alone and without my jacket, freezing. I had a large bump on the back of my head and my face felt awful — not as bad as it had when Rinco had beaten me in Brian's apartment, but it was a similar throbbing sensation. I felt dejected, but I was lucky on one count: I'd intentionally left my passport and airline ticket at the hotel.

I sat up. As the blood rushed from my head, I felt three distinct pains: swelling in the back of my head, a welt around my right eye, and my hangover.

I looked down at my feet. Whoever had robbed me had also taken my shoes! I wanted to condemn my bad luck, but I still had my life.

Source, why would you lead me here? I thought you had my best interests in mind.

We told you not to fly to Croatia, but you have free will, Ardor.

Yeah, but you told me to take this walk!

Well, now that you are here, there's still wiggle room to avoid a certain amount of pain.

I don't understand. You're telling me that I had to get robbed because I came here?

It's not quite that simple, but yes, that's not a bad way to look at it. Your best plan was to stay in America, but since you came here, you are now on a different plan. All my advice is designed to get you back on a better plan, but to get there, you have to give in to flow.

I stood and said aloud, "OK. So what do I do now?"

A gravelly, heavily accented voice asked, "Oh great. It is an American?"

I spun my head left and right, but couldn't detect the source of the voice.

Behind and above you, Source said.

I turned and looked up to see a white-haired man on a balcony, smoking a pipe. He was older, but looked strong. His chest was built like a torpedo and his thick, white hair was groomed short to match an equally well-manicured beard. I was surprised I hadn't smelled his tobacco. I wondered if the cold affected scents.

"You sure took hit, boy!" he said again in English with a smirk

"Who are you?" I asked, only I didn't wait for him to answer. Instead, I pinged him: His name was Josip. He was a native Croatian in his late sixties. He had worked for the USSR's KGB, in espionage. His education had included intensive language courses in America. Now he was a lone wolf, satisfied to have escaped the Cold War, free to smoke, drink, and wait for the Grim Reaper's scythe.

This aging man shook his head and said, "Boy, I don't know why you ask me who I am if you have Source tell you." He knocked his pipe on the balcony's rail and flakes of burned tobacco fluttered around me.

"What?" I asked with wide eyes.

"You know little for big psychic brain, boy. It might blow tiny mind to hear what I say, but some of us can know when someone like you have psychic ability. That is main side effect of silly Cold War. Both sides were desperate for 'win' that we embrace, how do you say, 'woo-woo science' for *any* chance at success."

His eyes twinkled as he continued. "We try everything! Non-locational visualization of top-secret factories and documents. We investigate all of quantum reality!" He arched his eyebrows. "Something you actually have, but must master."

I felt my face redden. "Yeah. I'm new to this, but... how did you *know*?"

He pointed his pipe's stem at his right eye to indicate where I had been punched and chuckled. "You look hurt. Pity you Americans are so soft."

I wanted to argue, but he was right. I was soft.

Source interrupted my thoughts. *Ask for help.*

I smiled weakly and said, "I need help. I have no shoes, no coat, and no money. You know my abilities, so you know I can make us rich. I just need help first."

He shook his head and turned to go inside.

"Money for your people!" I shouted. "I can help poor people! I want to help the poor. I was only offering you compensation, um, for your help. I can use my ability — you know what I mean? … And I can start a charity. But I need your help!"

He shook his head, but also smiled. Without a word, he turned and went back inside. My feet were burning from the cold, and I had idiotically worn the parka over only a T-shirt, so my chest was numb. I looked at the sad, gray sky with no sun and I realized in hours it would be dangerously cold and I had nowhere to go.

That didn't work, Source! I pleaded, more afraid than I'd ever been in my life.

I heard a door behind me open and turned. Standing in front of an open door, a half-foot shorter than me, was the old man, Josip, with a big grin.

"OK, Ardor, Come inside," he said.

I recoiled with fear.

"How do you know my name?"

He put a finger over his lips and widened the door. "Shhhh."

16
Yet?

I followed Josip into his home. It wasn't much warmer than the outside, but I did stop shivering. However, it was dark and hard to see, as there was only one small lamp in the corner of the room and the blinds in the front windows prevented sunlight. The room had a staircase at the opposite end with no other doors or rooms. I was curious to see the rest of the place.

As my eyes adjusted, I saw a rocking chair next to a tall, narrow end table with a pouch of tobacco and a small ashtray full of ash on it. There was also a normal sized coffee table in the middle of the room with a larger, also full ashtray and two white statues of angels, but they didn't look special. Two more chairs were pushed against a wall with Afghan blankets thrown over them. The place reeked of pipe tobacco, a smell I have always sort of liked.

Source, How did Josip read my mind?
Who told you he read your mind?
He knew my name!
Why don't you ask him yourself?

Josip took a pipe out of his pocket, sat in the rocking chair, and packed it with fresh tobacco. I was impressed with his focus. He wheezed like a chronic smoker, but his fingers were nimble, and his concentration was even and practiced.

He finished and finally seemed content. He then took out a matchbook, lit a match, but stopped and looked at me. "Why for you stand?" He pointed to the chairs.

I walked over to them and carefully pulled a blanket off one to make room to sit down.

He blew out the match, put his pipe down, and approached me. "Why so gentle? Just take chair and have sit!" With his free hand he grabbed the blankets from both chairs, flung them onto the floor, then kicked one of the chairs towards the coffee table before hobbling back to his chair. I hadn't noticed his hobble before. It appeared to be an old injury.

"Friendly fire," he said, pointing at his bum leg. "And no: I am not psychic. I know who you are because we track you. You have sister, Alba. Your *Dedushka* — he is one who get you on list."

"Dedushka?"

"How do you say," he squinted, "You say grandfather?"

I nodded. "And, uh, what 'list'?" I used air quotes.

"Why you do not ask Source for these?" He coughed, spat into his hand, and rubbed his hand on his pants. "You are lazy psychic." He rolled his eyes.

I did as he instructed, and Source informed me that 'The List' was a speculative list of CPs and PCPs (Clairvoyant and Possibly Clairvoyant Persons). It had begun in 1956 in the USSR with a clairvoyant KGB agent, but was swapped and confirmed by the USSR and USA many times since the end of the Cold War.

I scratched my head and asked, "So you know… you *knew* my grandfather?"

He put the pipe on the end table and coughed into his hand. "I do not *know* any of you. I know *about* you. It is, was, my job. I run CP division of KGB. You, unlike most, actually *would* believe shit I learn. But most? They not ready for truth. Santa Claus and Spring Bunny sound more real to them than what you do."

"Are you psychic?"

He sighed. "Boy, if all conversation will be like this, I save us both stress and time and give you sweater and send you in taxi to airport. I already say no."

I stood up, my hands had become fists and my voice was shaky. "What did I do that made you so mad? I'm just trying to make sense of… look at me!" I pointed at my shoeless feet and jacket-less torso and winced.

He laughed and motioned for me to sit down.

"Gosh, gosh. I forget you have no father, so you have no man to be like. Sorry. I know what is like to be from shitty home." He grabbed his pipe, lit a new match, inhaled, and frowned. He emptied the pipe into his smaller ashtray and re-packed it. I was amazed that the new ash didn't cause the existing pile to spill.

"I asked Source about you, but it told me to ask you."

"It *told* you to ask me?"

"Huh?"

"Don't speak lie, Ardor. Source does not 'tell you' what to do. Try again."

I sighed and looked down. He was right. Source *communicated* with me. It didn't talk to me in a language and tell me what to do. I was simply giving it a voice and character. Really, I just knew things, but I liked to have conversations to feel less psychotic. I also knew this was because Esmeralda had explained it to me many times, but it had always been in anger, so I'd never considered why it was an important distinction.

I asked Source to explain it to me one more time. Source "said" it didn't have an opinion or motive. Source was pure knowledge, and I had access to it when I was in the right frame of mind. The reason Source sometimes ignored me was because I wasn't actually in a stable mindset and able to connect.

I nodded. "When I asked Source how you knew my name, it wouldn't tell me."

Josip slapped his thigh and bellowed with laughter. "A-ha! Now we get somewhere!" he leaned forward with mirth in his eyes. "Want to know how I do it?"

"Do what?" I asked. "And I'm not being lazy! We're having a conversation—"

"Don't explain so much. I like teasing. You will get used to my humor."

"You keep talking like you knew I was coming."

"I do. I mean, I do not *know* it will happen *here*, like this, or when, but, yes, there are, let us to say, 'lingering threads' from career that I cannot escape." He folded his hands and nodded. "There is a book, and I have read it," he said.

Source butted in, *Ask him now.*

"Will you tell me what you know about me?"

He laughed so hard he went into a coughing fit that tested my patience. When he finally settled down, he said, "You ask too much!" He then held a finger up and said, "I'm kidding. *Hold those horses*. I'll get to it all, I swear this for you. And this is not movie, so I do not die before I explain things." He laughed. "And I also am not your father, and we have no war with stars or light sticks. I only know *how* you do what you do, and I know," he leaned forward and squinted, "I know that you are, without doubt, to be best psychic of my lifetime. Maybe any lifetime. I also know this not always good for *you*." He shook his head. "But, is good for world."

I empathed a deep sadness that bonded me more than any words could. He knew I suffered and sensed the pain of my existence, the loneliness, despondency, and isolation. I smiled. I felt like he was on my side.

He cleared his throat and said, "Do not go soft again! That is last thing we need. I do not wish for to scare you, but you might be best psychic, *someday*, but today, you are not. You are shitty psychic, at best." He straightened his posture. "So, boy, if present is future that past once would be, we have very little time…"

Leaning forward, I asked, "If the present is the future that the past… *what*?"

"Do you understand how time works?" He looked annoyed.

I looked around for a clock in the room, but didn't see one. I frowned. "Huh?"

"You know of Mr. Albert Einstein?"

I didn't need Source to detect his sarcasm. I nodded.

"The great man was on cusp to explain facts of Psi science!" He held up a fist in the air. "Free will creates destiny, but as one exists, he cannot see this." He paused to draw on his pipe and continued. "Since before birth, is written, your birth, Alba—"

"Is Alba psychic?" I asked.

He shook his head and held up a finger. "Do not interrupt. Is not polite." He smiled, made me wait on purpose, then continued. "Not much of my work for government mattered. We study things, things that fascinate, but no reason is learned. People are psychic, but so what?" He shrugged. "Psychic does not start war. Psychic does not stop war. Psychic only say, 'War will happen, war will not happen.'" He closed his eyes like a tired guru and didn't move.

After a long silence I asked "Um, OK?"

Still smiling, he opened his eyes. "Why do you come here?" He laughed and held up a hand. "I ask rhetorical. I know answer already. You are here because mother of baby deceive you. It is told we meet after these event. But, mother is not *some girl you sex with*." He shook his head slowly, no longer smiling.

I empathed fear, which in turn made me anxious.

"Yes," he nodded. "It is told so, by someone like you, and it cannot change."

"Who said this?"

He sighed. "Book. It say, 'He green. She Orange. Orange-green war."

My body tensed.

He nodded. "Yes. You know of what I speak. You know this," his throat clenched, and his eyes narrowed to a slit, "this Esmeralda?"

"Jesus," I said. "You said this wasn't like a movie."

He laughed. "Joke. Good. You make good joke. Maybe I like you." He winked.

The wink was kind, but I couldn't relax while thinking about Esmeralda.

"I still have yet to say how I do it!" He rose. "Come. Follow me."

I got up and followed as he struggled to walk up the short flight of stairs. They twisted in the middle then opened up to a loft. He turned on a lamp at the entryway that illuminated a small room with a bed and a kitchen table with only one chair. There was a hand sink next to a counter with an electric two burner stove and an old-fashioned toaster. There were two closed cabinets and a windowed-door that probably led to the balcony. It had thick shades.

He saw my wide eyes and grinned. "Allow me to give *The American* my grand tour. Down the stair you have seen 'family room.'" He used air quotes. "Now you are seeing 'kitchen' and 'bedroom.' Ta da!" He held out jazz hands.

With wide eyes, I asked, "Where is the bathroom?"

He hobbled to the door and pulled back the curtains to point to a red bucket with a lid behind the wall of the balcony.

"Welcome to Croatia!" he put his pipe in his mouth and felt his pockets and frowned. "Damn. I leave matchbook in *family room*." He laughed at his joke.

"I'll get it!" I said, dying for a moment to process my dismay. I ran downstairs, grabbed his matchbook, and made a mental note to buy him a lighter, if not more.

When I returned, he was washing a plate in his hand sink and humming a vaguely familiar song.

I was about to ask what it was when he laughed and said, "I did not finish to explain you how I stop you from pinging! I can stop any of you! That is what I can do, and that is what *she* can do, but you? You cannot." He looked at the ceiling before returning his gaze to me, "At least not yet!"

"She? You mean Esmeralda?" I asked.

"What?" he shouted. "I do not now or ever wish to discuss *her*." He spit on his own carpet. "I do not even want to hear this terrible name again."

"Then who?"

"Who what?"

"Who is the she? Who else can 'stop' me from *pinging*?"

"Ping pong?" he asked with a smirk.

"Psychic! ESP! C'mon! You said you can stop me from using my ESP, and you clearly can, but you also said, 'she can!'"

"Oh. I understand confusion. Alba. Alba can, what is word? Hamper! Yes! Alba is different. She can *hamper* or *help* your powers. That is what is different now. It is special sibling bond." He looked excited. "And THAT is what SHE does not have."

"Alba?" I asked.

He laughed. "I see confusion now. No, I meant other one. Devil woman. What she does not have is an Alba." He turned away and pulled back the curtain from the balcony and looked outside. I noticed that his body was shaking. He turned back around, and his face was white. He exhaled smoke and said, "Yet."

"Yet?" I asked.

He pushed his stomach out to mimic pregnancy and pointed at it. "She does not have special battery, yet."

17
Pilot Wings

"Are you saying my son is some sort of lucky charm for Esmeralda?" I demanded.

Josip shook his head. "Such American oversimplify way." He grimaced as he walked to the stairs. "Follow."

He turned off the lights and I could barely see as I stumbled behind him. When we returned to the main room, the dim lighting allowed me to see a folded paper in his hand.

"What's that?" I asked.

"Come here," he said.

I walked closer to him and stopped; not sure how close he wanted me to get.

He smiled. His lips were cracked, and I could now smell vodka on his breath.

I recoiled. I was used to this smell on my parents, but it didn't mean I liked it, or missed it for that matter. It did give me a little insight into his life, however, which gave me a bit of compassion. I didn't know why he drank, but I knew that people who did it in the daytime were usually running away from something.

He threw his head back and laughed.

"Boy does not like drunk man?" His voice was full of joy and merriment danced in his eyes. "I like this," he announced. "I respect naïve American way." He put the folded paper on his narrow pipe table and packed his pipe and held it in his hand and marveled at it.

"My parents drank too much, but I don't care what you do." I rubbed my temples. "Also, booze is why Alba had to raise me until she left—"

"Bah!" He spit again. "You all have too much heart. Too much for war!"

"War?"

"Psychic war. Psychic games." He took out a match but didn't strike it. "Life is a terrible, awful game. So I drink!" He was shouting and sending spittle confetti into the air.

"How does drinking make the game less awful?" I asked, hoping I might be able to gain some insight into my parents. I'd never had a chance to talk to my parents about their drinking, and it occurred to me that I might be able to gain some compassion for them too.

"It makes game go quicker." He waved his hand dismissively. "Enough talk about emotions. We have things to do. Pay attention."

He smiled. "You are human, with mind. Everyone has mind. Even dog has mind. So what is consciousness?" He struck the match and held it up. "Consciousness is awareness. Flame is, but it has no awareness. You see flame."

146

"OK," I lied, pretending I had a clue as to what he was talking about.

He coughed and continued, "You have ability to communicate *with* Source. Normal man only catch glimpse, here and there, can only listen to it." He blew the match out, just as it was about to burn his fingers. "But sadly, you are idiot. You have special relationship with Source, yet you ignore it." He gestured around his apartment. "So bad things happen. To me, to you, to Universe." He smiled proudly.

I frowned. "Are you… uh, happy about, um, how you live?"

He leaned forward, "I am not always good man, so I accept shit life with vodka stipend." He drew from his pipe and exhaled with absurd satisfaction.

I wondered if I should try pipe tobacco. Source immediately said, *No.*

He continued, "Source is energy of all. Is in you, is in me, is even in tree and rock. But *you, Ardor, you* can communicate with it and know what can be known." He held up a finger. "Remember, not everything can be known, as not all is done having been decided!" He smiled, seemingly pleased with his English, but then broke into a coughing fit. He thumped his sternum with a fist until it stopped.

It reminded me of my mother's cough before Alba put her in hospice.

He continued, "To be Ardor…" He shook his head. "Is not easy. Not ever."

147

I asked Source, *What is he talking about?*
Your destiny.

I cringed.

Josip laughed and asked, "You OK?"

"I don't want a hard life," I muttered.

He rolled his eyes. "How long I wait for you stop to be sensitive?" He looked at his end table and walked to it. He picked up the folded piece of paper, stood up, and walked to the front door. "OK. Time up. I don't want friend, and I want to drink. So now I am finish." He opened the door and extended the note towards me.

I walked to him. He forced my palm open and put the note in my hand. "These instructions are from woman. Strong woman. Woman who know about you, your Dedushka, Alba, devil woman, and much, much more. She is dead, but this note, it will help future you. I hold onto to it for many, many years." He clenched his teeth and grabbed his knee then spat through the open door into the street.

The folded paper was weathered and frail. I wanted to ask if he always had it ready, or if he'd woken up that day and put it on the table, on a hunch.

I started to open it, but he shook his head and put his hand over mine. "No! Do not read until you are *on* plane. This is most important thing I tell you." He withdrew his hand and put his fingers in his mouth and produced the loudest whistle I'd ever heard.

A few seconds later a dreadfully old car with no signs or indication of taxi services screeched to a halt and a toothless man who looked like he'd already died smiled and nodded at us. Josip grabbed my hand and led me to the back of the car, and opened the rear door. "This is safer than taxi," he said. "What is hotel name?"

As I said the name, the driver's eyes widened.

Josip shook his head. "No wonder you get robbed. You stay at rich hotel like idiot." He smiled a knowing smile. "Oh well. You will learn." He coughed again. "You leave Croatia now. Go home. *Only thing is not read note yet!*"

"OK," I lied. I planned to read it the moment we pulled away.

"Ardor!" He shouted. "If you read note, you lose son!"

Those were the only words that could stop me from reading it.

He smiled, closed the door, and we pulled away.

***

At the hotel, the same concierge was working. He noticed my missing shoes and jacket and asked me what happened. I was so tired I didn't bother lying. When I finished explaining, he asked me what my plan was. I told him I wanted to change my flight and leave that night, but I didn't have any money. He told me I was unlucky to get robbed, but lucky to know him. His sister worked for my airline. He called her and managed to change the flight without a fee.

Was that luck? I asked Source.

149

When you follow messages, life flows. But, please, don't get cocky.

What do you mean?

There is a difficult road ahead, but humanity will benefit if you do your part.

I thought about Esmeralda's running away and getting mugged, and I didn't think anything worse could happen, but I tried to believe this to stay out of trouble.

The concierge wasn't done. He hooked me up with a free shuttle to the airport and by the time I boarded my flight I'd forgotten all about the note.

Hours later, I was asleep in my seat when I woke to the sounds of panic. The cabin lights were on, and emergency lights were blinking. There was a terrifyingly loud grinding sound and the plane's angle of descent was more severe than a normal landing. Before I could panic, Source said, *Read the note!*

I pulled it out of my pocket and nearly tore it in half as I rushed to open it. It was a page from someone's notebook with a heading that said, *Manual override on a Boeing 747.* I glanced at the plane's emergency card. I was, of course, on a 747.

I looked back at the note: the instructions seemed complicated, but my instincts took over. I stood, but a flight attendant standing in front of the cockpit screamed at me to sit back down.

I was about to obey when Source said, *Do not sit*!

I ran to the cockpit and when I reached the attendant, she put out a hand and yelled, "You must sit!"

I screamed, "I know how to save us!"

With an odd air of calmness, she said, "Passengers cannot enter the cockpit. No exceptions."

I shook my head and pushed her to my left and strode into the cockpit where both pilots stood arguing about why the plane wouldn't allow manual override. One of them kept screaming, "Computer is stuck!"

My instincts continued to guide me. Glancing between the note and the equipment, I followed the instructions and soon enough found the option for manual override, but the system required a passcode. I looked back at the note, but there was no passcode on it.

"What is the passcode?" I asked the pilots.

One shook his head and collapsed into his seat, and I smelled human shit.

The other slouched and said, "It is impossible. We need satellite to get code. Otherwise hijacker could override system!" I glanced down and noticed a dark wet spot across the front of his tan pants.

"So use the satellite," I said.

"Is impossible!" he shouted. "This is redundancy, er, step!"

The look of fear in his eyes nearly broke my spirit. I glanced behind me. The attendant was again blocking the door and using the speaker system to repeatedly tell the passengers to stay seated. I tried to ping Source, but all I could tap into were the panic-stricken minds of two hundred passengers.

I never should have screwed my secretary.

151

My son is going to find those videos I filmed.

Is this because I lied when I filed my taxes?

I never should have told Claudia I hate her. Why did I call her a slut?

I'm so glad I donated to charity. I hope God noticed that.

My whole family... all of them... they're going to find out... they're going to know!

I'm glad I prayed my whole life. I finally get to see my parents again!

I deserve this. I stole from people I loved, and I never even felt sorry until now.

Well, I guess bad things do happen to good people. I hope there's meaning in all of this.

I know this is just part of the great Karmic wheel. I will return.

I love my children so much. I hope my brother is able to take good care of them.

Ommmmmmm, Ommmmmmm, Ommmmmmm

I'm sorry I said God isn't real. I'm sorry. I'm sorry I'm sorry I'm sorry, please!

This mind chatter was distracting, but the sound of the plane's swift descent to certain death returned me to the task at hand.

The pilot said, "We cannot get code without signal, but UHF is off and sat-com signal keeps bouncing!"

The plane's angle steepened, and I grew dizzy.

The pilot shouted, "We're doomed!"

I gave up trying to think and felt my heart lift. If this was how I was to die, I was at least going to be peaceful about it. At that precise moment, Source said, *Alpha Eleven Tango Fourteen Six Foxtrot Nine Hundred.*

Without hesitation I entered the code into the computer and both captains shrieked with joy.

An hour later we made a successful emergency landing in Halifax, Canada.

I lied to the police at our arrival, saying, "I just sort of guessed," but there were reporters on sight, and like an idiot, I gave them my name, so when they ran a background check later, they were reminded of my recent mild-fame experience in Los Angeles.

The headlines the next day read, "Psychic Saves Plane From Certain Death."

18
1000 X 1000 is 1,000,000

We didn't spend much time in Halifax. The emergency crews sequestered all the passengers in a conference room to give us information for free counseling, before offering three options to get home: another flight, a charter bus to our original destination in New York City, or staying at a hotel to wait for someone to pick us up. I was impressed with the sincerity of the process.

I chose the flight. It was non-eventful, but I did laugh at the pilot — the whole time he thought about how he would have saved our flight if he'd been in charge. His Dad had died in Vietnam when he was baby, and he yearned to be a hero.

I had a six-hour layover in JFK, so I walked a lap around the airport. At one point I passed a bar with a Keno game. As I passed it, my empathy alarm screamed at me, the way it had when all those passengers had thought they were going to die.

The culprit was a man clutching a ticket, staring at the Keno screen.

I need this. C'mon, c'mon, please I need this, he thought.

Turns out he'd left his wife and kids for the weekend to collect returns on a land deal in North Dakota. Unfortunately, the deal had been a work of fraud, and he was powerless to prove it or catch the crooks who had fooled him. Even worse, he'd fronted his savings to make the deal and lost it all. He had no idea how to tell his wife that they were going to lose the house to the bank sooner rather than later.

I walked into the bar and sat two stools from him. A middle-aged woman came over and scowled while placing a coaster in front of me.

"What do you want?"

"May I buy a Keno ticket?" I asked, trying to smile my way to her good graces.

She looked annoyed. "What you drinking?"

"Huh?" I asked.

"What do you want to drink?"

"Can I just buy a ticket?" I asked.

She gave me a saccharine smile and said, "Sure you can!" She then thought, *Prick. You think I get paid from Keno sales?* She turned around and came back with a Keno form and a pencil.

"How much?" I asked as I filled in the winning numbers.

"Five dollars," she said.

"No, I mean the payout?"

She used a long, fake fingernail to point to the biggest graphic on the ticket that clearly advertised a $200,000 payout for picking all ten numbers.

I had only a twenty-dollar-bill left to my name, but I handed it to her and said, "Keep the change."

She didn't say thank you, but she did think, *Well, that's nice, I guess.*

I took the ticket and walked to the man. He looked up at me with sad eyes. He had a third of a beer left in his mug and he reeked of booze. I handed him the ticket and said, "Hey, I just realized my flight is about to leave! Want my ticket?"

He looked at the screen. It had a countdown that said three minutes left.

He shook his head and spoke to his beer. "I don't understand?"

I pinged him: He wasn't lying. He was drunker than I'd thought. I put the ticket on top of his hand and put my face in front of his until he made timid eye contact like a dog that did something wrong. "It's OK," I said. "Just take it."

His eyes bugged. "Do I know you?"

"No, but I want to help you."

"With what?" He slouched in his chair and relived fantasies of life with his wife after the shame of the land deal. He downed his beer.

"Listen," I said with confidence. "You take this ticket. Now."

He shook his head. "Buddy, I don't get it. Why are you doing this to me?"

I picked up the ticket and held it in between his empty beer and his face. "Dammit! Just take this ticket and see what happens!"

He shook his head and said, "This is very confusing."

I left him and celebrated my good deed. He was so drunk that he would forget me, but he would not be too drunk to notice the winning ticket and use it to avoid a bank foreclosure on his home. I spent the rest of my layover trying to sleep in a chair at my departure gate.

***

When I landed in Phoenix the next evening, I was sure that I smelled pretty foul from all the traveling. It had been two days since I'd left Croatia.

I thought I was hallucinating when I got to the security exit and saw Bill, my former handler, waiting for me in an expensive suit, wearing a broad grin.

He put his hand out and said, "Ardor! So great to see you're OK!"

"Bill?" I asked with narrowed eyes. "I'm definitely not re-entering public life!"

He held up a hand of protest. "Ardor! Please!" beads of sweat on his forehead threatened to drip. "I'm here to help a friend. Don't you at least want a ride?"

I asked Source, *What does he want?*

He isn't lying. He represents a friend.

I pictured the bus ride home and grimaced.

"OK. I'll take a ride."

He was short and overweight, and I was tall with long legs, so I strode as fast as I could to the baggage claim so he'd have to huff and puff to remain near me. My plan worked. He was too short of breath to talk.

After we got my bag, I asked, "Where are you parked?"

He smiled. "Oh, no, Ardor. I'm not giving you the ride. I'm headed to LA."

"What's this all about?" I asked.

"C'mon, kid. We all read the headlines. You saved a plane!"

I shook my head but continued to walk with him to the curb.

Minutes later he closed the door from the outside after I'd entered a long black limousine. He told me there was a very important man in there, but I was psychic, so I knew who it was. It was Charles Fay, *the* Charles Fay.

I sat in the limo and stared at him. He was old, but in person he looked even more charming than on television. He had just a few wrinkles and a thick mustache that only a man from his era could pull off. His hair was naturally gray, full, and healthy. He was thin and wore a nice suit.

He was famous in the generation before mine, but I knew him since he was still known as one of the greatest philanthropists in American history.

I also knew his reputation as a secretive man with a vague past. No one remembered him from childhood, and he hadn't even graduated from a high school. The world only knew that he had become famous for inventing a new valve for oil rigs that he patented, and that he never married or had kids. There were more theories about his upbringing than there were for the moon landing or JFK, including rumors that he had no home or office, just an endless supply of money.

He smiled. "Ah-dor Agopian?" he asked in a thick Southern drawl.

"Yup," I said, trying not to let his charismatic eyes affect me. I didn't have a bad feeling about this ride, but that was precisely what made me wary and nervous.

I pinged him, but there was nothing to read. It wasn't like Josip, who could block my pings. His mind was readable, but it was a vessel of stillness, the mind of a calm, worry-free man.

"I will, ah, cut to the chase," he said, still smiling.

The limo swerved. The driver thought, *Nothing but assholes in this city. I can't wait to get back to Dothan.*

I was about to ping the driver, but Charles said, "Ah-dor, I'm sure you know who I *am*, but I'm about to tell you something about what it is that I *do*, and then I will make you an incredible offer." He glanced out the window then continued, "That is, of course, assuming you are not one who practices fraudulence." His eye contact was intimidating, but I nevertheless empathed sincerity in his heart.

"Where is Dothan?" I asked.

His eyes widened. "Why did you ask that?"

159

"Your driver thought, 'I can't wait to get back to Dothan,' so I figured I'd ask."

He reached into his pocket and pulled out a strange-looking device. It looked like a remote. He hit a button and said, "Connect."

The window to the driver's cabin unrolled and the passenger asked, "Yes, sir?"

I recognized the voice. It was Robin, the guy who'd been my security guard in Los Angeles! He'd actually been the only person I'd liked in that whole experience, especially since whenever I pinged him, I always got the thoughts of an honest, good man. He was also funny. Surely his appearance here was no coincidence.

"Robin?" I asked. "No way!"

The driver shook his head and I empathed anger and bitterness. Meanwhile, Robin's vibe was as kind as ever. I relaxed a little in my seat.

Charles smiled. "I have been vetting you for quite some time, Ah-dor."

I pinged him. He wanted to take me to Dothan, Alabama, on his helicopter.

"I've never been in a helicopter before." I smiled with no humility.

He gasped. "So you can!"

"How much proof do you want, Mr. Fay?" I asked. "I'm psychic."

He shook his head and smiled. "Charles, please… call me that."

"Sir?" Robin asked. "You called for a connect?"

"Oh, yes, yes," Charles said. "We have a change in plans. I'm already, I am, ah, sure that…" he looked at me and blushed. "Take us to the helipad in Scottsdale."

"Sir?" Robin asked. "What about the screening seminar at—"

"There will be no need for that." Charles rolled up the window and looked at me. "So, Ah-dor, tell me everything. What exactly is it that you can do?"

"I can read any," I thought of Josip, "um, *nearly* any mind, and I can—"

Source interrupted me, *Stop!*

"And…?" Charles asked with even wider eyes.

I pinged him: *I want to understand. Please let me understand.*

I asked Source, *What is your problem?*

You need to be careful. You are still on Plan B. Watch your words.

Fine, I sighed. *How about you tell me what Charles wants?*

He wants the meaning of life, but money cannot buy enlightened wisdom.

I scrunched my face and asked Charles, "Do you want to be enlightened?"

He laughed and looked at the limousine's bar. "I'm sorry I didn't offer you anything to drink. I don't personally imbibe, but would you like anything?"

I pinged his memories and got flashes of extreme abuse, from both parents, alcohol-related. I thanked my lucky stars that my parents had never hurt me.

I nodded solemnly. "I'm not a drinker either. So let's cut to the chase. What do you want from me?"

He looked offended. "I have a story to tell you."

I nodded.

"You see, when I was a child, my parents abused me. They beat me and kept me in a closet for hours at a time, often neglecting to feed me. Later, they lied about homeschooling and made me work on their failing farm. One evening, when I was eleven, they left for a dance hall and," his eyes narrowed, "it caught fire and they *tragically* died.

"When the police came by the home to look for me the next morning, I was nowhere in sight, for that previous evening, a spirit had spoken to me in a dream. It had explained how to run away, where to hide, and how to survive. I followed those instructions and ended up renting a small room at a gas station house where I was hired to work the pump. I did that for years, until one evening, at sixteen, the same spirit returned in a dream with a vision for a new valve for oil rigging equipment. I again followed the instructions, precisely, but," he sighed, "the spirit has never returned."

I pinged Source, *Is he telling the truth?*

Yes. But please be careful. Telling the truth doesn't make him a good man.

He rubbed his eyes for what felt like an eternity then said, "So, Ah-dor, what do you think? Can you explain my own life to me?"

I was about to answer when Source said, *Don't tell him anything. This is a test.*

I smiled, "Thanks, but no thanks, Mr. Fay. It's not in the cards, so to speak."

He shook his head and reached into the chest pocket of his jacket and took out a sealed envelope that was about four inches thick and handed it to me.

Did you know that for eleven years, until 1945, The United States printed $1000 bills?"

I shook my head.

He leaned forward, grinning. "Want to see an envelope with 1000 of them?"

I couldn't hide my disbelief or my excitement at the thought of all that money.

He nodded. "So, ah, you will help me? I merely want to study what you do."

Source pleaded with me, *Ardor, this is just like Croatia. Don't do this. Just let him take you home. You were only supposed to meet him and prove you're not a fraud. Please listen!*

I pictured a life of poverty and grabbed the envelope.

"Charles, I'm in!"

19
Fays of Our Lives

Dothan, Alabama is a nondescript, unmemorable city that reeks of neither here nor there, unless you are lucky, like me, and got to visit Charles Fay's secret mansion. Then, you would think of it a bit differently.

On the flight out of Phoenix, I signed a forty-six-page non-disclosure agreement that obligated me to be a "lab rat" for two weeks, at which point Charles would deduce if I was or was not "yet another fraud with a knack for misdirection and deception." Either way, I got to keep the envelope of money.

It was already late when we began the two-hour drive from the Tallahassee Airport to Dothan, which had its own airport, but Charles explained that he took every precaution to hide his residence.

We were in an SUV with tinted windows. From the outside it looked like any other twelve-year-old car, but the inside had a flat-screen TV, which Charles used to show me interviews of others who claimed to have clairvoyance.

Watching frauds pretend to have the clairvoyance that Esmeralda and I actually had was embarrassing, and this was just the tip of the iceberg. He had a whole series of other videos with fraudulent non-local viewers, telekinetics, channelers, dowsers, ghost hunters, mediums, levitators, and more.

About two hours into our drive, Charles arched his back and drawled, "Ardor, I do believe it's quite late. You must be starving. I know I certainly am." He smiled and checked his watch. "I'll see that Rosie brings room service for us at the house."

I looked up from an interview with Barb the Kansas City Psychic. She was in the middle of babbling nonsense to the camera after a machine had just used brain scans and audio recordings to prove to her, beyond a doubt, that she was full of it.

Charles was smiling, but his eyes were sad.

Source said, *Don't trust him, Ardor! You shouldn't be here.*

Sorry, but *this money will change my life.*

If you demand to be dropped off at the Dothan Airport, it's not too late!

I longed for a 'Source Remote' to shut it off.

Charles' eyes twitched with concern. "Ardor, what are you doing?"

I looked at him and decided to play dumb. "Huh?"

"I asked what you were doing just now? You looked positively... far away?"

I pinged him. *This boy is not a fraud.*

I pinged Source, *Seriously. What are you so afraid of? What am I doing wrong?*

I got no reply, which worried me, so I tried a different strategy.

Is Charles lying to me?

He's not lying, but you must leave now. You don't want to be his lab rat.

Why?

This isn't a negotiation. Listen, or pay the price.

That sounds like a threat. Are you threatening me?

Do you remember anything you learned in Croatia? Ardor, you have a destiny!

The frustration I experienced from that reply ended any debate on my end. My shitty ex-girlfriend had run off with my son, and I was lonely and poor. Charles might be creepy, but he wasn't going to kill me or anything, and I trusted Robin. How bad could this really be? Two weeks for a million dollars sounded amazing.

I smiled at Charles. "Sorry. I was communicating with—"

He leaned forward with slightly manic eyes. "Source?"

I didn't like his look, but I hid my apprehension. "What was that you said before about dinner?"

He frowned. "Oh. We can choose our dinner…"

I read his mind: *He's a child. Be more patient. Why did he have to be so young?*

I put more effort into my glib attitude and asked, "What are you eating?"

He sighed, leaned back, and stared out the window. "I might just call it the night. I'm old now, and with all this traveling, I quite feel like a moth in a mitten."

I looked at his smooth skinned face and full head of hair. He had crow's eyes and had gone gray, but he didn't act or look old to me. "How old are you?" I asked.

"Why, I don't recall ever being asked that by a *psychic*." He smirked.

I didn't like his insinuation. "OK. You're eighty-two and you think I'm a child."

He smiled. "So you can infer facts *and* read my mind." He looked down and tried to hide his giddy smile. "Well, at least, so you purport."

He thought, *Incredible. I am so close. Finally.*

My palms grew wet. Was I making a big mistake?

I begged Source, *Tell me! What am I doing wrong? Not following advice, over, and over again.*

It was a good point. I had ignored its advice many times, and things had never worked out when I did. What if, thanks to my greed for that cash, I was making another terrible mistake? I tried to stifle my panic as I decided to trust Source and cancel my plans.

I pressed pause on the DVD and said, "Charles, I feel sort of sick."

He cocked his head, "I'm not sure I follow?"

"The car," I pointed out the window, "I get car sick. Can we stop?"

He looked annoyed. *He might be psychic, but he lies like a child.*

"I'm not a kid!" I shouted, like a child.

He called out, "Scott, please pull the vehicle over."

"Yes, sir," The driver answered from the front.

The car slowed, and we pulled to the side of the unlit country road.

I pulled on the door handle, but it was locked.

Charles called out again, "I'm afraid Ardor might have a touch of a gag. Do we have any receptacle for such an occasion?"

"What?" I asked. "I need to get out! I'm gonna puke!" I breathed quickly to help my case, which wasn't too much of a stretch given my panic.

He shook his head. "I don't think that's a wise idea for any of us."

"I'm sick!" I pleaded.

He smirked. "Ardor, I'm not certain about you. Why, I think you'd call an alligator a lizard. "

"What are you talking about?" I shouted.

He stopped smiling. "Are you really sick, Ardor? You seem to be just fine to me." He narrowed his eyes. "I know when I was a boy, I had a fancy for mendacity, if the occasion called for such. Are you certain about your, ah, what you say here is your *weak* stomach?" He donned an intimidating authoritarian smile.

"Let me out!" I screamed.

Robin coughed loudly. I empathed compassion from him, but a terrible fury from Scott.

Charles looked out the window at the dark night, seemingly lost in thought.

168

I wished I could attack him with an orange hue, like Esmeralda. I thought about it, and remembered what Josip had said about "Green versus Orange" and decided to try my take on it. I focused on Charles, not with my eyes, but with my mind's eye. I then visualized a headache and "sent it to him."

He winced and touched his head, but then smiled. *So he's got that too.*

I tried to increase the pain, but as I did this, he reached in his pocket and pulled out his remote again, twisted a dial, and I felt faint.

Source! Please help me! I pinged with desperation.

Nothing happened and my dizziness increased. I shut my eyes as I heard a whine, like from a mosquito, only it was certainly external and in no way from my mind. I squinted through a haze of disorientation and saw Charles wearing a goofy grin as he pointed his remote at me.

"Ardor, let's be more civil. Did you think I only had one oar in the water?" He twisted another dial and I felt pain in my temples.

"Stop!" I screamed. "What do you want?"

"I want you to help me. It's a simple exchange, really."

"Exchange of what?" I asked, pressing my fingers into my temples.

"I want a lot of things, but most of all, I want you to give me access to Source."

"You want… *what*? How can I do that? I can't give you Source!"

169

"Tsk, tsk. Still playing hard to get?" he growled. The whine increased, and I lost consciousness.

***

When I awoke, I found myself in a king-sized bed with silk sheets and bed posts in a glamorous suite of some sort. There was a lot of art that looked fancy, like what I imagined you'd find in European art museums, a large Chinese pot, and an armoire with a mirror. Through an open door, I could see a huge bathroom with a Jacuzzi. The place was larger than the penthouse in Croatia.

I felt groggy and would have stayed in bed and gone back to sleep, but my memories returned, and my heart raced. I jumped out of bed and ran to what I assumed was the door to escape from and pulled the handle. It was locked from the outside.

I tried to ping Source, but I heard the same whine from in the car, and felt some pain and disorientation. I stopped and it faded. My stomach growled. I shook my head and fought off tears of frustration.

I climbed back into bed and heard Charles' slow Southern drawl call out from a speaker in the ceiling.

"Good morning, Ardor. I do hope you are feeling rested, and you find your accommodations lovely, as intended. I also hope we can achieve a fresh start for our relationship, after last night's, ah, unfortunate commotion. What do you say? Can we recompense ourselves with civility?"

I looked around and saw what looked like an expensive lamp. I ran over to it, picked it up, and threw it as hard as I could at the door while yelling, "Your plan will never work!" The lamp ricocheted off the door with a thud and shattered when it hit the floor.

There was a long silence before Charles said, "Ardor. What are we going to do about your temper? Do you think I have the common sense of a goose?"

I shook my head and sat on the bed and sought Source, but the mosquito whine returned, and I lost consciousness.

***

When I awoke, there was an epic breakfast calling my attention from a table across the giant room. Most of the dishes were covered, but I smelled bacon, toasted biscuits, and other delicious, enticing aromas. I wanted to protest my imprisonment, but my feelings of dizziness, fatigue, and hunger took priority.

"There, there, Ardor," Charles' voice called out as I walked to the table.

I uncovered one of the dishes and grabbed a thick slice of perfectly crispy bacon and shoved it in my mouth. I then uncovered the other dishes and didn't even bother to plate any of the food, choosing to shovel different portions into my mouth with a fork.

"Atta boy," he mocked.

In less than ten minutes, I'd eaten the entire serving of eggs, potatoes, Texas toast with butter, a biscuit with honey and gravy, bacon, and something I would later learn is called a dumpling. I could've eaten even more.

I tried to ping Source, but when the whine returned, I stopped pinging.

The speaker crackled with laughter.

"Ardor, I do understand how it is possible for the two of us to have gotten off on what I would refer to as the wrong foot, so I'm going to take a far different approach than I would with an *adult*."

I shook my head with defiance, but I had no leverage to make a deal, so I didn't say anything.

"You are a *guest* in my home, and I take that privilege quite seriously." There was a long pause and when he resumed speaking, his voice was entirely devoid of its usual Southern charm. "Now listen to me once, Ardor, because a fog horn can only warn so much. You know what I want. Now give it to me."

"I don't know how to *give* you it!" I shouted.

He sighed. "What sticks in my throat like hair in a biscuit, is why you continue to lie to me, like I'm a fool. I don't give a lick about what you think. I want you to use your abilities to get me what I need!"

"Source?" I took a quick breath. "Look, I don't know what to tell you. Before I met Esmeralda, I didn't even know I had a connection to it. And now? Now, every time I try to even talk with it, you turn on that damn remote and—"

"Esmeralda?"

I bit my lip. Source had told me not to tell him anything. My face heated.

He laughed. "Now we're gussied up for the ball. Tell me about *Esmeralda*. How do you know her?"

"She's no one. C'mon, I *really* can't give you Source. Can't you just, um, like test me for two weeks, like we agreed?"

"I really thought you were smarter, Ardor, or at least a better clairvoyant. You are such a poor, trusting fool. You think I'm going to play with you and let you go? Come on now. Tell me about your relationship with Esmeralda, and maybe we can talk about leaving."

I had severely underestimated my situation. I wanted to ping Source, but I was afraid of his device.

"Don't cry. Tears won't solve anything. Here, tell you what." The speaker grew quiet and a minute later Charles' voice returned. "I have turned off the signal blocker. Go ahead. Ask Source for help."

I asked Source, *What the hell is going on?*

We warned you not to come here. But we cannot compel you to follow our wisdom. It is your human choice to trust and live in unity with Source, or to go your own way. You have been ignoring us at whim, and the consequences are what they are. What is happening is exactly what should happen when you act with selfish desire. You have a destiny, and it doesn't include selling yourself for a million dollars. Charles knows who Esmeralda is. Anyone interested in Psi science knows of

173

*her, but few know her. He wants her a lot more than he
wants you. And if he develops access to Source, it's bad
news for the world. We wanted so much for you to listen.*

*How could I give him Esmeralda? I don't even
know where she is!*

*Ardor, for your sake, and the world's, don't contact
Source again so long as you are in Charles' home.*

I felt a wave of dizziness and pain in my temples.

"That's enough." Charles said through the speaker.

I stopped pinging and the pain went away.

Charles said, "Why Ardor, I think I have *finally*
stimulated a light bulb in your mind. Now then, let's get
down to negotiations. What I can *offer* you is a million
dollars, and freedom, but I want contact with
Esmeralda. I can, and I will trade you for exactly that,
and I assure you that I'm a man of my word. But, Ardor,
I didn't become Charles Fay by playing nice."

"Trade?" I saw myself in a mirror. I had the
desperate eyes of a caged animal.

His chuckle died.

"Ardor, how much do you love your sister?"

20
Grandpa?

I didn't answer Charles, and he didn't bother to continue the conversation. I sat on the bed and began to figure out my options. Source had warned me against coming here, and had since warned me to be careful now that I was here, especially with connecting with Source itself. I inferred that Charles had developed some powerful Psi machine, but I needed Source now more than ever.

I heard a knock on the door and a moment later the normal-looking door slid horizontally into the wall to reveal that it was two feet thick and made of steel with a wooden façade. I was definitely only going to leave this place with permission.

Robin stood there in his usual attire: a black suit, white dress shirt, and black tie. A few gray hairs sprinkled his thick, black hair, which complemented his compelling, serious, brown eyes. I didn't need Source to know that he was my only hope here.

I didn't really know him, but that whole time in LA he'd always been professional *and* kind. He'd even managed not to roll his eyes at Esmeralda, despite being with the two of us in the penthouse for numerous "Esmeralda moments." I couldn't explain it with evidence, but I trusted him to toe an ethical line.

"Charles wants you to come with me," he said through barely parted lips.

"Where?" I asked, sitting up on the bed.

"To a lab." His gaze conveyed neither safety nor severity.

I glanced at the pistol holstered on his hip.

He noticed and rolled his shoulders back. "It's OK, Ardor."

While I trusted his vibe, he was also my guard, which meant he was an accomplice to my abduction. I lost self-control and pinged Source, *Help me!*

You can trust Robin, but no one else here. Especially the other one.

Scott, the driver, was the other one.

What should I do? I asked.

Stop contacting us. Please. You're putting yourself in more danger.

I sighed. "Hey Robin, I stink. Can I take a shower?"

The speaker crackled. Charles' voice said, "You think the sun rises so you can crow? You had ample time for hygiene. Instead, you elected to break a lamp, slander your host, and take a nap. If you behave like a child, you will be treated as such."

I appealed to Robin with my eyes.

He looked at the floor and said, "Let's go, Ardor." He stepped into the hallway.

I put on my jeans and tried to straighten my hair, but it was a greasy mess. I gave up and entered the hall, and the door slid shut behind me.

The hallway was sterile and well-lit. There weren't any other doors, but at the far end there was an elevator. When we got to it, a ball with a camera extended from the ceiling on a wire to perform a retinal scan.

The elevator was hospital big and when we stepped in, the doors closed, with what seemed like lethal force. There were no buttons. Instead, it surprised me by sliding in all directions: first horizontally, to the left, then down, then to the right, then up, after which the doors opened.

Robin stepped back and said, "Please exit."

I stepped out, expecting him to follow, but the doors shut behind me.

Ahead of me stood Scott, in front of a panel of equipment that reminded me of movie scenes with the NASA space center, only we were alone.

Scott was pale, bald and in his early fifties. He had his hand on his holstered pistol. His cold blue eyes conveyed a comfort with authority. He said, "Put your hands on your head."

I nodded and did as told.

He approached me and gave me a full pat-down.

"This is bullshit!" I said, as he grazed the sides of my testicles over my jeans.

"Language, boy," Charles said from a side room I hadn't noticed. He'd been wearing an expensive suit when I met him, but now he wore well-pressed khakis and a blue button-up collared shirt with a V-neck sweater. He looked like he was returning from a photo shoot for a family Christmas card.

"Who taught you to curse like that, anyway?" he asked, smiling like we were old pals.

I squinted, shrugged, and tried my best to look annoyed. "Movies, I guess."

He shook his head. "How sad. I truly believe our culture has lost its dignity. "

"What do you want from me?" I asked.

"Ardor." He pursed his lips. "This acerbic tone of yours: what purpose does it serve? Now tell me, let's start with this, where is Esmeralda?"

"I have no idea! She left Phoenix without me, and that's all I know."

"Hmmmm. I believe you, so maybe we need to try a different angle."

I kept my mouth shut.

"Tell me about your sister, Alba. Is she like you?"

"No. She's a girl, and a nurse, and she's smart enough to not get into a car with a stranger with a lot of money. Next question, please?"

He cracked his knuckles and shook his head. He then pulled out his remote and tapped it with his long index finger. "I'll remind you that there are two ways to procure information, Ardor."

I involuntarily shuddered and he smiled.

"I'll be more direct. Where is your sister?"

178

"Where? I don't know! I just came back from a shitty trip to Croatia, and I couldn't find her, even with my so-called powers, so you tell me!"

He smiled, "So you think she's in Croatia?" He nodded at Scott.

Scott smiled with beady eyes, walked to a laptop, and typed something.

I pinged Source, *What can I do?*

I heard a cackle from Scott before he announced, "It's working! It said, 'What can I do?'"

Charles' head snapped and he glared at him.

Scott stopped smiling, cleared his throat, and returned to his laptop.

"What are you trying to do, exactly?" I asked.

Charles cracked his knuckles. "I ask the questions, Ardor." He motioned to the door he had entered from, near Scott. "Please follow me."

Scott closed the laptop and stood, placing his hand on his gun.

When we reached the door, another slim camera extended from the ceiling and scanned his retina. The door slid open to reveal a cozy dimly lit study with two plump armchairs. The walls were lined with books and the floor was made of dark oak panels, mostly covered with a beautifully woven red rug.

Charles entered and pointed to the rug. "It's Persian, so please check your shoes. In case they're as dirty as your mouth." He took a seat in the chair that faced the door and motioned for me to sit in the one facing him.

"How much was the lamp?" I joked, taking a seat in the absurdly comfy chair.

"Chump change. Thirty or forty grand." He rolled the 'r' in grand like a true Southerner. "An aide got it at some Sotheby's event."

I nervously tapped my fingers on my knees, trying to look at him, but each time we made eye contact, his complacent smile either made me nervous or angry, at which point I'd look at the bookshelves to try and read the titles.

Charles let me stew then asked, "When did you first know you were psychic?"

"When I was seventeen."

"How?"

I told him the story about Veronica in high school.

He chuckled. "That's great. Now tell me, where is Alba?"

I slapped my thighs. "What is your problem? Are you deaf? I don't know!"

I felt pain in my temples and the mosquito whine returned.

"Please answer my questions." He held his smile.

"OK! I get it!" I shouted.

He nodded and glanced above my head. The pain and noise vanished. "Scott, please come here. We're going to accelerate things and go with Plan C."

Scott entered with an intimidating needle gun, like the ones they use in the military. He pressed my neck with brute force, pushing my head to the side so he could stab me with it. It hurt worse than I feared. I bit my lip until it bled.

After six pulsing stabs, he let go and left the room.

I rubbed my neck while Charles stared at his watch. After a while, he smiled, pulled his sweater back over his wrist and asked, "Where is Alba?"

I felt normal, so I was surprised when I replied, "She's with the Red Cross, in Croatia. I flew there to find her, but couldn't. Then I met this guy Josip—"

He smiled and held up a finger. "Excellent, but please slow down. We're not in a hurry." He again glanced above me and said, "We are recording?" He waited, then said, "Please continue. More about this Josip. What did he tell you?"

I proceeded to tell him everything. *Everything*. I had no self-control.

After I caught him up to speed, he asked, "So Alba is indeed a battery of sorts, for your powers? The source for your Source?" He laughed at his own joke but when I didn't smile he frowned.

I remained quiet. I wasn't in a trance, but I had no desire for anything. I was complacent in a way I'd never felt before. I didn't have a care in the world.

He smiled again and asked, "How are you feeling?"

"I feel nothing."

He leaned forward. "Excellent." His eyes revealed a desperation I hadn't seen before as he leaned in further and whispered, "Tell me then. When am I going to die?"

"Very soon," I said.

He gasped and his face went white. "What? Impossible! You are a fraud!" He shook his head a few times, then stood and walked to a bookshelf. He removed a thick tome. Grunting with effort, he returned and handed it to me.

The book looked prehistoric. It had gilded golden cursive on the front. I had to stare at the fading letters in order to make sense of them. They said, "For Those Who Decided Long Ago." I didn't understand what that meant, but it sounded serious.

"Open it," Charles said.

I slowly opened it to the first page and Charles said, "Go to page 763."

I did as instructed. Page 763 had a sketch of a woman who looked just like Esmeralda, but she was dressed in old-fashioned clothes and the caption said 'Hecilda the Wicked' with the dates 1884-1968. I looked up at Charles and his grin made me cringe.

"That is Esmeralda's mother."

I let out an audible sigh and my eyes grew wide.

He seemed please with my shock. "Turn the page."

Page 764 showed a sketch of a man, and while I'd never met him, I instantly recognized him from memories of trips to my grandmother's house where she had photos of this man. He was her husband, my grandfather, who'd died just before my birth.

The sketch had a caption that read 'Jarkavkiel Agopian' with 1875–1987 underneath, a death date from well *after* my birth. Something was off.

I asked, "Is that…?"

Charles nodded. "Your grandfather. He was a legend, before and during his time. He was the only one who was able to stop Hecilda the Wicked. He became so famous that he had to go into hiding, but, well, it wasn't enough."

He put his hands out and nodded at the book.

I closed it, gave it back to him, and asked, "I don't follow?"

"Esmeralda killed your grandfather."

"She *what*? When? How?"

He glanced at the ceiling. "She was quite the prodigy. Acquired amazing skills at a precocious age." He cracked his knuckles. "She also killed your father."

My mind replayed the details of my father's car accident, as the papers had written it, and I realized that something about the story had never sat right. He'd been a drunk, sure thing, but he'd never really had a problem driving and he wasn't even on a highway near our home that day. A lot of the details hadn't made sense, but I'd written them all off to alcoholism.

He nodded. "Go ahead, ask Source."

I didn't like his smile, but I asked anyway. *Source, Tell me everything.*

183

Source acquiesced. It was true. All of it. Charles was a tyrant, but not a liar. Esmeralda had used mind control to force my father to drive into all those cars. She'd also killed my grandfather, and she'd been tracking me since birth. I didn't know how to process any of this. I asked Source, *Why is Charles asking about Esmeralda if he already knows about her? What is he trying to achieve?*

We told you to not to come here, but the answer is—

Charles clicked his little device, I heard a whine, and Source went away.

21
What, Me Murder?

Charles put the book back on the shelf and spoke to the ceiling. "OK, Scott, we're done here." He looked at me. "Wait here. Scott will return to escort you back to the comfort of your suite." He wasn't smiling as he left.

As soon as he left, I tried to ping Source, but the whine returned, so I stopped, but then I thought that maybe his device only stopped my connection to Source, so I tried to ping Charles' mind, and it worked.

He was a lot more upset than he'd let on. He was thinking, *The boy surely can't be right about everything. I am not to perish soon. It's mere hogwash. He's trying to get in my head, to trick me. I know I am not to die soon. This is nonsense. Nonsense!*

Scott entered. I tried to ping him, but he wasn't thinking anything. He was a man of few thoughts, so I empathed him and felt a disturbing, unfamiliar fury that frightened me. His anger had no boundaries.

He was holding a large, multi-belted restraint device and grinning.

"What's that for?" I asked.

He held the belt above me, cocking his head and squinting his eyes, as if to size me up. He whispered, "You better make this easy."

I hoped he was joking, but I knew better. I'd felt his rage. I smiled, hoping to calm him down. Bad choice. My head whipped to the right as he elbowed me in the cheek. It was hard enough to sting, but probably would not leave a bruise.

"What the hell?" I yelled. The next strike came from his other elbow, this one harder. The chair didn't fall over, even though I had been slammed hard into its side. Tears welled in my eyes. I struggled to hold them in and sit up.

He laughed. "I told you to make this easy, but that doesn't seem to be your style. I'm not a doormat. I'm wise to you. You're not going to mind meld me."

"*Mind meld*? What are you talking about?"

He put his index finger over my lips and gave me a goofy grin.

I shook my head but didn't utter a complaint.

He untangled the restraint and wrapped various straps around my torso. He used smaller bands to adhere my arms to my sides. It wasn't a straitjacket, but it had the same effect.

"This protects all of us, especially you, from yourself," he explained.

I shook my head and tried to speak, but his eyes became clouded with fury.

"Ardor, it will be my pleasure to do anything that is asked of me, including the *full use* of self-defense." He leaned in and I smelled tooth decay. "I take pride in stopping people like you."

I exhaled any remaining pride, closed my eyes, and gave a submissive nod.

"Stand up," he snapped.

I obeyed.

"Turn around."

I did as instructed, and his shoe nailed me in the back of my leg, sending me flying. My head slammed into a wall, and I fell to the ground. My head hurt, but my hip hurt worse. I was blinded by tears, but I heard the door open, then Robin said, "What's going on?" He sounded a bit scared, a tone I hadn't heard before.

"Go away," Scott replied.

I felt a breeze as Robin crossed over me.

"Scott, seriously, what are you doing?"

"We got another one of the problem ones. Kid decided to act up, again."

"Act up?" Robin repeated.

"He tried to escape," Scott said. He sounded giddy.

"That's bullshit!" I yelled.

Scott shouted, *"Shut up!"*

"What *exactly* did he do?" Robin asked.

Scott's voice had an edge to it, but I felt he was trying to play it cool as he said, "Do I have to remind you I'm a full level above you in threat-protocol?"

"OK, Scott. Point taken. But I don't think Charles would approve of this."

I wriggled but the restraints made it impossible to sit up. I yelled, "He elbowed me, twice, and he kicked me to the ground, and I didn't do anything, Robin!"

"Shut up!" Scott yelled again.

"C'mon, Scott," Robin sighed. "He's just a kid. You think you need restraints?"

I twisted my neck so I could see them from the corner of my eye: they were standing close. The frenetic energy was making my empath senses go off the charts.

"You saw what the other one did!" Scott said.

"I spent a lot of time in Los Angeles with both of them. He's a good kid."

"That's enough. I don't care what you think. I don't like to pull rank, but I guess I have to." He raised his voice and said "Initiate threat level 3. Repeat: threat level 3, Psi suppression."

"Are you kidding?" Robin asked.

The lights dimmed before flaring. I then heard what sounded like a loud air-conditioning system start, and the floor hummed, and the mosquito whine came on.

Robin's voice was panicked.

"Scott! He's restrained and not even moving!"

My temples began to squeeze, and a sense of panic flooded my heart. It felt like Esmeralda's mental attacks, but without any colored hue.

I clenched my teeth in pain and said, "Robin, trust me. I didn't do *anything*!"

Robin didn't answer, so I empathed him and was surprised to feel that his heart was strongly connected with mine. This felt nice, but it didn't do anything for the pain I was experiencing. I shut my eyes and used all my strength to listen.

Scott yelled, "Get out of my way!"

"I can't," Robin replied. Protocol or no protocol, this is basically murder!"

"That's your take."

Robin shouted louder. "Seriously. Stop! I won't stand for this!"

"That's not a problem I can't handle, if you force my hand."

Robin's voice became conciliatory. "Scott, this is being recorded on camera!"

"Also not a problem."

I heard the sound of a gun cocking. Robin grunted and I felt a strong vibration on the floor that accompanied the sound of them falling into it.

The crushing pain in my head was constant. I tried to connect with Source, but couldn't.

Still able to empath, the results were not comforting. Robin was giving into fear, and Scott's anger gave him a rush that enhanced his strength.

I gave up hope and this somehow led me to focus on an awareness of my heartfelt connection with Robin. I felt a surge of love and trust, and the next thing I knew, my mind's eye could see the room, as if I were a fly on the wall. It was surreal, but it also felt natural and intuitive. I had never even heard of this ability, but I had it, and it was easy to control.

Now that I could 'see', I saw Scott reaching into his pocket to grab a small knife. I panicked as my mind's vision waned, but I mustered the strength to shout, "Robin, he's getting a knife!"

Robin grunted and used his elbow to hit Scott on the head, which bought him enough time to twist the gun out of Scott's hand. He flipped over and aimed the gun right at Scott's head, and said, "Freeze!"

Scott pulled a small pistol from his left pocket.

Before Scott could fire, I envisioned great pain in his head and he screamed and lowered his gun for a moment, which gave Robin enough time to act.

He squeezed and fired, and Scott fell back to the floor with a dazed look of surprise, then his eyes lost all life, and he slumped over.

Relieved, I gave into the pain from the device, and lost my ability to 'see' the room. The pain worsened, but just as I was about to lose consciousness, Robin yelled, "Terminate level C!" The pain vanished, and the lights returned to normal as the sound and vibration murmured and shut off.

Robin came to my side, and I whispered, "Thank you," but instead of answering me, I felt his hands on my back accompanied with clinking sounds. After a few seconds I realized he was tightening the restraints.

"What are you doing?" I asked.

He kneed me hard in my back.

I winced and asked, "Robin? I thought you were helping me?"

He pressed the back of his hand into my back and leaned into my ear while pulling hard on a restraint, then whispered, "We're on camera. Follow my lead, or we're both dead. I'll save you, but you have to play along." He yanked a restraint so hard I yelped like a dog.

I moved my neck forward just enough to acknowledge our conspiracy.

"Don't you move!" He yelled, hitting me, only not with much force.

He pushed me into the ground then pulled me up by the straps so that I was crouched on my knees. I felt the barrel of a gun poke into my back and next thing I knew he was manhandling me to my feet.

He marched me out of the study, into the main lab room, and over to the other side of it, where there was another door, also made of glass. I hadn't noticed it my first time in the room, not that it would have helped. It led to a rubber room.

He shoved my face into the door and squeezed his head next to mine to hold me in place as he reached across my body to punch a code into a panel. He was clever and whispered each time the button made a noise, so the microphones couldn't hear him. "Just keep playing dumb. I'm not on Charles' side. Never was."

The door pulsed as the lock released. He opened it and threw me with brutal force into the room. He locked me in it and turned around. I squirmed against the wall

191

to get into a sitting position in time to see Charles enter, holding a pistol.

The glass door prevented me from hearing what Charles said to Robin, but Robin looked apologetic as he backed up against a wall. Whatever he was saying didn't seem to work. Charles raised the gun and fired twice at Robin and Robin slumped to the floor.

I pinged Source for help, but got no reply.

22
This Book is Not So Great

My hopes for an end to my imprisonment slumped along with Robin's body as he fell to the floor. Charles glanced at Robin's body before locking eyes with me and smiling. He then turned around and walked to the laptop that Scott had been using. He set the gun down next to it, flipped it open, and typed.

I tried to ping his thoughts, but I couldn't. I had been able to use some sort of energy to hurt Scott and I'd also been able to ping his mind before that remote had done its thing, so I assumed that my chamber was under the same power of that remote and similarly affecting my connection to Source.

After a few minutes, the far wall of my prison vibrated and a thin panel near the ceiling slid open to reveal a flat-screen monitor. The monitor then turned on and smiling into the screen was Josip!

A speaker somewhere in the vaulted ceiling crackled and Josip's voice spilled into the room, providing me with a small sense of relief.

"Surprise?" Josip asked. He had on a loose-fitting button-up dress shirt and was in some sort of expensive looking leather chair in what appeared to be a well-lit office — I wondered if he was still in Croatia. I thought for a minute it might be an impostor, but then he pulled out his familiar, worn pipe and took a deep puff.

With merriment in his eyes, he said, "Charles show you Great Book, yes?"

Through the same speaker, Charles' Southern drawl interrupted us: "Indeed, Mr. Krzyinski, despite our divergence of *strategy*, I adhered to your request."

Josip laughed. "You followed orders, for once!"

I was in no mood to laugh. "Josip, what is going on? Charles is a madman! He killed Robin, and Scott tried to kill me, and—"

Anger flashed across his face before he regained composure. "You must be mistaken. Calm down."

Normally being told to calm down upset me, but I remembered Robin's words, to "Play along," and I decided to trust Josip and do my best to follow his directions. I nodded. "Sorry."

He returned my nod. "Charlie, give him book!"

I heard several beeping noises as Charles punched buttons into the panel on the door of my cell. He had the same book from before in the crook of his armpit. He was a slender, elderly man, so the heavy tome seemed to bother him a lot as he tried to punch buttons.

After entering the code, a panel next to the door slid open. It was slightly larger than a mail slot. He tried to push the book through it, but it was too big.

I had to stifle a grin as he huffed and puffed like a frustrated child.

He muttered, "Well doggone it, this damned thing won't fit!" He tried again to cram it through, a laughable effort in futility.

Josip laughed derisively. "Just open door, silly!"

Charles looked embarrassed and angry. I recalled from earlier that the device he'd invented couldn't stop me from empathing. I empathed Charles and was surprised to find out that he wasn't angry with me. He carried an intense hatred for Josip. I wasn't even on his emotional radar. They must have had some history and it made me trust Josip even more.

Josip said, "Stop wasting time. Open door and give book to boy already!"

"I will do no such thing!" Charles shouted.

"Ohmygosh!" Josip rolled his eyes. "I spend hours with boy in Croatia shithole with no protection, and no problem. But you need to lock him in cage like animal? Fine, Charlie Fay. Be coward and turn on Psi block device like Hollywood movie." He nodded at me and smiled. "What a big, scary boy he is. Woooooh!"

I smiled at Charles, with pure smug, and asked, "Are you scared of me?"

He pressed his remote and said, "Don't act like you don't fear me, boy!"

I winced from the pain from his device and took a step back.

Josip cackled. "See? Boy is scaredy-cat."

"I don't see you taking any chances!" Charles shouted. "So safe behind your monitor!"

Josip's face grew serious, and his voice lost all its melody. "Mr. Fay, you will not shout at me again. Remember, you work for us, not other way around."

Charles flung his hands over his head and let go of the book. It landed on his toe. He shouted, "Damn it!" and slammed his fist into the window between us. The Plexiglas quivered.

Josip's voice resumed its normal sarcastically sparkled lilt. "See? If you did not kill Robin, you would still have someone to help carry this *big, heavy* book!"

Spittle flew from Charles mouth. "Robin murdered Scott, and the boy helped him do it! I do not intend to give him the chance to do the same with me."

"That's not true!" I shouted. "Scott was trying to murder us!"

Charles kicked the book into the frame of the door and pulled at his hair. "I am not one to tolerate disorder!" He pointed at Robin's body. "You think I take any sort of satisfaction in losing Robin?" He shook his head and glared at me. "Nothing is worse than a wolf in sheep's clothing." He glanced at the book and straightened his posture. "Besides, Josip, Why keep him alive? I got what I needed. He told me *everything* we wanted to know about Esmeralda. I got the info you requested, so now I get him, right? A deal's a deal!"

Josip put his hand in front of the camera so I could only see the edges of his room and whispered to someone off screen. He eventually removed his hand and said, "Charlie, it is not OK to kill boy. We agreed that you could run tests, but is not OK to hurt him. OK?"

Charles nodded and swore under his breath.

Josip's eyes briefly glanced away before he returned his gaze to the camera. "Good. Also remember that boy must know full stakes, or we all suffer, right?"

Charles smiled sarcastically. "Yes, yes. Of course."

Josip nodded. "Good. Now open door and give book. Let's get show on road!"

Charles shook his head and returned to the laptop where he'd set his gun. He picked it up and returned to my cell door. He nodded at me. "OK, Ardor. Step back against the wall."

I squinted and reluctantly followed his instructions.

Josip said in a mocking voice, "Lady and Gentleman, introducing Mr. Charles Fay!"

Josip was pushing his buttons and I liked it. I empathed Charles and got pure rage.

Charles punched a code into the panel and the door lock clicked. While keeping the gun pointed at me, he tried to use his shoe to push the book to the side in order to make room to open the door, but thanks to the weight and size of the book, and his frail, aging body, he was going to need his hands to move it.

He looked at me and said, "Turn around!"

Remembering how I had earlier been able to witness the room from my mind's eye, I turned around and tried to do it again and succeeded. I could now see

Charles as he walked in the room, using both hands to move the book.

In this same vision, I was able to see Josip silently mouthing something on the screen. I could tell he was trying to talk to me, but I had never tried to read lips. It wasn't easy, but after several tries, I finally got the gist. He was mouthing something like, "His gun has blanks."

Charles' attention was focused on moving the book, so I turned my head slightly towards the TV and my vision returned to normal. I winked at Josip.

Josip flashed a quick smile of acknowledgment.

Charles dropped the book on the floor and pointed the gun at me. "Stay put while I exit."

If I'd read Josip's lips wrong or he was lying, I was sure to die, but this was my only chance, so I went with my intuition and trusted Josip. It was now or never!

I turned and ran towards Charles at full speed. I was lanky, with nearly no muscles to speak of, but he was old, so I wasn't scared about one-on-one combat. I was only scared of my possible failure at reading lips.

He saw me coming and looked surprised, but also happy. I empathed an excitement for an excuse to kill me and felt even better about what I had to do.

He squeezed the trigger three times and the sounds of three shots created a ringing in my ears, but nothing struck me.

He looked shocked, but not enough to give up. He swung the gun into my face, hard, and the blow sent me flying back into the rear wall of the poorly padded cell.

My pain was severe, and I felt sort of spacey. Instead of feeling a rush of adrenaline, I wanted to fade into the pain and go to sleep. I knew this was not an appropriate response, and figured it was from the drugs he'd given me earlier. I *knew* that deep down I wanted to live, so I fought against the pain and fatigue and ordered my feeble body to stand. It worked, but as I rose, the edge of Charles' gun again struck me in the face, and I fell back to the floor.

I put my hands over my face to protect me from what I assumed would be more gun smacks when I heard Charles say, "Good thing I have a backup!"

I opened my eyes and saw him aiming a much smaller pistol at me.

"Oh no! We do not know of this!" Josip shouted.

I kicked my leg out and tried to trip Charles as he fired a real bullet at me.

He lost his balance and missed, but stayed on his feet. "Nice try." He sneered, aiming the gun at me again.

I shut my eyes and braced for death, but instead I heard Charles scream. I opened my eyes to see Robin putting Charles in a chokehold. He was wriggling with great effort, but Robin was an absurdly fit, expert bodyguard, so it wasn't going to work.

Charles dropped the pistol on the ground, just a foot from me. I leaped forward and grabbed it. Robin wasn't having any trouble securing him, but I'd just nearly died and decided to let my emotions take hold of me. Watching Charles kick and scream produced a terrible surge of anger in me. It felt hot, foreign, and forbidden, which made it even more tantalizing. I raised the pistol and aimed it at his chest.

Josip shouted, "Ardor! No! Stop! Don't do this!" with a sense of urgency that might have worked a few moments earlier, but it was too late. I wasn't willing to listen to anyone.

I squeezed the trigger and fired a bullet into Charles' chest. He winced and his body flopped loose in Robin's arms as thick blood soaked into his shirt.

Exhausted, I took a seat on the floor, still holding the gun. I felt like I was dreaming and wondered if it was from the drugs, or what I'd just gone through.

Robin let go of Charles' and stared at me with disappointment.

Josip's voice crackled on the speaker, "Boy… oh boy. We did not expect this."

Robin nodded and looked down at Charles' body and sighed.

Josip said, "Yikes. This is not good."

"He was trying to kill me!" I exclaimed.

Josip sighed. "Yes, but he was also only person who create and operate a very important machine."

"You mean that thing that almost killed me? Who cares?"

"That machine was going to change the world. It was going to prove our science. It was to provide peace. To stop wars. To end generations of violence!"

"You're telling me that Charles was *helping* us?"

"Yes, Ardor. That is what I am telling you. He was not a good man, but he worked for us and, well, when Charles died, his machine did too."

23
Incomprehensible

I was in shock. I never thought, in a million years, that I would kill a man. It had been self-defense, but my mind and body were not on board with any of this. I was a murderer. I had killed. I felt tremendous remorse, even though I knew Charles had intended to kill me.

After minutes of icy silence, Josip told Robin to take me back to the elevator, where he took me to a wing I hadn't seen. He sat me at a giant table and offered me lunch, but I shook my head. I was too emotional to eat.

He then spoke aloud to some sort of microphone system and a large flat-screen TV slid into view across from me with Josip's absurdly large face on it.

He said, "Hello, Ardor. I know I make jokes about how you are sensitive, but even though I am upset that Charles die, I do not think it is easy to kill man. So we have to move on and do the best we can. I mean, we know this will happen, it was just eventual, after, not before, we finish machine and use it to—"

From the corner of my eyes, I saw Robin make a discreet gesture to Josip, and he stopped talking. I pinged Robin and it worked. They must have shut the machine off. He thought, *He didn't read that chapter*.

I rubbed my eyes and stretched my face in a fake yawn, trying to feel human. Everything felt strange. Even speaking felt strange. I had killed someone. I didn't care about what they cared about. I didn't care about any books, not even one with my family in it.

I felt a tug in my heart, a gentle, sad one, and gave in to its demands. I cleared my throat, because that's what people do in the movies before they say serious things. "Guys, I'm sorry, but this isn't for me. I can't join you in whatever weird super hero movie you are making here. I'm not your guy, I'm just—"

"We know!" Josip said with disdain.

I pinged him, but it didn't work. I forgot he could block me. "You know what?" I asked.

He frowned. "Baby! You are big baby. You are bad at Psi, you are bad at following instructions, and you make bad decisions. In psychic world, you barely crawl. Esmeralda is rocket scientist, compare with you. You are not even close match, but," he gave a classic smirk, "you are next best thing. So we need you."

I shook my head. "Again, sorry, but I'm not your guy. Especially if I'm a *baby*." My voice sounded more agitated than remorseful.

"We do not care!" he shouted.

Robin shot him a look to shut up, but it didn't work.

Josip continued, "I do not care for feelings! I care for mission!"

203

I slammed a fist on the table. "I'm not helping you on any mission! You say I make bad decisions? Well, here's my first good one. I'm going home."

Source piped in, *Ardor! They don't need your help.*

What are you talking about? They just said they need me!

They need you for publicity, but nothing else. You're a pawn.

Josip shook his head, "Ardor! You understand nothing! Foolish boy. We do very much work to keep you *away* from Alba. So you can complete prophecy."

I pushed my chair back and stood. "You know where she is?"

"Of course we do," he said with a stoic face.

I lost my balance and fell back into my chair. I'd lost my will to exist, and my body was following suit. I was so tired of dealing with people. And now, to learn that I was a pawn, and everyone was using me? I'd rarely felt this angry.

I asked Source to explain things to me and it said, *When I told you not to go to Croatia, it was to prevent a bad timeline from emerging. But you went anyway. The FRH is a worldwide organization, and they have agents everywhere, so they stepped in to prevent you from finding Alba. Charles was a part of that plan, but—*

The FRH? What is that? And what plan? I asked.

It will be easier if you let Josip explain things to you. You can trust him.

I shook my head, sighed, then said to Josip, "Tell me everything. Now."

Robin took his hand off my shoulder and nodded at the screen.

"What you want to know?" Josip asked.

"Let's start with *the FRH*: What the hell is that?"

He rolled his eyes. "Oh, so now you are back on team? No more pouting?"

"I'm serious. Fill me in. And start with this FRH thing. What does it stand for?"

Robin chuckled and Josip smirked.

"What's so funny?" I asked with narrowed eyes.

"It is nonsense name, so it is funny joke. FRH has no meaning. It's just the name someone picked long before any of us were alive. But it is a group of, how-you-say, interested minds. It is group that tries to keep balance in the Universe."

"This sounds insane. Do you hand out tinfoil hats?"

Josip didn't smile. He looked at Robin and said, "OK. Time for more book."

***

Two hours later, my mind was clear, but my heart was heavy. Josip had counseled me as Robin flipped to and pointed at various parts of that same book from before, which they all called 'The Great Book'.

Apparently, the Universe has always had humans with the ability to mentally intercept and isolate the variables of time and space. It is no coincidence that every culture had intuits, prophets, and seers. Of course, many faked it, but not all of them did.

There had always been people just like Esmeralda and me, born with a sense of how to use Psi energy the way a sculptor knows how to use clay. Many of us had been able to read and even harm minds, to empath, and do all sorts of other 'tricks' that people marvel at or fear, and often pay for. The weird part was that every human had this innate ability, and could thus master these same elements, they just weren't born into a family or culture that encouraged them or helped them, so I was one of the lucky few who had that encouragement, as well as some highly sharpened abilities at birth. It was just like how some children knew how to play musical instruments without lessons, but most humans learn to play them with training.

The green energy I was tapping into was one part of a spectrum that was balanced by other colors, like Esmeralda's orange. For no reason anyone could understand, orange energy had been typically used for what we judge as evil purposes, but my green energy was just as capable of harm, which explained how I'd hurt Scott. All energy was equally capable of harm and good. The user made the difference.

The Great Book had many prophecies in it, but the one that concerned me was the only one the FRH cared about, and I could see why. It said I was supposed to prove to humanity that my powers were real, so the cynical, modern world could accept it, before it was too late. And as if that wasn't enough pressure, I was supposed to do all this before Esmeralda could use my son as a battery to enhance her powers in order to wreak havoc on the world as no one had done before her.

I felt a lot of pressure, and I didn't like any of it. I'd never asked for any of this, and I was now so far into it that I felt like I had no choice. It felt ironic. I was here to prove to humanity that free will exists, and we should be using it with our intuition to make our lives more meaningful, yet I felt like I had no free will of my own.

Esmeralda and her clan were bold, innovative, and, in my opinion, quite evil. They'd figured out how to kill my grandfather and father so Esmeralda could find me, seduce me, and use me to procure the ultimate weapon that no human should have, an allegiance between orange and green energy for malignant purposes.

Our child would be the first child ever born unto an orange and green practitioner. And Alba was also important. She was not psychic, but she was a powerful battery for all things Psi. She was supposed to support me and enhance my powers to help me stop Esmeralda. No other psychic in recorded history had ever had a sibling so powerful. It was the Universe's attempt to even the odds in the battle between orange and green.

Meanwhile, Charles had been working on a machine that could "prove" I was psychic. The machine detected quantum material that is released when humans use Psi powers, and he'd been in the final stages of development. I thought his work was detestable, since it had led to the machine that disabled my powers *and* caused me pain, but those had been pet projects. They hadn't been sanctioned by the FRH.

I didn't want to admit it, but I had finally been convinced that Charles had been working towards a goal that would help me, and when I killed him, I'd killed that hope. Like it or not, his life had been tied into my prophecy, and I'd ruined that part of the plan.

The good news, if you wanted to call it that, was that even without Charles, the prophecy maintained that I was still supposed to bring Psi science to the masses in order to promote world peace. The idea was that if everyone could read minds, then no one could lie, and that would end most of the wars and oppression that plagued humanity. I was supposed to end deceit!

***

"You are on same page now, Ardor?" Josip asked.

"No." I smiled. "But I'll go along with this if it means I get to leave this place."

"Good."

"So what's next?" I asked.

I heard a cough, off screen, and Josip looked away from the camera before saying, "OK, Ardor, I think we are done now. Uh, yes. We are done."

The screen went blank, and I looked to Robin for help.

He rolled his eyes then shut the book and tugged it out of my arm's reach before sitting down opposite from me at the large table. He rubbed his eyes and said, "Ardor, I don't know what to tell you."

"Excuse me?" I asked, jaw slightly agape.

He pulled out his phone, checked it, then frowned. He stood, avoiding eye contact. "I, uh, I gotta take this. Just sit tight." He then left me alone with The Great Book.

I waited for what I thought was a minute, to make sure he wasn't rushing back, then opened the book and looked for its Table of Contents, but it didn't have one. I couldn't remember which pages Robin had flipped to, and the book had more than 8,000, so I closed my eyes and asked Source for guidance.

Are you sure you want to know your full destiny?

I thought I did. I'm supposed to save the world.

Yes, but are you sure you want to know how?

Of course. How can I save the world if I don't know how to do it.

You could listen to us and follow your wisdom.

I shrugged. *Yeah, that sounds great and all, but I'll just read how to do it, if you don't mind.*

It is fine to do it this way, but once you know this, it's going to change you.

What do you mean?

Some things are not fun to know. Sometimes it's easier to be surprised.

Yeah, yeah. Whatever. I don't care. I can handle whatever it says.

OK. Then turn to page 6,453.

I looked at the door Robin had left through. I wasn't going to get any warning if he came back, but I figured he was the moron who'd left me with the book, so I opened it to page 6,453.

It was a new chapter. The title said: *How the World Ends.*

I got a strange feeling that I was about to understand *exactly* what Source had been trying to get at, but I read on, curious as ever.

It is decided that no one human shall inherit the predetermined fates, and only the free will of a soul can opt in or out of predestiny, but if green and orange energies wage war without balance, it is such that the world must start over, and all souls must re-experience the balancing of a retro-cyclical experience.

I looked up and shook my head. I wasn't a great reader, but even if I was, I doubted this made any sense to anyone. It sounded like nonsense.

What the hell...? I asked Source.

If you don't find your son and you don't stop Esmeralda from corrupting him, everyone is going to die. This isn't really a big deal, in a Universal sense, for Earth is but one planet in one dimension, but with your help, the human race has a fresh chance for peace, happiness, and an end to human-caused suffering.

Um, I feel like that's a lot of pressure! I replied.

Not really. All you have to do is listen to us and things should work out.

I looked at the book and flipped the pages until I got to the end of the chapter.

Source said, *No Ardor! Don't read more. You've learned enough.*

Look, if I'm supposed to save the world, I don't think there should be any secrets. So either I read what I want to, or I'm going back to Phoenix.

You have free will, but you sure don't understand cause and effect.

Yeah, yeah. I get it. Over and over again, you're such a broken record. Just leave me alone. I got this.

I looked down and read the last page.

For all to end well, it is ordained that green must stop orange, at all costs, or the Orange-Green child will succeed to destroy all that is. No exceptions.

24
Alba Returns

My first reaction was to give up hope and guzzle a mug of cynicism. I was pretty sure I'd read the last part correctly, so I was confident that the book had just told me that if I didn't kill Esmeralda, my own son was going to destroy the human race.

Source had been trying to tell me this for a long time. That my life purpose was not about me, but for the world. I was to make sacrifices, like it or not.

I was OK with trying to stop Esmeralda, but to think that my son was evil? That was too much. I had been hoping since his conception that we would be able to spend life together, as family, but now that seemed impossible, and I spiraled into despair. I felt a longing for love. I wanted to be loved and to have someone to love. But when I thought about it, the truth is there was no one in my immediate life to love. Alba was God-knows-where, and I was trapped in this bizarre mansion.

Tears welled in my eyes as I revisited my past to search for meaning and hope. I'd once had a grandma who loved me, but she'd succumbed to cancer.

Then there were my parents, who'd basically been vague characters in my life. I could describe them and their mannerisms and the basic facts of their lives, but neither had ever shown any capacity to love me, or Alba, for that matter.

I reflected on other fleeting moments of love in my life. Brian had loved me, as only a good friend can, and I felt like I'd also blown that relationship. If only I'd been able to keep myself in line, he wouldn't have been scared by my powers, and maybe I could have avoided moving in with Esmeralda. I wondered what he was up to and if I would be able to track him down when all this was over to rekindle our friendship.

What was love, and why did I need it? I knew this question was above my paygrade, but I still wanted to know how it worked. Instead of feeling bitter or walking into another bout of self-pity, I thought calmly about all of this and came to a natural understanding that love wasn't something any of us were entitled to, but it was certainly to be valued and respected, and that was going to be my take away from all of this. I needed to work harder on cultivating love in my life.

Since my grandmother's death, only Alba had loved me, but she was my sister, so I'd somehow discounted it, even now. Her love was great, but I wanted to be *in love* with someone. I wanted someone to confide in and gain support from, someone who chose me, and I chose back. It felt terrible to think that I was supposed to save the world without any help or support, with no one to love me and to love in return. I needed to change this. Even if it was a friend, I needed more love in my life.

I looked at the door Robin had left through and hoped he'd return. I felt like I was going to suffocate from this loneliness. I needed a friend.

I asked Source, *Why am I all alone?*

You don't have to be. You are young. Give it time. Until then, you must find your son, before it is too late.

Too late?

To stop him.

I sighed.

Source said, *Ardor, it's less complicated than you think. This life is not for you. It's for others, but you'll be rewarded in many ways you cannot currently conceive of.*

I was crying when Robin returned. He was smiling until he saw my face and his jaw quivered. I empathed him and felt a rush of compassion, exactly what I'd been seeking. I guess I did have some support.

I sniffled and dabbed my tears with my sleeve.

Robin said, "You OK?"

I sniffled and faked a smile. "I guess so."

He turned on the TV, and Josip appeared.

Josip said, "Now you cry for good reason. You understand value of human life." His smile was tender, and I couldn't empath him, thanks to his blocking abilities, but I nevertheless felt his support and it stoked a small fire in my heart.

I wiped my eyes again and said, "Guys! I'm ready now. I, uh," I glanced at The Great Book. "I cheated and I did a little extra reading."

Josip's eyes widened. "You did what?"

I smiled, feeling like I was finally in the big leagues and allowed to play ball.

Josip shook his head, bit his lip, and whispered to someone off screen.

I looked at Robin. "What did I do wrong?"

He looked down at his hands.

Josip said, "So it is… is understood, yes? You… understand all? You read all of it?"

I nodded. "Yup. I'm heir to a legacy of psychic shit, so is Esmeralda, and—"

Josip looked like he was on the verge of tears.

"What on earth?" I asked.

He didn't move a muscle.

"What's wrong?" I asked. "I know it's a big task, but I can handle it. I'm in!"

"I am… Ardor, I feel real sadness, for you. I am sorry you have life where you know… where you know your future. To know that your own son must die…I can't imagine how that feel."

My heart sank. "What?" I hadn't read anything about killing my son. I entered into a trance.

"Ardor?" Josip asked.

I continued to stare into space and said nothing. When I'd read "at all costs," I thought that meant killing Esmeralda, not my son. I didn't know what to think.

215

Josip cleared his throat. "Ardor, it has to, it had to be this way. In order for—"

"*What* are you talking about?"

Josip's eyes showed remorse I'd never seen before.

"This is awful!" I screamed. "I'm screwed at every turn. First I fall for some psycho, and then she uses me to 'create' my son! My one shot at…" I trailed off.

My one shot at what? I'd never really thought about why I wanted to know my son. I just instinctively knew that he was someone I wanted to care for and love, and protect, especially since I'd never been protected. But what was I really angry about? I guess I was just upset at another twist and turn in the increasingly dark story of my prophetic life. Why couldn't I be normal? Why couldn't I just get a job, fall in love, make a family, and enjoy my life, like every other person on Earth?

I felt so much self-pity. I'd suffered from drunk, absentee parents, both of whom had died when I was pretty young. I felt like life was one unfortunate event after another, and nothing more. I felt so empty, yet also so full of emotions. And these emotions were overwhelming me now when I most needed perspective and an ability to remain calm.

I took a deep breath and thought about my anger. It was warranted, but it was still pointless. I could get as mad or sad as I wanted, and it wasn't going to change anything. There was a prophecy that said I had to kill my son, but I'd read it differently. Was it possible that the prophecy was open to interpretation, or was I just a bad reader?

According to 'fate,' I'd been born in order to impregnate the world's *latest* evil psychic so I could later battle her and kill my own son. Was I really supposed to accept all this "for humanity?" Surely, there had to be an alternative, within my control.

A coldness consumed me, and I felt a bitter hatred for 'How Things Are' when compared to 'How They Should Be.'

I was about to ask to leave when Josip said, "Ardor. I think I know what can help. Would seeing Alba help?"

"Alba?" I asked. "What do you mean?"

The camera zoomed out to reveal Alba sitting next to him. She was dressed in a suit with makeup that was starting to run, thanks to some big, lumpy tears.

I was consumed with confusion, but seeing her did remove a shred of ice from my heart. But then it occurred to me that if she knew Josip, it meant she probably knew about a lot of other things that had been hidden from me.

My humiliation from her betrayal was too much to handle. I shut my eyes, and said, "You're in on this too? Are you kidding me? I flew all the way to Croatia to find you, and all that time, you were hiding from me?"

"Ardor, wait," she said. Her voice sounded painfully constricted.

I shook my head and refused eye contact.

"Ardor... please, listen to me," she begged.

I looked at Josip and said, "This is too much. My own sister is some sort of… some sort of spy?" I didn't know what else to say. I wanted to give them an ultimatum, but I didn't have one. I took a long, deep breath, and looked down and talked to the table. "I think there's been a mistake. When I said I read ahead, I—"

"You let him read *everything*?" Alba asked Josip with wide eyes.

"What the hell?" I screamed again. "Why does everyone treat me like a child?"

Josip's voice became angry. "Because you are child! You act like child, you talk like child, you think like child, you cheat and read book like child. You are exactly definition of child. Many child is less child than you, especially in East. You finger-point like child. You act actual age, we talk different." He shook his head then coughed loudly into his fist.

I looked at Alba, accidentally, as a reflex, even though I wanted to ignore her, but I'm glad I did, because the atonement in her eyes was the only cure for my suffering. The heat in my body waned and wave of relief replaced my fury with a calm sadness. I'd never thought I'd feel this way, but I preferred this sadness to the fury I'd previously felt.

I slowly nodded. "OK, guys, I'm calming down."

Alba exhaled slowly and I saw Josip try to hold back a smirk.

I said, "I'm going to give you a chance." I looked at Robin then back at the screen. "All of you. You have

218

one chance to explain how I'm supposed to think it's OK for my sister to collaborate behind my back. But either way, there is no way in hell I'm going to kill my son."

No one spoke and I sensed confusion all around.

Finally Josip broke the ice. "Look, Ardor. I understand that you feel duped, but Alba has been following her own prophecy, so what we tell you next, you have to understand, that it was all part of, it is all part of plan for whole world. A good plan."

"Let me guess, you want to kill me too?" I asked, staring off screen with anger.

"No. Of course not!" Alba interjected.

Josip broke in. "But there is more. Much more than you seem to know. Your sister, she can block what you do, what Esmeralda does, what anyone does with Psi energy. And she always know this. Since she was child because your Babushka, I mean, Grandmother, she tell her everything." He reached into his pocket, pulled out his pipe, and cleaned it.

I stared at Alba like she was a space alien. "Granny told you everything?"

"Everything," Josip confirmed, looking at his pipe.

I looked at Alba. "So why would you lie to me? All those times? I asked you so many times about this!"

She nodded. " I lied, Ardor, but I wanted to tell you, and now I can tell you everything. With no secrets."

"What more is there to tell me? Am I adopted? Is Josip Santa Claus?"

No one laughed.

Alba asked, "Are you calm enough to hear the truth?"

I contemplated then nodded. "I guess so."

The television went blank, and Josip and Alba entered from a side door.

25
Interesting Times

Alba's face revealed little emotion, so I decided to dive inside and see what was going on. However, when I tried to ping her, I was blocked. Instead of sulking, I paid attention to what it felt like to be blocked and realized how often Esmeralda had been doing it to me. I had a lot of catching up to do.

Alba took a step forward and said, "I'm sorry, Ardor. I'm so sorry."

Hearing her voice created a heaviness in my heart. She was family, and the only family I had, so there wasn't any point in holding a grudge.

I looked her right in the eyes and asked, "How could you lie to me about all of this?"

She looked at Josip.

He nodded and put out his hand like a host guiding his guests into his home.

Alba took a step towards me and said, "I had to."

"But my son!" I started to cry. For the first time in my life, my own tears didn't embarrass me. "I just want to raise my son! How could you have known all along that I was not only going to have a son, but that I'd have

221

to kill him, and not tell me? That's some seriously evil shit, Alba. I thought we were family."

I was met with defiant eyes that warned me to watch my words. "Ardor! I did no such thing. I simply did my best to uphold the prophecy and keep Esmeralda away from you, from killing you. Besides, are you saying your son was more important than the balance of our Universe? When did you learn to be so selfish?"

I felt my skin get hot. "Hold on. You just said 'was,' like he's already dead. I thought the prophecy was that I had to kill him?"

Josip blurted, "Alba, we were supposed to give him time."

"Give me time for what?" I shouted.

Alba and Josip exchanged uneasy glances which I took as a confirmation of my worst fear: Someone had already found Esmeralda and killed her, with our son in her womb. I was speechless.

Josip put a finger in the air. "Look. We are very, very far off track. We need to get back on same team."

My hands formed fists, and a terrible anger brewed inside me. I tried my best to speak without shouting and managed to say, "This is unbelievable. I can't believe you've been lying to me for all these years, Alba. And to find out now, that someone already killed Esmeralda, and my son? This is just too much. Too much."

Josip nervously patted his pockets to search for his pipe, Robin stared at a wall, and Alba looked like she was trying to hold back tears, but I didn't care about any of them. I wanted to crawl into a hole and die. My son was dead, and my whole life was a lie. I saw no point in continuing this conversation.

"Let me go," I said. "I want to go home."

"Guys," Alba said, looking only at me, "I want to talk to Ardor alone."

Josip opened his mouth then shut it and he and Robin left through the side door.

When it shut, Alba burst into tears. She sobbed so dramatically that it sounded like she was dying. Her chest heaved in a way that almost seemed like she was acting. She even leaned on the table for support.

I ran to her, to help hold her up, and it turned into a hug. She was heavy in my arms. Her heaving became heavier, at first, until she seemed like she was forgetting to breathe, but then she let out a long, loud sigh and cried a little softer, the way she'd cried at times when we were growing up.

She removed herself from my arms and sat.

I sat next to her, and she took my hand and held it firmly and looked away.

"Alba?" I asked, finding myself overwhelmed with empathy for her sadness.

She whispered, "You don't understand."

"Try me," I whispered back, squeezing her hand.

She returned the squeeze. "Do you really want to know *everything*?"

"There's *more*?" My chest tightened.

"Well, for starters, Grandpa didn't die when we were young."

"I know. I saw it in the book."

"No. You don't understand. Even that was a front. They were getting too close, so we had to fake it."

"They? We? What the hell are you talking about?"

"The FRH. The team. We had to hide him to protect Dad, you, and me."

I tried to ping her and was again blocked.

She squeezed my hand and smiled. "I can block you easily, Ardor. Always could."

"So you're telling me Grandpa is still alive?"

"No. Esmeralda found him and killed him. I thought you read the book?"

"I did, but this is confusing. Why'd you say I don't understand then? And...wait a second. For just how long have you been working with the FRH?"

"Since a little after Dad died."

"*What?* When we were still in high school?"

She looked at the floor and blushed.

"So what about nursing school, the Red Cross, and Croatia...?"

"They were real, but also a cover-up. I had to deceive a lot of people, not just you. And it worked. Esmeralda didn't think I was psychic until we became friends, and that was also a ploy, so we could keep tabs on her, which was working until—"

"Wait! Hang on. Back up. I mean, you just said... you've been talking to Esmeralda?" I felt myself starting to tremble with anger.

She let go of my hand.

"Please ping me," she said. "I can't... I don't want to talk about this."

I pinged her and her mind erupted with a flood of information.

When they met on my birthday, Esmeralda had tried to get Alba to switch sides and work with her. Alba had pretended to agree, but it wasn't a choice. The FRH had ordered her. The FRH wanted a double agent. The only other person who knew was Charles Fay, also a double agent, who'd worked with Esmeralda to build his machine.

So when Esmeralda was looking for a place to hide after she left me in LA, Alba had encouraged her to come stay with her in Croatia, where she was also working, undercover, as a nurse.

Alba blocked me again.

"What?" I exclaimed. Why'd you stop letting me ping you? I want to know what happened next?"

"That's too recent. Too painful. Sorry."

"Was it you? Did you murder Esmeralda?" I asked.

She shook her head. "I've said too much already."

I frowned and turned away. I wanted to know, once and for all, about my son and Esmeralda, but no one was being straight with me. I felt annoyed and angry, but

225

there was nothing I could do to discover the truth since Josip and Alba could block me. I had to trust them.

Alba took my face with one hand and forced me to look at her. "Look. It wasn't easy, and it wasn't fun. All these years, lying to you. Especially when we made plans for your twenty-first birthday, and I had to pretend when I visited you at the mall that I didn't know... I mean, do you have any idea what it's like to lie to *you* Ardor? You're not only psychic, but a *legend* in the community. You've been prophesied for centuries in The Great Book! However, if you knew any of that, then Esmeralda would've pinged it, so we had to repeatedly deceive you, to keep us all safe. Even Grandma's training was risky."

"How are you keeping me safe? I just nearly died in some freaky lab, and you knew I was here, I mean, hell," I gestured at the door, "you were one room away this whole time! I seriously almost died, twice!"

She threw her hands in the air. "You don't get it."

"No, I think I do! I only don't get how lying to me all my life and going behind my back to help my enemy, who is also apparently the world's enemy, is helpful. I mean, I just found out that my son is supposed to become evil, so he has to be killed, and that my grandfather was murdered, and our dad was a psychic, not a drunk. Everyone has lied to me, my whole life!"

"That wasn't fake!"

"What do you mean?"

"Dad. His drinking wasn't fake. He couldn't handle the pressure. He and Mom really were that depressed. Sure, Esmeralda manipulated him to crash the car, but he was still an awful drunk! We didn't make up any of that. No one did. Dad was hopeless. Mom too. He was fired from the FRH in his twenties! A total disgrace!" She entered into a fit of sobs.

I lost my anger and tried to stroke her back, but she jerked her shoulder.

"Alba! I'm sorry!" I lowered my eyes and voice. "But, c'mon! Give me a little break. I'm overwhelmed. I just got into this Psi stuff, and don't understand how to use it and what to trust. Can you tell me the truth? Are Esmeralda and my son alive?"

The door burst open, and Josip and Robin entered.

Josip was wearing his trademark smirk. He glanced at Alba before looking at me and saying, "Petulant boy is back! Yay. Boy who think life is *so* hard!"

I stood. "Are you kidding? You're laughing at me?"

I pinged Robin. *Don't have thoughts. Don't have thoughts. Don't have thoughts.*

"What the hell?" I shouted. "How come no one wants to help me?"

Josip grinned even more and said, "We do want to help. But you only care about yourself and right now. Instead of future, and what you can do with it." He scowled.

I pinged Source. *Tell me about my son! I know you can't lie to me.*

227

This is not for you to know.

What do you mean?

This isn't yours to know.

Josip's phone rang. He picked it up and motioned for us to be quiet. "Yes? Yes! I see. Now?"

"What's going on?" I asked.

He put a finger on his lips and pointed at the phone.

I said to Alba, "What's the big deal?"

Josip scowled, covered the phone with his hand, and said to Alba, "I need silence, so I leave you alone with child brother now. Maybe you can get him to grow up, despite his knack for to be idiot." He left.

I tried to ping Alba. She blocked me and shot me an annoyed expression. "Can you stop, please? It takes effort to block you, every time. Don't be a drain. Do you have any idea how annoying it was, growing up with you? You were constantly pinging everyone, without knowing it, all day long, and I had to multi-task and—"

"Have you always been this weird?" I asked.

"We're not weird, Ardor."

"Um, I think we are. I mean, I talk to 'Source' for Universal knowledge, you work as an agent for a global psychic network, which ordered you to get my psycho ex-girlfriend to fly to Croatia, all for some psychic spy war, all of our destinies are written in some 'Great Book,' and now you're telling me that, as a *battery*," I used air quotes, "you spent most of our adolescence fooling me into thinking I didn't have psychic powers." I smugly smiled. "I'd say we're off the charts weird!"

She frowned. "I didn't always stop you from being psychic. I let you cheat on your homework, and what I'm saying is that." She frowned. "What I'm saying is that we're not weird. It's worse. We're *cursed*."

My heart raced.

"What do you mean we're cursed?"

Her gaze became grave. I'd never seen such intensity in her.

She said, "What I mean is that the future, for most humans, is good and bad, but for us? It's mostly bad."

"Then tell me what's so bad. Right now. Tell me."

"Right now? Nothing is bad. But that's only because you're acting like a spoiled brat and denying your destiny. *Our* destiny. But either way, it doesn't matter for us."

"For us?" I asked.

She sighed. "We're cursed, no matter what we do or don't do. And that's why you might as well give up, give in, and play your part. The world needs you, and if you aren't willing to help, well, don't expect any favors in return."

"Screw that." I looked her in the eyes. "And screw you."

She shook her head and rose from the table. "I know you think you know *everything*." She exhaled a long breath. "But you don't." She walked to the door.

"Wait. Where are you going?" I didn't want to be alone.

"I'm leaving. I'm tired of your lousy attitude."

I crossed my arms. "Fine. Leave. See if I care."

She winced slightly, then shook her head and left.

229

I felt like crying, but now that I knew I was probably under tremendous surveillance, I did my best to look calm, cool, and collected, but even without a mirror I knew I wasn't fooling anyone.

26
The FRH

I stayed in that room stewing for quite some time until I eventually calmed enough to ask Source for help, but all it said was, *Stop fighting your destiny.*

I didn't like its reply, but knew deep down that my grandmother wouldn't have lied to me, and she'd told me to always trust it, so I stood and spoke to the closed door. "OK, guys. I give up. I'll go along with your plan, whatever it is. Can someone come back in here, and maybe bring some food?"

The door opened and Josip and Alba returned.

"Thank gosh, boy finally lets fate be," Josip said.

"Well, at least for now," Alba said with sarcasm.

"Enough of the teasing," I said.

Josip looked like he was choking on a good joke, but kept quiet.

I nodded and said, "So what now?"

"Come with us," Josip said, pointing at the door.

"Where are we going?" I asked.

"You are ready to help, right?" Alba said.

I nodded.

"Then follow us," she said.

Josip shook his head. "Jesus, this boy never makes anything easy."

"We're lucky," Alba said. "It took him fourteen years to agree to eat a vegetable."

I walked to the door and waited for them to open it.

Josip held up a hand. "You must wait for retinal scan." He looked into the small device above the door and the door unlocked. He walked through it, but before I could follow him, it shut behind him.

Alba did the same thing, so I waited until she'd left, then stared at the thing, but nothing happened.

"What the hell?" I muttered.

Source said, *You must agree to your fate.*

What?

Once you enter, you are entering into a new, negotiated path.

Negotiated... what?

All humans have free will. This door requires that you use your free will to choose a new course, which is the right course. This is a big step in your life. Can you accept this? If you do, great things await your world.

And me...? I asked, even though I kind of knew the answer.

Source didn't reply.

I stared at the stupid device and stopped resisting my fate. My heart sunk as I did, but at that precise moment, the door opened.

Source said, *Truth lives and speaks from the heart.*

Thanks, I replied with sarcasm. *I'll remember that the next time I find out everyone I've ever known has been lying to me.*

I stepped through the door and was surprised that it didn't lead into a room. It led to a hall with an elevator at the end of it. I walked to the elevator and peered inside. It had no buttons. I shrugged, stepped inside, and the doors closed. For a moment, nothing happened, but then the thing took off at a chaotic speed, and it wasn't moving on any tracks. It was floating. It went on and on, and at one point, my ears popped, and right as it slowed, I was afraid I was going to vomit.

When the motion stopped, the door opened, and I saw a plain, ordinary looking conference room with a large oval table. Three men and four women in dress clothes sat at it, as well as Alba and Josip. I entered the room, and the elevator closed behind me.

This room had several giant windows that showed a stunning view of some body of water, yet Charles' mansion had been in a landlocked part of Alabama.

"Where am I?" I asked no one in particular.

A woman who looked to be in her early fifties stood up at the end of the oval table. She was thin with curly hair clipped below her ears. She had a large golden pendant draped around her neck that overshadowed the rest of her clothing. Her eyes were intelligent and sharp, but they conveyed no warmth.

She gave me a weak smile and walked towards me with her hand out for me to shake.

"Hello, Ardor. I'm glad we get to meet after all."

I heard Josip harrumph then heard a familiar chuckle from behind. I turned and steady as always stood Robin, clearly on duty. I nodded and he returned it respectfully, with a slight smile.

I shook the woman's hand and empathed a reserved detachment that wasn't familiar to me. It wasn't bad, but it wasn't good either. It was pure indifference.

"My name is Suzanne." She pointed to the rest of the men and women. "And this is the board of the FRH." She nodded at Josip, who was stuffing a pipe, "Of course you know Josip, who *knows* not to smoke here."

Josip scowled. "This is modern idiocy! No one has any rights any more."

Suzanne rolled her eyes. "I would introduce you to the rest of the team, but there's no point. You can ask Source for anything you want to know." She stifled a yawn. "I'm sorry, but this recent ordeal has kept us up a few nights."

I noticed the sun was blazing outside, which didn't make sense. I'd woken up in Charles' mansion that morning, and there was no way only a few hours had passed between now and then. There was no way the daylight could be this strong.

"Where are we?" I asked. "Was that really an elevator?

Everyone looked puzzled.

Alba said, "Give him a bit, to adjust. He's new to this, and a little stubborn."

234

The room chuckled, and my face got hot.

Source, please help me out, I asked.

That was not an elevator. It was a transportation device, designed by Charles Fay. You were transported here once you agreed to your fate.

So I time-traveled?

No.

Then I teleported?

Also no, but that's probably the easiest explanation to satisfy you. There aren't words in any language to explain what you just did. Not yet.

I looked at Alba. "OK. Let's get on with this. I want to know about my son, and Esmeralda. Are they alive?"

"Here we go one more time again," Josip said.

Alba stood and glared. "Ardor, if you continue to play victim, the Universe will suffer. I don't understand how you can't understand that this is so much bigger than you, than me, and all our petty desires, besides—"

Suzanne said, "It's simple, Ardor. If Alba had refused to kill Esmeralda, someone else would have. Esmeralda killed your grandfather and father, and she was going to kill you. Stopping her saved many lives."

I pointed at Alba. "*You* killed her? And my son?"

Source said, *Ardor, you need to calm down. Hold back your anger and listen.*

I didn't like that advice, and even if I wanted to follow it, I was too angry to do so.

I crossed my arms and shouted at Josip, "What the hell is going on?" I then turned to Alba and asked, "Did you kill Esmeralda and my son, or not?"

She looked at the floor and Josip coughed into his hand. I heard Robin clear his throat. Suzanne stared at me like I was a specimen in a petri dish.

I looked around the room and said, "How many more times are you people going to lie to me? What is the point of this? Just give me some damn answers!"

Alba gave me a look that made me feel like I was being difficult, but I didn't care. "Oh, OK. I see how it is. I guess *I'm* the jerk, since I should be thankful, right? Thankful to all of you, and especially Alba, for killing Esmeralda. Oh, and my unborn son, who is evil and was going to kill us all. Am I right?" I produced a fake grin, but it wasn't easy. My body was shaking.

Suzanne's eyes crossed ever so slightly for a second before she resumed her blasé demeanor, so I pinged her to cut to the chase. Words angered me.

Nothing happened.

I pinged Josip and felt him block me.

I pinged Alba, and felt her block me.

I pinged a random woman at the table. *He's too young and immature for this.*

I pinged Robin. *Don't have thoughts. Don't have thoughts. Don't have thoughts.*

I pinged Suzanne again. Nothing happened.

Suzanne pursed her lips and said, "It's impossible, right? It's like I don't exist, yet here I am. Talking. Breathing. Listening. Aware."

I empathed her and got nothing. She had no emotions. I pinged her again. I wasn't blocked. There was nothing to ping. She had no thoughts.

"Are you a robot?" I asked.

Josip chortled. "So American with robot fetish. No will to think outside box."

"Would someone please tell me the truth?"

No one spoke.

I looked at Josip. He looked at me like he wanted to say something but was stopping himself.

I gave up and asked Source, *Help me. Please?*

My vision went dark, and I heard a swooshing noise. After a brief spell of darkness, I appeared in an unfamiliar room with drawn curtains and dim lighting. I looked down at my hands. They were middle-aged. Consciously, I felt like myself, meaning I had my normal brain, but I *felt* older. It was like I was in someone else's body, but with my regular mind.

I looked around. The room was huge, with marble floors, a four-poster bed, and an enormous fireplace. The room was bigger than the house I'd grown up in.

I heard a knock at the door.

"Come in," I said. My voice was surprisingly mature. It didn't have its normal nasal-whine pitch to it, and I liked it better. As the door opened, I recalled memories from random public speaking tours featuring

237

me, 'Ardor the psychic' wherein I had explained 'Psi science' to packed lecture halls. At each engagement I remembered Alba and Robin close by. The memories didn't make sense, but they felt real. My best guess was that I had somehow time warped into my own future.

An older Alba entered. She still appeared youthful, but she was well into her forties. She conveyed the same sisterly warmth as always. It comforted me.

I *knew* she was my loyal sister and that she loved me. Neither of us had married, and we lived in this mansion, as housemates. This was my bedroom. How was this possible?

I looked at her and could tell she'd been crying.

"What's wrong?" I asked.

"Ping me," she said, tears flowing.

"You're not going to block me?"

She shook her head and loose tears fell to the floor.

I felt a crushing pain as I looked at her. She was so innocent and loving. She was my favorite person. She'd protected me, all these years, as a battery. She'd risked her life to kill Esmeralda and even protected me from the FRH during my youth so I could have a semi-normal childhood and enjoy my life for a bit.

I walked to her and took her hands and tried to make eye contact, but she continued to look at the floor. She didn't want to be touched, so I let go.

"Ping me," she repeated in a whisper.

What came next was terrible. I can't convey the pain I felt as I learned from her mind that she had lied to me, all these years. She'd never killed Esmeralda. No one had. It had all been part of the FRH's plan to orchestrate a strategy to avoid the prophecy. They'd deceived me in order to let Esmeralda raise my son, so he could grow up in the Orange clan until he was old enough to be contacted, and turned. They wanted him to be the ideal double agent, and thought that they could pull it off.

Josip had been the only person in the FRH to oppose the plan, insisting that my son would never come to our side if he spent that much time with Esmeralda, and that we'd end up destroying the world by giving the Orange clan too much power. His plan was to train me to kill Esmeralda after our son's birth and let me raise him.

But no one had agreed with him, not even Alba. And his resistance to the FRH's plan was not taken well. After repeated warnings to get with the plan, he'd been killed. They'd hidden this murder from me, saying it was a heart attack, and I'd believed them. The FRH had gotten away with all of this thanks to Alba's incredible ability to block my Psi powers.

Alba had been the precise instrument of my betrayal, but now she and the FRH were fully aware that their plan had failed, so she was coming clean.

My son had become even more powerful than anyone could have imagined. He'd eviscerated the prophecies in The Great Book and done something no one saw coming. He'd killed Esmeralda, and now was on his way to kill me and Alba.

I stopped pinging and looked at Alba, a portrait of remorse. Before I could say anything, the room melted and I returned to the conference room, in my current twenty-two-year-old body, but with those memories from the future. I had this new insight, and now understood why Source had told me to listen.

Yes, Ardor, Source said. *You get it now. You can prevent all of this, but you can't trust Alba or the FRH, and while you can trust Josip, you can't let him know that you know ANY of this. It's important that you keep this all to yourself. You must play along.*

Suzanne looked at me with concern. "What happened?"

I looked at Alba. She looked apprehensive, and I felt her blocking me, in case I tried to read her mind. I needed to work on my awareness of being blocked.

I looked at both of them and smiled.

"Nothing," I lied. "Nothing happened."

Alba looked like she didn't believe me, but didn't say so.

I said, "Look everyone, I'm over it. I talked to Source, and it told me that what you did was right. I'm sorry I yelled at you. I wanted my son, so badly, but I know you did the right thing. I understand why you killed Esmeralda, and him." I pretended to gulp and tried to look as sad as I could.

Alba looked relieved. "Oh thank God. You have no idea how relieved I am," she said with genuine solace. "I'm so glad you understand."

I nodded. "Me too."

Suzanne said, "Well then. Let's get busy training Ardor for service."

I smiled and nodded. "Sounds good!"

Suzanne faced the table. "Meeting adjourned."

27
Pants on Fire

I was more than happy to lie to the FRH, because my vision of the future, and Source, had each confirmed that my son was going to live, and that's all I cared about. I could handle anything else, including a prophecy that said I had to stop him, because I knew that part was open to interpretation. I didn't have to *kill* him.

What I couldn't ignore was the fact that standing in my way was the FRH, including Alba, and how I had to pretend to believe that Esmeralda and my son were dead. The road ahead would require a lot of patience and tact on my part, two things I'd never been great at.

I didn't have a plan, but I knew one thing, for Source had been clear. I had to trust no one and keep this all to myself. I vowed then and there to pretend I didn't know Esmeralda was alive and do whatever it took to find her before she could nurture our son's powers. That was the most I could do, for now.

As the various attendees from the meeting collected their things, Alba approached me and asked, "Ardor, are you OK?" She seemed genuinely concerned.

I flashed a decent fake smile. "I'm just tired."

"Oh." She looked down. "You seemed lost. You said nothing happened, but…" she looked up then at her hands again. "I guess… never mind."

I felt something I hadn't felt since living with Esmeralda. I was being pinged, and it was obviously Alba. So Alba was capable of reading my mind? I was about to ask her to fess up, when Source stepped in and said, *Don't let her know you know.*

I blocked Alba from reading me then asked, *Are you suggesting I lie? I thought that was immoral!*

Morality is different at higher perspectives. Do you want to succeed?

I mentally shrugged then used the same trick I'd used with Esmeralda to respond to Alba's latest ping. Instead of blocking it, I gave her a fake thought. *"I wish my son had lived."*

I then asked Source, *What's the real deal with Alba? Is she psychic?*

She is your battery, so she can read your mind, but only yours.

When she blocks me, I can tell. Can she tell when I'm blocking her?

Yes.

Well that complicates things.

***

After the meeting we used Charles' crazy elevator to get back to Dothan, and from there the FRH sent Alba,

243

Josip, and me on a private jet to New York, for a press conference. The FRH felt that the world was ready to receive me, but I didn't agree. I remembered my experience in LA. No one liked a psychic, especially a real one.

"Do we really have to do this?" I asked them both for the third time in an hour.

Josip twirled his pipe. He'd packed it at take off so he could light it the moment we landed. "Yes! Stupid press knows that idiot boy landed plane with miracle, and that same boy previously claim to be psychic. Then next day, boy mysteriously disappear, so now, whole country is bananas. They want to know what happened to you. We must return you to light of lime with good excuse before speculation goes out of control." He yawned. "Is simple matter."

Shaking my head, I asked, "What excuse could I possibly have for vanishing?"

He sighed and looked at Alba. "Can you make dumb boy less dumb?"

"Ardor, we already went over this. The press will bombard you about your disappearance, but all you have to do is prove you are psychic, and they'll forget."

I slapped my leg. "Alba! Everyone in LA thought I was psychic until they concluded I was a fraud. They aren't going to believe me again. This is dumb."

Her face soured. "This time they'll believe you."

Source contacted me, only without words. I suddenly *knew* something, and it was big: I *knew* that a major earthquake was going to happen in two days and an entire soccer stadium in Chile was going to fall in on itself during a packed game. At least three hundred people would die.

"Oh my God!" I yelled.

Josip jumped in his seat. "What? What happened?"

"In Chile, a lot of people, they're going to die from an earthquake!"

His face relaxed. "Oh. Sorry to hear." He looked at his watch and grinned. "Only forty minutes until we land!" He put his pipe in his mouth and wiggled it.

"What is wrong with you?" I glared at him then turned to Alba. "How can he be so ho-hum about this?"

"Ho-hum?" She smirked and cocked her head. "Where'd you hear that?"

I let a smile creep across my face. "I heard Josip say it earlier. I kind of like his weird phrases. Anyway, we have to do something about this!"

She held steady eye contact. "No we don't."

Josip laughed. "Tsk, tsk. Boy thinks he is so smart."

Alba said, "Ardor, if we warn people, it will just pay the consequences forward to another group of people. Everyone has to die at some point."

I scoffed. "That's ridiculous. If I prevent those people from dying, they're not all going to have the Grim Reaper go after them like in some dumb movie—"

"Correct!" Josip took the pipe from his mouth. "But still exist consequences!"

I rolled my eyes.

245

Alba said, "You should take Josip more seriously."

He wagged a finger at me. "Sister is smart. Wish she were not just battery."

She shot him a dirty look. "I'm not *just* a battery!"

"Sorry. I know. But brother is so stubborn. All he has to do is trust!"

It was not lost on me at this point that I sat with two conspirators. Both had lied to me about my son (and the woman who had murdered my father *and* grandfather), and now they were belittling *my* issues with trust? I swallowed my pride, kept my cool, and remained silent.

"Ardor," Alba put her hand on my knee. "I know the laws of the Universe sound funny, at first, but how can you be so skeptical? Think about it. You're psychic, you just escaped near-death at the hands of an insane billionaire with magical machinery, and now you're flying in for a press conference as 'The missing boy who landed a plane'. On what grounds are you questioning how fate works? When did you become so arrogant?"

I didn't trust her, so I checked in with Source.

They're right, Ardor. If you reveal the future to people and they don't balance out the equality of all that must be, then those consequences manifest elsewhere. No one gets a free lunch. You can't stop consequences.

"Fine," I nodded. "I trust you guys."

Josip smirked and leaned forward. "Don't forget, boy. I am no battery, and I am no psychic, but I feel Psi energy when it is used. I know you just ask Source. I know you do not trust *us*." He leaned back with his hands behind his head and sighed. "But, this is good sign. You *should* trust *only* Source." He raised one furry eyebrow. "Of course, what do I know? I am old man. Put pasture on me." He winked, checking first to make sure Alba didn't see it.

Source, why can't I trust Josip?

You can. You just can't let him know that you know the FRH is lying to you.

I wanted to ping him and tell him I knew I could trust him, but I let it go.

"OK. Fine. I'll just shut up and follow orders, yet again." I rolled my eyes.

Alba said, "The laws of the Universe do not have to make sense. If you tell those people to avoid that soccer game—"

"Match," Josip said.

She rolled her eyes. "If you stop that *match*, a child will be born with a peanut allergy, or something like that. It's incalculable, but not beyond our comprehension. We know that intentions create consequences, and the energy of those consequences is real, and it must manifest, some way—"

Josip raised a finger in the air. "Or somehow!"

Source said, *They're right. You can shift the flow of energy, but you can't stop it. It's like a river.*

I nodded, and Alba assumed it was for her.

The plane lurched, reminding me of the nearly fatal descent of my last flight. I got nervous and pinged Source, and received a vision of a safe landing.

247

I relaxed, and soon, as predicted, our plane landed safely, and even though we'd flown into a private airport north of New York City, in a place called Westchester, there were armies of people waiting for me. As I got off the plane, I felt Alba's Psi energy increase my psychic and intuitive awareness. The book was right. She was like a battery. I was more powerful with her at my side. I was able to ping people with more speed, confidence, and accuracy, and I felt less fatigue as well. It was too bad she wasn't truly on my side.

We entered a small lobby, packed with reporters. It was quieter than I thought it would be. In the movies, press conferences seem so hectic and loud, whereas this one had a lethargic feel to it. Some reporters were even yawning. I pinged a few to test the crowd.

Geesh. It took them long enough.

Wow, he's scrawny and looks like a kid.

No way this big-nosed kid has secret powers. I can't believe I got this shitty assignment.

His nose is so big, but his eyes do look sort of...

Who is that chick with him? She's beautiful!

I pinged Josip. He was scanning the room to detect Psi use. I'd assumed Alba and I were the only psychics, but he wasn't so sure, and we had to be careful.

Source elaborated for me, *Everyone can do what you do, but few believe they can, and even fewer accept they can, and from that lot, only a fraction nurture it to any sort of fulfilling fruition. But others do exist, and the FRH does not have all of them registered or on file.*

I noticed an attractive reporter in the front row and hoped she would like my upcoming statement so I could use it as an icebreaker. Naturally, I pinged her. She was thinking about how trivial this story was and desperately hoping that by doing this dumb story she could get her boss to give her better assignments. I was nowhere in her mental world. She hadn't even looked at me yet.

At some point I felt Josip's hand on my back, guiding me to a podium. I got in front of the crowd and felt a rush of butterflies. I looked behind me, hoping to get some support, but he and Alba were now standing far behind me, and they seemed preoccupied with something other than me. I guessed I was on my own.

I tapped the microphone and heard a dull thud echo in the back of the room. I gave a sheepish smile and said, "Uh, hi. I'm Ardor. We've met. A few times. You guys have questions I guess? I'm nervous. I think I have to pee. I also want water. Shit. Did I say that out loud?"

The attractive reporter giggled and looked amused, and I heard a few more people chuckle. I literally *felt* the room relax and start to like me.

I smiled. "So, aside from having a big nose and scrappy hair, I'm also psychic. I can like, read minds and discern futures. I turned around to look at Alba and said, "And my sister here—"

"Enough!" Josip barked.

I'd forgotten that I was only supposed to talk about myself. Luckily, the room wasn't well-lit, and few could see Alba so far behind me. I turned back to the crowd and pinged them. Their mental chatter featured nothing about Alba, except one lewd thought I ignored.

"So, I guess now you can ask me, um, about me, the plane I saved, or—"

Josip coughed loudly, and I got the hint. Talk less.

The attractive reporter stood, as did many others, but I called on her first. She held up a badge and said, "Shirley Winters, Free Corps Press." She smiled. It was a genuine nice, warm, pretty smile. I really wanted her to like me. This felt weird.

I empathed her and received a passionate energy for seeking the truth, but no passion for me. I tried to let it go and sound casual as I said, "Ask away, Shirley."

She blushed when I said her name, then recovered. A true professional. She said, "Can you verify a report that your pregnant girlfriend ran away from you and has recently been mysteriously murdered?"

The crowd gasped and became eerily silent.

I had no idea what to do, but thankfully, Josip did. He came up to the podium, pushed me aside, and said into the microphone, "Interview over!"

28
Associated Mess

After Josip ended the press conference, I heard vague complaints, but the general atmosphere returned to what it had been, bored and complacent.

Josip led us to an SUV outside the airport, where Robin waited to whisk us away to some house on Long Island that the FRH owned.

No one spoke about what had just happened. I knew better than to ask any questions, especially because I was worried that if I did, I might let on that I knew that Esmeralda was still alive.

When we parked at the house, Josip announced, "I have spoken to Mizz Shirley Winters from today. Nice girl. She wants to interview you tomorrow. Big day. Sleep tight and no bedbug warning for spoiled American, but you get gist." He blew me a fake kiss, for his own merriment, then left me with Alba.

"You OK?" she asked.

"I'm fine."

"Don't lie."

I thrust a finger at her. "Me? You're the liar!"

She put her hands on her hips. "Excuse me?"

"You lied to me for most of my life. Like all of our childhood, like, when—"

"Ardor, we went over this."

"Don't interrupt me! I'm talking about lots of things. Not just Mom and Dad, or the FRH. It's small stuff too. Like why do you block me all the time, huh?"

Her eyes narrowed, and I felt her trying to ping me.

I continued to pretend that I couldn't tell. Besides, my inner thoughts were matching my words. I was angry and holding nothing back.

She motioned to a couch in the far corner of the room and walked to it and took a seat.

I followed her, but refused to sit.

She sighed. "Fine. I do block you a lot. So then, what do you know?"

I collapsed on the couch. "Never mind. What difference could it make?"

Josip returned. "Holy smokes, you two are still fighting? Will you just give up and agree to not agree? You remind me of old married couple. Why not do as the kids say, and hug it out?"

Alba and I laughed at his attempt at pop culture as he left the room.

She yawned and stood. I'm really tired, and I'm going to assume you are as well, Ardor."

I yawned and smiled. "Yeah, you're right. I definitely need some sleep."

She pointed at the couch. "Don't fall asleep here. You have a bedroom, OK?"

I nodded and watched her leave. A minute later, I stretched and fell asleep. I could agree to disagree, but I didn't like being told what to do.

***

I woke up alone on the couch with the vigor one only gets from truly restorative slumber. I felt like my soul had taken a hot bubble bath with scented candles.

I was about to shut my eyes and go back to sleep when I heard some faint kitchen noises from afar. My stomach growled, so I got up to locate the source.

I followed my nose and eventually found the kitchen where I saw Alba and Robin collaborating over an expansive six-burner stove with many sizzling pans and pots. The room smelled amazing.

"You'll love it, but you'll also have to wait!" Alba said without turning around.

Robin smiled and shrugged.

"Where's Josip?" I asked. I wasn't sure why, but I missed him.

Alba continued to face the stove and said, "Probably on the phone with the FRH. He had to finish up a report after the conference. You feel better now?"

Before I could answer, Josip entered. "I'm back! And with good news!"

I turned to see him hobbling into the kitchen. He had not been all that limber when we had met in Croatia, but now he seemed remarkably older.

"You OK?" Robin asked with a frown.

"Arthritis is like American death and taxes." He shook his head and smirked. "Anyway, good news, boy! FRH approves of interview. Mizz Shirley can ask things, you can say stupid things back, and then you will," he used his hands to mock an explosion, "blow her mind, with soccer match prophecy."

I pictured the beautiful reporter from the conference, and recalled my verbal gaffe and felt my pulse quicken. I didn't want an interview, even with her.

"I'm doing what? Maybe this is a bad idea."

"Grow up," Josip growled.

I waited for him to smile, but he instead swiveled and left the room.

"Did you hear that?" I asked, shaking my head.

Alba laughed. "He's right."

"What?"

"Grow up, Ardor. Accept fate. You're obviously afraid of what comes next."

I wasn't nervous about fate. I was nervous about Shirley. I again pictured her, and this time my memory lingered on her lithe figure, auburn hair, and her sharp, intelligent eyes. I'd never felt this way about anyone, even Veronica. I didn't know why, but I really liked her.

I pinged Source for odds of impending romance.

Don't be selfish. Focus on the task at hand.

I shook my head and left the kitchen to find my room. I took a shower, and imagined all sorts of fake scenarios in which I'd win Shirley over. Soon enough

254

Alba called me to dinner, which ushered me into a pleasant food coma. After dinner I went back to my room and quickly fell asleep.

***

A knock at the door woke me up the next morning along with Josip's mocking voice. "Wake up and get heck out of bed. Time to meet pretty girl for interview. Try not to be usual shabby self. Be in car in twenty minutes. No tardiness!"

I looked at a clock on the wall. It was six a.m. I groaned, hoping Josip would hear it.

Source said, *If you are truthful, this will go well. Think of your son.*

Before I could think of my son, I wanted to focus on my shabby self. Did I dress poorly? Did I look like a slob? Was I supposed to worry about these things?

You're supposed to worry about the Universe.

I sighed and thought about my son. I thought about that little future world-destroyer and smiled. I wanted him to thrive, with goodness, and I felt a surge of pride. I knew that if I listened to Source and stopped making selfish mistakes, I could find Esmeralda and save my son from the prophecy. He didn't have to die.

I realized that I didn't have to worry about the FRH, Alba's lying, or any other scenario that would usually wrack me with anxiety. My life wasn't about any of that or any of them. My life was about my son, and I didn't know what my odds were, but I knew my job was to find Esmeralda, put an end to her mission, and save my son.

With confidence mainlining my veins, I walked to the car.

It only took ten minutes to get to the diner. Alba and Josip didn't come, and Robin was silent the whole ride, so I spent the time fantasizing about how things would go, but every time I did, Source said, *Stop daydreaming. Be present.*

Robin parked and said Shirley would be in a booth in the back. I got out of the car, and as soon as I entered, I saw her sitting in the rear, looking over some notes.

She didn't notice me until I was in front of her. When she looked up, her eyes were soft and startled, but she adjusted them to 'on duty reporter'.

She put out her hand. "Mr. Agopian, thank you for coming to meet me."

"Ardor, please." I shook her hand, and instead of being self-conscious and bashful, I seamlessly stepped into my new role of "Psychic Designated to Save the World" and was surprised to find myself say, "Why did we have to meet at this ungodly hour?"

She smirked and her fingers slightly fidgeted.

I pinged her. *He's different one-on-one. Not as rigid. Maybe this won't be a bust.*

"Why would it be a bust?" I asked.

Her cheeks flushed, and I hoped she was feeling something for me.

I folded my hands and said, "Look, I'm psychic, but I know you don't want to believe that, or at least that you aren't inclined to believe it, and that it's your job to prove I'm a fraud."

She pulled her head back and gave a puzzled look.

I continued, "So, you can try to pretend that I didn't just read your mind, but what's the point in that? I mean, what do you want to get out of this interview?"

She bit her lip. "Who said I didn't believe you?"

I pinged her and discovered that she did believe me, she was just really upset by some argument she'd recently had with her sister.

"Oh," I said. "I didn't realize this was about a fight with your sister. Sorry."

Her eyes widened then relaxed, so I empathed her, expecting to feel a surge of trust. I was instead blown away by an anger basted in a broth of mistrust.

"What's wrong?" I smiled, but my cheeks felt hot, and the smile felt strained.

She frowned, so I pinged her. *What an arrogant jerk*, she thought.

"You think I'm arrogant?" My heart sank and now *my* hands were fidgeting. "Can we start over?" I asked.

She didn't say anything.

I kept quiet, waiting for her to answer, but she remained silent. Eventually she stopped frowning and a look of amusement crept into her eyes. This expression sealed the deal for me. I was in love. This was the woman of my dreams. I was destined to meet her, to fall in love with her, and to trust and love her! And I didn't want or need Source to confirm it. I didn't have any proof, except a feeling, but this feeling was stronger than any physical evidence I could imagine. I didn't need proof. I was *sure* of this. This was the person I was supposed to be with.

I was about to take a chance and flirt with her when her face returned to reporter mode and she said, "Tell me about your ex-girlfriend, and this kid of yours."

I didn't know what to do. Josip had told me that under no circumstances could I talk about anything outside of the plane landing and my abilities. I pinged Source and it said, *Tell her the truth, but be sure to say, "Off the record!"*

But Josip told me I couldn't tell her anything about Esmeralda!

Josip isn't omniscient. Source is. Please follow our instructions. What matters is that you tell Shirley the truth, but just her, not the world. You can trust her, but no one else. Say, "Off the record." OK?

Shirley looked like she thought I was having a seizure. "You OK?" she asked.

I empathed her and felt a sense of compassion. It made me feel accepted, like it was OK to be me, and I wanted more. I was totally falling for this woman.

"Can I tell you two things?" I asked. "I need to get them out before I have to leave."

"What's the rush?" She looked at her watch. "Your agent said I would have an hour."

My eyes scrunched. "*Agent*? There's an *agency*, but I don't have an *agent*."

Ardor! Stop saying things you will regret. Play the game. Say, "Off the Record."

I smiled. "So, I want to tell you two things, one on the record, the other off."

She looked flustered, but nodded anyway. "Well... I guess I'll take what I can get."

I pinged her, *At least it's a scoop, whatever it is.*

I smiled. "It's definitely a scoop."

She rolled her eyes, so I pinged her. *What a jerk. He could at least ask my permission instead of just invading my personal thoughts.*

I wanted to argue, but she wasn't wrong. I was just desperate for her to like me, so I was having trouble giving her privacy.

"OK, first, on the record. Ready?"

She nodded.

"Right. OK." I took a deep breath and exhaled. "There's going to be a disaster during a soccer game, um, match, and it's going to occur by the end of this weekend. It'll be in South America, and it's going to be specific enough that if you publish this news in our time zone, then it will come out after the match will already have started, but before the earthquake, so it will be an undeniable fact that I was able to foresee this 'unforeseeable event'. Will you please wait until Saturday to publish this news? I assure you this will be worth whatever you have to go through with your editor to do it. Your career will take off."

I waited with tension until she sighed and said, "If this is a scam, so help me God, Ardor!"

My heart froze when she said my name. I wanted to hear her say it over and over again. I was now wearing a magical smile and it was so big it hurt my muscles.

"It's not a scam! I assure you. You will never regret trusting me."

A few patrons turned to observe the commotion.

She said, "My issue isn't with trusting you. I know you're psychic. My issue is with your agency. They won't give me a name, they won't tell me where they are located, and I had to spend all sorts of time filling out paperwork just to get this interview."

I smiled. "Yeah. Trust me. They're the worst. I hate them, actually."

She wrote something on her notepad, and I shouted, "Wait! That's off the record, what I just said. You can't report that."

She screwed her eyes then nodded. "Fine, but this is a terrible interview."

I smiled, leaned forward, and whispered, "Well, here's the off the record part. Which is something no one knows, not even my own sister, and this is why you can trust me."

She raised her eyebrows and waited for me to continue.

I raised my finger in the air. "Remember, this is off the record, right?"

She gave a solemn nod.

"OK," I closed my eyes and said, "You're right. I do have an ex-girlfriend, only she isn't dead, and she's still pregnant with a boy. My son. That's why I can't let you go public. She's hiding, and I have to find her before she—"

"I know," she said, looking like she was about to cry. "I know."

29
Psychic Spy Games

She knew? I couldn't believe my ears, so I pinged Source for the truth.

It's true. She knows about Esmeralda. But she doesn't know about the FRH.

How could Shirley know about Esmeralda? And what did she know?

A worn-down looking server arrived with a pot of coffee and an empty mug. She topped off Shirley's and offered me a cup.

I'd never been a coffee drinker, but I wanted Shirley to think I was sophisticated, so I took the mug but declined the offer of cream and sugar. I figured real men, the kind Shirley dated, drank their coffee black.

The server filled my mug, and I wrinkled my nose. It smelled like burned paper. She dropped off two menus, saying she'd return in a few minutes.

"It's OK," Shirley stopped her. "He has to leave. We'll just take the check."

"No! I changed my mind," I said with inappropriate enthusiasm.

The server gave me an annoyed look then shuffled to the counter to talk to another patron.

Shirley smirked. "I thought you had to leave?"

"I didn't know you knew," I lowered my voice and whispered, "about Esmeralda." I took a sip of the coffee and wanted to spit it out, but swallowed.

She eyed my mug. "First time at the rodeo?"

"I'm a fraud." I paused for dramatic effect, then leaned in. "I can read minds, empath emotions, and predict the future, but I don't like coffee."

She chuckled and it was the sweetest sound I'd ever heard. I couldn't imagine anything more pleasant. Falling in love was great. I took her laughter as a good sign and decided to ask her out. But I was still scared, so I decided to empath her and was surprised to sense deep sadness that subdued my happy-go-lucky feelings.

"What's wrong?" I asked.

I continued to empath her and felt her compassion for me, only this time I felt how burdensome that could be. She felt sorry for me, and was powerless to help me. I'd never thought about empathy and compassion as two separate things, but they were. I had endless empathy, but little compassion. I realized that empathy was a selfish asset, while compassion was an asset for others. It made me appreciate her even more. I decided I would start to work on my compassion.

But what was she so compassionate about? What did she think I was suffering from? Instead of asking her, I pinged her. She was thinking, *No matter what you do, you won't be able to stop her. She knows what she's doing, and she's going to get away with it. She has power that people with money want, and she's playing all sides. You'll lose. There's just no way to stop her.*

I couldn't believe her negativity! I asked Source, *Why didn't you tell me this?*

It was best to learn this now, from her. She's on your side, so you'll listen better.

Shirley squinted. "Are you pinging me?" She put her things away.

"Please don't leave!" I pleaded, holding my hand up for emphasis.

Several diners looked at us. The waitress, who'd been coming to take our order shrugged and turned.

Shirley looked at me with lovely, but unloving eyes. "Ardor, I came here to interview you, not to have you read my mind and empath me. I don't like it."

"I'm sorry!" I exclaimed. This time no one stared.

She shook her head but maintained eye contact. "If you want people to help you and like you, you have to develop some tact with your abilities. No one wants to be around someone who doesn't respect their privacy."

I nodded, hoping to look as contrite as possible. "I understand."

For once, I was stumped. I had gone there expecting to announce the soccer stadium tragedy, with hopes of starting a romance with her, but her knowledge of Esmeralda and my son had thrown me way off course. I didn't know what to do now. I really liked her, and without Alba, I needed an ally to confide in.

I must've looked really depressed or anxious, because she stopped putting away her things and asked, "You OK?" with a soft expression.

I shook my head and my eyes teared up. *Please don't cry*, I thought to myself.

She sighed. "I'm sorry, Ardor, but the future, it's not something you can stop."

I broke eye contact. It didn't matter whether she was talking about Esmeralda *or* my abilities, it was true. It was the story of my life. I was a victim of destiny.

"It's not like you're a *victim*, Ardor."

I blushed. "Did you just read my mind?"

She took a sip of coffee, which was a light tan thanks to her generous dose of cream and sugar. She shook her head. "No. I can't do that. I just know all about you. I know that you're a hero, or at least you're supposed to be one. But," she glanced at the table, "being a hero doesn't mean things will work out. Sometimes the villain wins, and in your case, our case, I think that's what's going to happen."

Her gaze met my eyes, and I felt a powerful connection. I wasn't just attracted to her. It was obvious that she also liked me. I was again about to ask her on a date when she checked her watch and said, "Look, I'm going to do it. I'm going to get my editor to publish your prediction, which will propel you into fame, but—"

I waited and didn't ping her, which was akin to ignoring an itch on my nose.

She looked down at her notes and said, "I don't know how to say this, but…" she returned her eyes to meet mine. "It's just that… We're not on the same side."

My skin heated. Was I doomed for deception? "What?" I demanded.

"I don't mean I'm *against you*," she quickened her pace. "But it's your son… he's just… it's that, he's…" she leaned forward and whispered, "*evil*."

"No he's not!" I shouted. I started to stand, but she reached out and touched my arm and I felt a wave of soothing energy envelop my body. I sat back down.

With a blank look in her eyes, she continued to hold my arm and my anger dissolved. It felt magical. Her eyes remained vacant as she continued to hold my arm, and I relished the joyous energy. Eventually she let go, and the feeling stopped.

I felt like I'd just spent hours lying in bed with a lover, and I wanted more.

"How did you do that?" I asked with a goofy smile.

She closed her eyes and exhaled out of one side of her mouth. "Maybe you're not the only special person in this Universe." She opened her eyes and smiled.

I returned her smile with my own toothy grin. "Will you marry me?"

She blushed, laughed, and patted my hand, avoiding eye contact.

I felt nothing special from her touch, but her sudden shyness was intriguing.

She registered the disappointment on my face and cracked another smile.

My heart melted all over again. That smile!

She said, "So look. I like you, and I can tell you need a friend, but I can only do that if you learn to behave. Think you can cultivate some Psi etiquette?"

I laughed and sent her a pinged message. I'd only done that with Esmeralda, but wanted to see if it could work with her. *I want you to like me, Shirley.*

"We all want to be liked," she replied. "But you should know how much what you just did freaks out normal people. We have hundreds of thousands of so-called schizophrenics locked up thanks to telepaths like you sending them messages."

"I'm sorry," I said. "I just thought pinging you would be easier."

Her face scrunched. "Easier?"

"Yeah. I guess I figured if you felt my thoughts, you'd like me more?"

She shook her head. "You should educate yourself on the paranormal. There's a whole field about us, including etiquette and protocols for interaction."

"Really?"

"Really. It's called Psi science, and you're about to make it famous." She looked at her notes. "I mean we are." She blushed and glanced at me.

"Huh?" I sounded so dumb. I hoped she didn't think I was stupid.

"You're supposed to bring it to the masses." She grabbed her pen and notes and stuffed them in her satchel. She stood and put a ten-dollar bill on the table. "And that's why I'm going to publish this article. But I hope you understand that this is the last chance for you."

"Last chance?"

"Yup."

"I don't follow."

"Once you go public and become famous… It will never be the same."

Smiling, I fantasized about fans begging me for autographs and giving me all sorts of attention, but Source jumped in and said, *It's more like constant negativity, death threats, fear, and hatred… You need to approach this with caution.*

I felt my stomach drop and stared at the mug of black coffee.

Her tone lightened. "It's OK. You're fulfilling your life purpose. Besides—"

I looked up and flinched at the sight of her adorable smile. "Yes?"

She patted my hand. "I like you. So, there's that."

I was at a loss for words.

She shrugged, squeezed my hand, and left.

I pinged Source, *What just happened?*

You fell in love.

***

Hours after my interview, Josip told me Shirley's editor had called to let us know that he would *reluctantly* print my prediction, but it had to be very specific.

Josip asked me what to tell him, and Source delivered me a brief, but "very specific" prediction, including the exact death and injury toll.

I then asked, *Why can't I predict everything?*

Predictions come from Source, and we only reveal information for good purposes.

Is that why you won't speak about my future with Shirley?

No. That's because you don't need Source to know. That answer is in your heart.

Wait. If Source only helps a psychic who has good intentions, then how is Esmeralda capable of so much evil and destruction?

Esmeralda cannot manipulate Source. No one can. But she can use Psi energy for destructive purposes, and this is due to her lack of connection with her heart. Source is information, not Psi energy.

Where does Psi energy come from?

It's universal, but one must be connected to it to use it on a grand scale.

So Esmeralda is connected to Psi, but not Source?

Exactly.

So why is she so powerful and feared? How'd she get so much power?

Batteries.

Like my son?

Exactly.

Then how can I stop her from destroying the world?

Follow instructions and maintain a good heart.

OK then. What's the next instruction?

Stop Alba.

Alba? I shook my head. *I thought I was supposed to play along.*

You are.

Then how can I stop her?

Just play along.

I let my mind drift and thought about my son and The Great Book's prophecy, of him being the first human hybrid, a psychic-battery, and the FRH's fears made sense. If he could give himself unlimited energy and had access to Source, he would be a force to reckon with. But evil? Nothing was certain. Not now, not ever.

***

The next few days were a blur. The article was published on Saturday morning at a time that made it an "impossibly accurate" prediction of an earthquake unlike any previous prediction in the history of recorded prognostications. There was no precedent for what I'd done. I set the mold. The earthquake happened just after the article was published, and every American news agency was begging for my time.

But we didn't do anything until Monday, after every newspaper in the world — not just in America and Chile — made me the subject of their front page, I went from being a nobody to being the A-list star of headlines like "The New Nostradamus," "The Contemporary Cayce," and "Roll Over, Rasputin!"

I had been so accurate I'd quelled nearly every skeptic's explanation for how I did it. The story about my appearance on MTV came up, but the plane landing did as well, so only a few people accused me of being a fraud. It was official. I was famous. But Source was right, fame was different than I'd imagined it to be.

30
In War We Trust — Six Years Later

The first few years of fame were intolerable, thanks to how little it helped me with the only thing I cared about, finding my son.

Even with my abilities, Source was relentlessly defiant. It kept telling me to stop worrying about finding my son, and to instead worry about teaching the world about Psi energy. But that wasn't fun, and didn't seem fair. However, with no alternatives, I did as asked, traveling around the world to help the FRH promote Psi science.

And it worked. Slowly but surely, the world acknowledged and even practiced cultivating an awareness of what they called "intuition," which is what I called connection with Source. No one was reading minds or moving forks across tables, but many checked with Source before making decisions, and the net benefits were good.

The best news for me, however, was that in the years that followed my famous 'Chilean earthquake prediction', I cultivated a serious and healthy relationship with Shirley, who supported and helped me mature.

I learned a lot in those years, like how the FRH wasn't the only organization involved in Psi. There were rival groups, like the one that had contracted Shirley, for her energy skills. This of course explained how she'd known about me that day in the diner.

The FRH was a collection of psychics and batteries, while her organization, the World Energy Collective, featured energy workers or 'healers', like her, who used energy to heal and assist others who couldn't run their own energy effectively, which was the root cause of physical and mental stress.

Those six years were eventful. I fell in love, I developed expertise, but not mastery of my abilities, and I spent a lot of time doing PR for the FRH to publicize the benefits of Psi science.

But things got really interesting when I was asked by the U.S. President to help him avoid a war.

***

I was nervous as I entered a room in the basement of the Pentagon. I'd been famous for six years, but nothing could prepare me for meeting with the President. So there I was, in the notorious war room, after a hellacious six hours of screening.

I was grumpy when I was finally let in, having spent half a day in interviews and waiting rooms, which I considered an unnecessary government power play.

I tried to shrug my anger aside as I entered the war room, which didn't look like the ones I'd seen in the movies. It was neither dark nor well-lit, and while it did have an expensive oak table with a bunch of fancy chairs, there were no flat-screen monitors or art on the clean, white walls. The one thing that caught my eye was that at the head of the table, where the President sat, was an old-fashioned landline phone. I wondered if this relic from the past was perhaps the best way to secure a connection.

I made no effort to put up any pretenses. I walked in looking like I always did, a poorly postured, eat-some-more, lanky twenty-something, with unkempt hair, blue jeans and a plain black T-shirt. This was part of my appeal with my fans. I acted like a regular guy.

"Mr. Agopian," the President said with a smile, standing. He looked at my shirt and his eyes twinkled. "Please, take a seat," he said before sitting.

I sat in a chair between two hard-ass-looking generals. The one on my left was built like an anvil, stout with pure muscle. He stiffened when I sat next to him and held his breath, as if I had a virus. The other general I nicknamed 'silver hawk'. He was tall and thin, with a full head of bright silver hair, and about as warm and welcoming as a scorpion poised to strike. He sneered when I made eye contact and spread his papers

274

out to cut off the space I was supposed to have in front of my seat.

I smiled, trying to ignore their obvious hatred.

I'd been nervous until I felt that energy. How could I be nervous when I understood how childlike their hatred was? They hated me because of fear — imaginary fear of what I could do — and how I could influence the President, a man of peace, whom they didn't like nor trust. These men wanted war.

Each general had a folder in front of him. Most were open, with packets of unstapled documents scattered about, but there was nothing in front of me. I closed my eyes and used non-local vision to read the title on one of the files.

It said 'Agopian, Ardor' with my social security number. I smiled and waited for someone to start, but no one did. I finally asked, "Mr. President, what can I do for you?"

The President smiled exhaled charisma. "Welcome, Ardor. we're thankful you could make it."

Silver hawk coughed then sneered and several generals smiled at him.

The President ignored the distraction and continued, "I want to know your thoughts on the upcoming Manila Conference, Mr. Agopian."

"Ardor, please," I said.

"Ardor." He nodded.

"The Manila Conference?"

With a thick drawl, a general across from me turned to the President and said, "Sir! With all due respect, The Manila Conference is ultimate clearance!" He turned to me and chuckled. "Besides, what on earth could *you* possibly know about foreign diplomacy?"

"He—" the President said.

"Source knows everything, sir," I interjected in a submissive, dutiful tone.

"Source? What source?" a general with sharp blue eyes asked with a nasty frown.

The anvil to my right huffed and shuffled through his papers, using his elbow to shield the documents, as if they could solve the problem of 'Ardor'.

I said, "I'm not concerned with your papers."

He stopped moving and looked away.

I looked at the general who'd asked about Source. "If you want to challenge me, I'm fine with that." I nodded at him. "I'll start with you, you know, to clear your skepticism. Then, if anyone else wants me to prove myself, they can go next. OK?"

No one answered, but I had their undivided attention. I cleared my throat. "For starters, you don't use your real name. You legally changed it fifty years ago then removed the evidence as you ascended to power, to avoid a small crime from the past."

He squinted then tried to laugh off my accusation.

I shook my head. "You want me to continue?"

He squinted harder, but didn't speak, so I said, "OK, but I'm warning you, I don't need to do this. I don't need to talk about this. You know, the thing you're desperately trying not to think about right now?"

He scowled. "I'm not afraid of you."

"OK. Fine. I'm talking about that girl, the one who was seventeen when you met her?"

His eyes widened and sweat appeared on his brow.

"Yes. Her," I said.

His face turned bright red, and he held up a hand. "Please. Stop."

The President said, "That's enough," then eyed each of the generals with a stern expression. "No one will interrupt Mr. Agopian again." He turned his gaze to the general I'd spoken to. "And we will be discussing this matter directly after this meeting."

The President picked up the telephone in front of him and pressed a button then said, "Mr. Detticus, please tell my next appointment I will be delayed by fifteen minutes. I must meet with General Minkshoff. Thank you." He hung up. "Ardor, please, give me your take on the Manila Conference."

"Thank you, sir," I said with genuine deference. "Look, we're in a unique situation. You know everything you want to know about Russia's goals, but let's be realistic: If there were a race between our two intelligence agencies to see whose nose could out-Pinocchio the other, it'd be a photo finish."

No one laughed. I blushed and became self-conscious. I was trying too hard to fit in and my voice sounded insecure as I tried to recover. "My point is that everyone is full of it, and the more you publicly vilify Russia, the worse things will get for everyone. If our goal is to avoid war—" I paused and stared at Silver Hawk, who was trying to bore holes in my face with his angry eyes. "If our goal is to avoid war, then we want to come out publicly as soft as we can."

I paused, knowing the next thing I had to relate would not go over well. It involved trusting ESP, which was a pretty big leap for these war-hungry generals.

"What I know, thanks to my abilities, is that the irony of our situation is that the Russians think we are stronger than we are, and we think they are weaker than they are, but if we shift into a policy of diplomacy, even if feigned, it will steer the consciousness of both nations, which will reduce the threat of war."

I expected interruptions and angry pushback, but instead, the generals sat in silence, each pretending to focus on the papers in front of them.

Stunned, I pinged them. Most were resonating with my message, even those who desperately wanted to test their fancy new military war toys.

"Any questions?" I asked the room.

Silver hawk coughed twice and meekly said, "Thank you."

I sat down, but I wasn't done. I had one more task to complete. I'd checked in with Source before the meeting, but what I'd learned in the last six years was to always check back in with Source after I'd used Psi powers, to ensure I'd spoken accurately.

I checked in, and was pleased to receive the all-clear. I'd said the right thing (Although Source did convey that I could have been less sarcastic about it.)

I said, "I think I've done all I can. May I leave?"

The President smiled. "Yes. Thank you. You may."

I left the room full of twelve stunned men who'd spent their lives scoffing at every facet of the science I regularly relied on now scratching their heads with wonder. They weren't exactly on my side, but I'd given them a lot of things to think about when I'd made an example out of that general. I hoped they'd follow my advice and avoid a deadly conflict.

31
Ping Pong

I was feeling pretty cocky after that meeting, and why not? I was coming into my own and no longer felt like a kid. I'd been in a healthy, committed relationship with Shirley for years now, and I was pursuing quality goals that felt good, like saving Earth from a brutal war. I couldn't wait to see Shirley and tell her all about it.

The only variable that hadn't changed in those years was my obsession for finding my son, whom I'd never named, preferring instead to cultivate a sound, a reverberation, a mantra, "my son, my son, my son."

Every day I woke up to this mantra with a war-drum rhythm in my head, and every day Source rejected my pleas to help me find him.

To be fair, it's not like Source was playing phone tag with me. Source never ignored me. If I felt like it, I could ping Source all day, every day with, *Where's my son?* And all day, every day, it would respond, *Serve your life purpose.*

Shirley would shake her head when I complained. She didn't care how stressful it was, she was of the world of energy and only cared if I was helping humanity to choose good energy over bad energy, which was in the prophecy about me and my potentially evil son, as recorded in that damn Great Book.

So there I was, a man on a mission, or as Shirley had said it, a week before as we were lying in bed, "It's like that old song. You know, 'If I could teach the world to *ping*, in perfect harmony!'"

I smiled at her, but I wasn't buying it. I was sick with anger, and as soon as she turned off her bedside lamp, I returned to my incessant nightly ritual of thinking, *How do I find Esmeralda*? I thought my obsession was normal. I even thought it was OK to pen revenge fantasies in my head, all of which ended quite violently.

Shirley and I lived in New York City now, in a small apartment in the Upper West Side that the FRH owned, so they'd booked a hotel in DC for me to stay at for my meeting with the President.

I normally traveled alone, since Shirley had her own job, but I'd been so nervous about this trip that I'd begged her to come so I'd have her support. Even though Source had assured me nothing would go wrong, when I met the President my anxiety had hit a fever pitch.

I was therefore happy when, on my ride back to the hotel, I was able to text Shirley and ask her to meet me in the lobby bar for a celebratory drink.

I still didn't like drinking, but tonight was a real reason to celebrate, and Shirley did like to drink, which had been an occasional issue of contention. She didn't care if I drank, but she cared if I, even unintentionally, made her feel bad for liking it.

Happy to be on her side for once, I got to the bar before her and ordered a bottle of Champagne. I took a moment to reflect. I wasn't doing so badly. I'd met the woman of my dreams, and the FRH had given me an apartment and a comfortable salary. However, that wasn't enough to make up for lying about my son.

Plus, the FRH was getting their money's worth. They needed me for their mission, and moreover, they knew that in my prophecy was a career full of lucrative speaking tours with sponsorships. I was an investment to them, not a near-and-dear ally.

As I continued to wait, I thought about Alba, whom I rarely saw now. After my earthquake prediction, the FRH had a lot of bad PR to fight when fake psychics came out of the woodwork to make money off my fame, so Alba had moved closer to the FRH's PR office in LA to help with the negative fallout from these con artists.

I wished I could have her and Shirley there to celebrate, but that wasn't a good idea, since Shirley did not appreciate Alba for her complicity in 'The Esmeralda Lie' and I was always nervous that Alba would sniff this out if they spent enough time together. I was lucky that Alba couldn't read other people's minds — just mine, since they'd met a handful of times before Alba had moved to LA.

I snapped back to reality as Shirley appeared in the bar in a sequined dress that matched her hair, which was now shoulder-length. She sat and I motioned to the bartender to uncork the Champagne and fill two flutes.

When he'd finished, I handed Shirley one glass and raised the other and recalled that the last time I'd had Champagne was with Esmeralda on my twenty-first birthday. It was sure nice to paint over that memory with this. Life was capable of so many twists and turns.

"To World War Three — the war that never happened!" I said.

The bartender shot us a peculiar look.

I swallowed my glass in one gulp and pinged him. *We get the weirdest sorts here.*

I laughed.

Shirley cocked her head. "What's funny?"

I blushed and lied. "Oh, nothing." Shirley was cool about most things, but she was stringent as can be about following the ethical codes of Psi science, which involved never pinging another human without a noble reason. It was unethical, but I liked to do it when I was bored, or curious, and this was one of those times.

"OK," she said with a flat tone.

I was seized by a vision of the two of us in an argument outside in the rain. I would normally have paid attention to it, but I figured it was just my imagination, and not Source, since it was raining in the vision, but the sky had been cloudless all day. I looked

283

outside to double-check. Sure enough, it was dark, but there were no signs of impending rain.

I shrugged it off and looked at my empty glass. I got the feeling Shirley wasn't in a celebratory mood, but I was, so I took the bottle, refilled our glasses, and took a swig from my glass.

"You OK?" she asked with concern.

I didn't feel like myself. It was the alcohol, but I didn't want to admit it, so I gave into some self-indulgent pity and said, "Fine, I'll tell you. I just pinged the bartender." I made a face to show her I was annoyed. "Cause I'm unethical, unlike you."

She rolled her eyes but stopped midway. "I didn't say you were unethical."

Before I could respond, the bartender came by and asked, "How is everything over here?"

We were interrupted by a loud clap of thunder and the lights briefly dimmed.

Shirley jumped in her seat.

The bartender smiled. "Don't worry. It's an old hotel. Happens in every storm."

I frowned at the achievement of part of my vision. Now I was certain our fight was going to happen.

The bartender asked, "Is something wrong, sir?"

I glanced at Shirley then dead panned, "No. Everything is perfect. It's the best night of our lives."

Shirley looked at me with her head tilted. "Ardor, are you trying to get into a fight?"

The bartender turned to leave, then cocked his head and spun around. "Wait! Are you...Ardor?" he grinned.

Six years ago, public recognition had been exciting, but over the years I'd had a few issues with stalkers, so now it wasn't much fun. In order to protect me, and Shirley, the FRH had appointed Robin as my full-time bodyguard. He now lived in the apartment across the hall from us in New York City, and he was also here in DC, staying in the room across from ours in the hotel.

This had become protocol after the last stalker, who'd sent us death threats and tried to break into Shirley's car while she was grocery shopping.

When I'd checked in with Source about what to do, and why this was happening, it had been *very* clear. It said if I followed the ethics of Psi, with no wiggle room, there was no need for concern, but if I stayed the course, especially to pursue Esmeralda, anything was fair, including assassination. This was why Shirley was strict about toeing the line. She was certain that selfish pinging was dangerous, and while she had a point, I needed to relax from time to time.

After the supermarket incident, Shirley had gotten so scared that I'd tried to resign from my public life, to protect her, but Suzanne had said, "You must fulfill your prophecy, and the prophecy says to embrace fame and teach the world about energy. That's your job. If you die, it's still worth it."

Shirley agreed with her, only her take was a little different. She thought it was her job to ensure that I

285

didn't mess up, which had created a sort of cat-and-mouse game between us when I failed to check in before pinging strangers, like I'd just done.

I returned my attention to the present and realized the bartender was staring and waiting for my reply.

I nodded without smiling. "Yeah. I'm him." I wanted him to go away so I could argue with Shirley about letting me play around a little from time to time.

His smiled widened and his jaw jutted. "So, uh, can you read my mind?"

I empathed his zeal as well as Shirley's apprehension for how I would reply.

A new image of Shirley and I arguing in the rain near a taxi flashed. I swallowed more Champagne then said to the bartender, "Yeah, I see no tip."

He narrowed his eyes before looking down and hunching his shoulders.

Shirley put her palm on her forehead and said, "I'm sorry. He's in a bad mood. We'll take the check."

I didn't need empathy or ESP to know he thought I was a jerk.

When he was out of earshot, Shirley said, "Ardor, what's wrong?"

"It's just—" I thought about what was wrong, and I was disappointed to realize that the only thing wrong was with me. Shirley had nothing but our best interests in mind, and I was being immature and looking to fight. I looked at the Champagne glass on the table and remembered why I wasn't a fan of booze. It made me act out and give in to immature impulses.

The bartender returned and dropped the bill.

I gave him a big tip and wrote, "sorry," and signed it. I looked up. "I'm sorry, Shirley. I'm just not feeling like myself. I need some time to think."

She reached for my hand. "Let's go to our room."

I withdrew my hand, still feeling off and sullen. "No thanks. I'm hungry."

"Our flight is early. Let's get room service."

I stood. "What? C'mon! I just met with the President, and I want to celebrate!"

She shook her head. "Ardor, I'm sorry, but I'm really tired. I just don't have it in me."

I shook my head and felt a wave of self-pity. I *deserved* a chance to celebrate. "I understand, but I'm going out. I can sleep on the plane."

I started for the lobby as Shirley took a second to grab her purse and follow me. When I got there, I told the bellhop to hail a taxi.

He motioned to a cab outside. "No wait, sir."

I strode ahead of Shirley to the cab then turned around after opening the door to let her in.

She shook her head. "I told you; I don't want to go."

I rolled my eyes. "Fine." I got in and turned to face her. "I'll be quiet when I get home tonight."

She started to say something but then stopped herself. "OK, Ardor, but… please be careful."

I smiled with sarcasm. "Have a great night."

I closed the door and the driver asked, "Where to?"

"Take me to a bar."

"Which one?"

"Any one."

He said, "Okey-dokey," and we pulled into traffic.

32
Stupid Human Tricks

The cabbie dropped me off at a bar in Adam's Morgan.

The bar was small with few seats and a pianist playing softly in the back. It smelled like fresh paint, but the walls were old and peeling. I was the youngest person there, by far. I felt drunk, but the mirror behind the bar told me I didn't look like it and no one paid attention as I sat on a stool. I was still wearing my shirt and jeans from my attempt to look cool at the Pentagon, but it seemed OK for this part of DC.

I pulled out my phone and turned it off, hoping Shirley would call, get my voicemail and worry. I was upset at her for being right about, well, pretty much everything, and I was still taking offense from the incident with the bartender for the same reason any partner does. I was displacing my anger with Esmeralda, the FRH, and Alba on her, because she loved me, and I thought I could.

The bartender was an aging man with a mean face, so I was surprised when he smiled warmly as he asked, "What'll it be?"

As soon as he was done asking, his face fell back into a frown, so I pinged him, and learned that he was a victim of a bad resting face: All I got in my ping were the complacent thoughts of a good-natured man.

This was my first time ordering just for myself, so I got stage fright when the bartender expected me to know the name of a drink. I'd only tried beer, wine, and Champagne, so I asked him to make me something with what the guy on the other end was drinking. I didn't even look at the guy's drink. He just seemed cool.

The bartender nodded pleasantly and asked, "Anything you don't like?"

"Yeah, my life," I said, forgetting to accentuate the half-joke with a smile.

The man on my right faced me, smiled, lifted his beer, and said, "Amen."

I didn't know how to make conversation, but I was lonely, so I tried, "Got that right," mimicking my best recollection of how people on TV talked.

The man trained his eyes on me and asked, "What's your story?" He looked tired, or drunk, or both, but not intimidating. I felt like we could get along.

"Same old, same old," I lied. "I'm just trying my best to figure life out."

He laughed derisively and said, "Well, kid, it doesn't get much better if you're wondering what it's like on my side." He burped, shifted his weight and leaned forward. He smelled boozy, but I didn't mind.

Without Shirley there to scold me, I pinged his memory and learned he had been left twice, both times for being a drunk. But he had no history of abuse, nor a mean bone in his body. He was a sad case. A man who couldn't hold down a job or a relationship.

He'd never married, but both women had tried to make things work with him for a decade each. He'd been single for a third decade, eking out a living on a graveyard shift at a storage facility, watching monitors for break-ins. He drank on the job, but not enough to get caught. It was a good fit for him.

He gave me a puzzled look when I stopped pinging, and I sensed that he had 'felt' my presence in his mind, something few people sensed. It meant that, if so inclined, he could easily develop his Psi abilities. One of my projects with the FRH had been investigating theories like this. We were performing research on 'normal' subjects to see if I had exploited a common gene, or if I had special talents. Both were true.

"Sorry," I told the guy. "Just lost in thoughts."

He nodded. "Not a problem." He put his hand forward. "I'm Hank."

I shook his hand, trying to exert manly strength, but I failed and instead, it felt like he was crushing my hand.

"And you are?" he asked, looking confused again.

"I'm Ar-Arthur," I lied, hoping to remain anonymous.

"Nice to meet you, Arthur." He smiled and took a swig. "Lemme guess, woman gotcha down?"

The bartender returned to hand me a martini glass with a gold-colored drink and a bright red cherry floating in the center. I took a sip, and it was so bitter I wanted to spit it out. It made Champagne taste like fruit juice.

Hank and the man to his right laughed.

The second man said, "First Manhattan?"

I didn't get the joke. "Yeah, I'm from the Upper West Side."

They briefly shared a look.

Hank pointed at my glass. "He means the drink."

I laughed and took another sip. "Yeah, I come from a family of drinkers, but I'm just learning now."

The man to Hank's right lifted his glass but didn't wait for me to take his sip.

I raised mine and took a third sip, and realized it wasn't so bad once you knew what to expect.

"So, what's your story?" Hank asked a second time.

"Well, I had a big meeting today, and it went great, so I asked my girlfriend to meet me to celebrate, and she was—" I shook my head. "She was a real wet blanket."

Hank looked lost in a memory, then said, "Yeah."

I pinged him. He had nostalgia for the first ex, who had been a total wet blanket.

"It's OK," I said, forgetting my plans for anonymity, "If you want Helen back, just go easy on the drinking and call her. She misses you too."

He sat up straight and coughed. "What the hell?"

The man to his right said, "What's wrong?"

"This kid. He just… I swear, he just read my mind."

The guy looked at Hank, then squinted at me, and said, "Say, are you…?"

I took another sip, a bigger one, and smiled. "The one and only."

"Ardor! You don't say. Wow." He finished his drink in one gulp and waved his empty glass in the air.

The bartender came over. "Another round, Eliot?"

"Yeah, and another for the kid." He nodded at me and winked. "The psychic!"

The bartender looked amused before he looked at me and did a double take. "Wow!" he exclaimed, looking back at Eliot. "Is that *him*?"

The energy of the room shifted. The piano player had just ended a song, so it was quieter and the whole bar could hear jubilation in my corner. It didn't take long for others to see me and connect the dots.

"Do me!" The bartender said, as if this were a normal question to ask.

I let the Manhattan and my angst at Shirley's rule-following get the best of me and smiled. These parlor tricks were easy, and I wanted this night. I'd earned it.

I rubbed my temples for effect, like I'd done when I worked for Esmeralda in the mall, and said, "Let's see: Dan, from Centerville, you always wanted to be a carpenter, but the modern economy said otherwise, so you bartend at night, and—" I was about to say he masturbated a lot, but I was afraid of how he'd react. I pinged him, and gleaned pure puppy dog enthusiasm, so

293

I said, "Let's just say you like to whittle your own wood, um, a lot." I looked down from shyness.

The bar erupted in laughter.

I looked up. Even the pianist had come to check me out. A man pushed his face over Eliot's shoulder. "Tell me! Will my kid make it?" He wasn't smiling.

Jolts of terror and sadness hit me as I pinged him and got an answer, but not the one he was looking for. Before I could try to lie, he started crying. My face had said enough. His five-year-old would not survive the next round of chemo. I thought about my son, and for the first time, I felt lucky.

The next two hours flew by as I gave free psychic readings to everyone while other patrons came and went, all the while getting free drinks and shots.

I told a man the gender of his ten-week pregnant wife's baby. I told another man about an upcoming inheritance from an unknown relative, and I even told one guy where to find the parents who had given him up for adoption twenty years ago. Eventually I got so dizzy from the booze that I excused myself to breathe into a toilet. I ended up puking, and Hank had to help me walk to the sink when I was done.

I don't remember much else, except a flicker of the bartender calling me a cab, and a hotel employee assisting me to my room as I said, "Gosh I'm sorry!"

***

I woke the next morning to an empty bed and no sign of Shirley. I didn't need Source to perceive that when she returned, I'd have a lot of explaining to do.

Source interrupted my throbbing headache. *You really did it this time. You shouldn't get drunk in public now that you're famous.*

Huh? I asked.

Look at the paper.

What paper? I asked.

Check the front door.

I walked to the door, every step sending daggers of pain to my temples. I opened it and saw a copy of *USA Today*, with a huge font that read, "Congress Demands Testimony from Ardor after President asks for reversal on War request."

What is this? I asked Source.

There are consequences to failing to adhere to the ethics of Psi science. Be glad this is all that happened.

I left the paper by the door and returned to bed. Desperate for rest, I pulled a pillow over my head, but before I could drift back to sleep, the hotel phone rang. I picked it up then immediately hung up, but it rang again right after, so I picked it up and said, "Hello?"

"Ardor!" Josip's angry voice was on the other end.

"What?" I asked, throwing the pillow off my head and sitting up.

"Get body downstairs *now*!" he screamed in a tone he'd never used.

295

I hung up and was in the lobby five minutes later to find him standing with arms crossed and a sour look.

"Get in car!" he said.

"What about Shirley?" I asked.

"She does not want to come."

I put my hands on my hips. "Well, I want her to come."

He didn't say a word. He turned around and led me to an idling SUV out front with Robin in the driver's seat. I slumped into the backseat and stared out the window as we left, checking my phone every so often to see if Shirley had texted or called.

33
Alba's High Heel

As we drove, I didn't ping Robin or Josip. I instead spent the time stewing over the hypocrisy of the Universe and its demands. So what if I'd had a little fun with my Psi talents? Why was I being punished? Ultimately, I realized that what really had me down was the fact that Shirley had not called.

Hours later, as we pulled into the FRH's estate in Armonk, New York, I was startled by a surge of energy from Josip. It was a blizzard of sorrow and trepidation.

He had the ability to tell if I was reading his mind, but he couldn't stop me, so I probed him. I was expecting anti-Ardor thoughts, but instead felt gut punched upon learning that he was festering with anxiety for his impending death.

I teared up as I learned he had late-stage lung cancer and didn't want to go just yet.

He eyed me briefly before gazing out the window as Robin entered the driveway to the compound. When we pulled in front, I was shocked to see Alba standing on the front porch, and she did not look happy to see me.

Exiting the car, Josip fumbled for his pipe and took a puff before entering into one of his patented coughing fits, which until then had seemed amusing.

I shot him a look of concern.

He squinted at me and shook his head.

I hung my head, but before I could enter a state of pity, Josip pinged me!

Is not so bad, Ardor. I had good life. I did much good, and less bad. I did not want to forgo certain pleasure, the tobacco, so it is like this and so it goes. But now that I am near end, I must prepare you in secret for final stand. You must listen.

I didn't reply. My heart felt thick and heavy. I was overwhelmed with an urge to heave and sob, not just cry. I knelt down on the ground. It was early morning. Birds were chirping and they somehow made it worse.

Alba turned around and shot me a strange look.

Josip pinged me, *Tell her nothing! Nothing!*

I pinged, *Why did you hide your ability from me?*

We are not discuss this. It may not be safe as we want. I will approach when at good time. For now, you do normal Ardor things. But just in case…

He hunched over and grabbed his chest.

I empathed terror. *In case what?* I begged.

He couldn't reply. He was suffering from something nasty. I empathed him and sensed a familiar energy. I wanted to stop, but continued and felt the terror Esmeralda had inflicted on me many times before.

This pain was just as brutal, only the hue was yellow, not orange. Someone else was attacking him with Psi.

Josip hung his head lower but managed to ping, *Trust only Shirley!*

I wanted to rush to his side, but was frozen with fear. I knew he was about to die, and I could do nothing about it. This helpless certainty was terrifying.

He removed his hand from his chest and crumpled to the floor. His body smacked against the wooden porch and all the birds flew away in a hurry.

Robin turned around and sprinted to Josip's side. A moment later, Alba ran towards him, but something seemed off — like she wasn't surprised.

Robin tried to do CPR as I stared at a tree and asked Source for guidance.

It said, *Things are unraveling. Keep your integrity.*

Alba broke my concentration by yelling, "Ardor!"

I turned from the tree I was staring at. "Huh?"

She was standing over Josip's body with her arms crossed, wearing a scowl. "What are you doing? Get inside. Now!"

I didn't like her tone or demeanor, but before I could object, Robin zipped in front of me, pistol drawn, as if we were under attack. I spun around to discover what he was looking at, but couldn't make out any foe.

"Ardor! Get inside now!" Alba screamed from the doorway.

I backed my way to the front door and bumped into her. She grabbed me, pushed me inside, then slammed the door, leaving Robin outside. Her behavior was off. She seemed upset, but somehow, I could tell it wasn't related to Josip.

"What the hell is the danger?" I asked.

"Be quiet!" she replied.

The lights in the house dimmed, and the power shut off. It was light outside, but the entryway had no windows, so we were immersed in pitch-black.

The front door opened, and Robin ran in and slammed it behind him.

"All clear outside, but we have some funky energy. I haven't seen this since Esmeralda."

Before I could ask what was happening, that same yellow hue crept into my mind's eye. I trembled with panic. It had been years since I'd felt this type of energy, but now that I was feeling it again, I was certain that while this felt the same, it wasn't. It wasn't orange and it wasn't Esmeralda.

"Stop it!" I screamed.

No one answered and nothing happened.

"Robin? Alba?" I shouted.

The pain increased and I remember wishing I had Shirley and her healing powers as I lost consciousness.

***

I woke on a couch to the sight of Alba and two strange men in lab coats standing over me. Alba looked furiously worried, another new look.

"What… what happened?" I asked.

She shook her head. "It's not good, Ardor."

I sat up, felt a head rush, and fell back on the couch. "Is Esmeralda back?"

Both men flinched when I said her name.

Alba shook her head. "No. That's impossible. She's dead. You must've hit your head really hard."

I sat up again, still feeling dizzy, but this time I was able to get into a normal sitting position.

"Right. Duh. So then, what the hell is happening?"

"We're under attack — from inside."

I felt butterflies in my stomach. "Who is it?"

She narrowed her eyes and pointed at me. "We think it's you. You're the only person who could've done this, only we don't understand why. Somehow, you just killed Josip, then almost killed the rest of us, and we're lucky you passed out."

Her words stung, but I knew they were false. Josip wouldn't have confided in and warned me if I were dangerous, and I would know if I'd used Psi energy. Either Alba was lying, which I could no longer put past her, or she was misinformed and paranoid.

I was about to argue when I felt my pocket vibrate from my phone. I pulled it out. Shirley was calling and it said I'd missed three calls from her.

Alba snatched the phone and denied the call. "You are not to talk to anyone!"

"Give me that back!" I shouted, lunging at her.

She dodged me. "Let's take him to the secure facility. This is too risky."

"What?" I asked.

The men put their arms under my armpits to help me stand, but I pushed them away and shouted, "What is going on?"

I pinged Source and felt a terrible pain accompanied by a yellow hue. Was I going crazy? Could this yellow source somehow be coming from me?

What the hell? I asked Source.

The pain increased and I again couldn't connect.

One of the men approached me.

I raised two shaky fists and yelled, "Stay away!"

He backed off and the other grabbed a walkie-talkie, but Alba held up a hand and he put it away.

"He'll cooperate," she said with a thin smile.

"The hell I will," I snarled.

She shot me a look I knew well. She was my older sister, and my mistrust was insulting.

Her appeal to our familial bond worked. I said, "OK, I'll go, but I want answers on the way!"

She nodded and the men gave me space. "Follow me." She turned and walked down the hallway that led to the kitchen.

I followed her, shocked to see Josip's pale body lying on the dining table with Robin standing over him, a pistol still in his hand at his side.

I felt a pang of devastation as I again contemplated the loss of one of my only friends, but I also remembered his final words: *Trust only Shirley.*

I looked at Alba. She was staring at the body. I empathed her and she didn't have an iota of remorse about Josip's death. I could no longer fool myself. She was not an ally and most likely an enemy.

I cleared my throat. "Give me my phone."

She looked at me and shook her head.

"Alba, I'm a second away from telling you and the FRH to take a hike. I don't care how serious this is. I'm not an enemy, or a prisoner. Give me my phone."

The painful yellow hue returned. I shut my eyes and winced. "What the hell is going on!" I screamed. The painful hue doubled, but when I tried to stop it with the trick I'd learned with Esmeralda, it didn't work.

Robin shouted, "What's happening?"

I opened my eyes and saw Alba shake her head then faint to the floor. I mustered all my strength and said to Robin, "I don't know, but this is bad."

"Help!" one of the men shouted. He pushed at his temples as blood oozed from his ears then collapsed. The other man shrieked as he too fell to the floor.

My phone rang. I prayed it was Shirley, my only hope. I crawled to Alba's limp body, grabbed it, and shouted, "Hello?" My pain vanished, but when I heard the reply, my heart seized with dread.

"Hello, Ardor," a familiar voice said. "How are you?"

"Esmeralda?"

The voice cackled. "So you *did* know."

"I've been waiting a long time to hear from you."

She laughed again. "And why is that?"

What do you want?" I said.

"You know what I want."

"Actually, I don't! You already have our son. What more could you want from *me*?"

"It's not enough." She sounded happy.

"What else could you possibly need?"

She giggled. "You, Ardor. I want you."

"What? That's insane. I don't even know what that means, but I assure you I'm never coming near you again!" I glanced down and grimaced at the sight of Robin and Alba's limp bodies beneath me on the floor.

"Oh yeah?" she taunted.

Before I could reply, Alba reached up, pulled my leg, and I tripped and fell. Before I could react, she grabbed my arm and twisted it so that my head bent forward. She then used her other arm to press my face into the floor. Her hold was so tight I couldn't wriggle.

"Come with us, and make this easy," she said.

Source pinged me, *Save your strength.*

I fought an urge to resist and relaxed. "Fine."

Alba released her grip enough for me to side step Robin's body and stand.

She bent over and removed the gun from his hands and poked it into my back. With no emotion, she said, "Walk ahead of me and don't try anything."

I nodded while repeating Josip's final words in my head. *Trust only Shirley.*

Finally, a test I could pass.

I spun around and clocked Alba in the face with my phone, hard as I could. She flew back as I hit her, tripped on Robin, and fell, still clutching the gun.

She pointed it at me, but her fall had awoken Robin.

His eyes darted from the gun to me and back to Alba. He frowned then twisted her arm so that the gun popped out and flew across the floor.

I stared at it until he yelled, "Ardor, get the gun!"

I grabbed it and stared at him with wide eyes.

Alba stood, squinted her eyes, and Robin screamed.

I felt the same pain, and now it was clear to me that this yellow-hued attack was coming from Alba, and had been the whole time.

She had murdered Josip.

Robin mouthed, *kill her* as he writhed with pain.

Alba walked towards me, my pain increasing with each step. "Sorry, not sorry, bro," she said with a smile.

Trust only Shirley. I aimed and fired once. The sound hurt my ears, but the painful yellow hue vanished as my sister collapsed against the wall. Blood oozed into the front of her blouse, and she slumped to the floor.

Robin stood but looked unsteady and weak, like a drunk. With great effort he threw his keys to me and said, "Take the car."

"Come with me!" I shouted.

His eyes rolled back in their sockets as he squeezed his temples and blood trickled from his ears. "I can't," he winced.

"No way!" I said. "I need you. Shirley will fix you!"

He nodded at Alba. "The FRH is on its way and they're not going to believe you. You have to go. I'm too weak. Just go."

I stood still, mouth agape, trying to think of a plan.

"You must go *now!*" he shouted

I nodded, ran to the car, and pulled out of the driveway, but waited until I got on the main road before tossing the gun on the passenger seat.

The phone rang a moment later. The caller ID said 'Suzanne'.

I picked it up and shouted, "Suzanne, you're not going to believe what happened!"

Esmeralda replied, "Ardor. You have been very bad, and I'm sorry to say that there is no longer any hope for you. I am going to find you and kill you."

I didn't answer.

"Ardor? Are you too scared to answer?"

I hung up then pinged, *I hear you, but you're the one who should be scared. And you don't need to find me. I'm going to find you and take you out. You got that?*

34
The Lam Scam

I wasn't familiar with this part of New York, but I was armed with adrenaline that helped me make my way back to the highway out of Armonk. But what now? Josip was dead. I had one ally left, Source. Well, at least I was all in on trusting it, finally.

OK, riddle me this, Source. I just killed my sister, Esmeralda wants to kill me, and apparently, the FRH is also against me. What can I do? Help me!

Congratulations, You get it. Luckily, we're still on a timeline that can work.

I nodded. *So the world isn't doomed?*

Barely, but yes. Thanks to your incredible ability to ignore Source and Psi ethics over and over again, you almost failed, but you got it in the nick of time.

I chuckled. *Harsh, but fair. Go on. I'm all ears.*

First and foremost, continue to heed Josip's warning. Trust only Shirley. The FRH is monitoring her, and this car, so you must ditch it for public transportation and avoid contacting her until further notice.

My heart didn't like this, but I remained composed. *And Ez, can she find me?*

Yes, and no. She can try to locate you, but you can deceive her.

How?

Pretend to be where you are not.

C'mon, Source! This riddle stuff is getting old. What does that mean?

Pretend to be where you are not.

I took a breath, thought about it, and it made sense. If I pretended to be in Hawaii, my mental stream of consciousness would indicate that I was in Hawaii. *The world is as you are.* Anyone pinging me would only be able to ping what I considered my reality. Esmeralda didn't have GPS or radar tracking. She could only intercept my thoughts. Come to think of it, this was just like the time I'd tricked her by cultivating false thoughts about my day when I'd tried to meet Alba and came home late on the bus.

OK, Source. I got this. Over and out!

I got on 684 North while imagining I was on 684 South, headed back to my apartment in the city. I didn't think about anything else as I actually drove to Danbury, Connecticut, the nearest city with a major bus line.

Forty minutes later, I was parked at a Greyhound station. I looked at the gun on the passenger seat and realized it was a murder weapon, with my prints. I felt like I should bring it along, but it was too big for my pockets, and I didn't have a bag.

What should I do?

Grab the gun and stick it in your pants. Walk carefully to the back of the dumpster behind you. You'll find a discarded backpack there. It's muddy and looks like it belongs to a junkie, but it'll do. Put the gun in it, buy a ticket for DC, and bring it on the bus.

I obeyed. Minutes later I bought a ticket to Washington DC, and in an hour my face was pressed against a window as I faked sleep to avoid talking to the elderly woman next to me who was emoting desperation for conversation.

Two people had stared at me in the station, but when I'd read their minds, I'd discovered that while they had recognized me, the notion of Ardor with a muddy backpack taking a bus was so preposterous they'd assumed I was merely a lookalike.

As the bus traveled south, I doubled down on my misinformation campaign, and imagined myself getting on a train at Penn Station to head to DC.

I desperately wanted to ping Shirley, but I knew it was a bad idea. The less she knew, the safer she'd be. I trusted that Source would help us reunite in time.

Meanwhile, I was terrified about the gun going off. I didn't know anything about guns, so I was worried that if we hit a speed bump it might go off. I also knew that I had no idea how to use it. When I'd killed Alba, I'd been lucky. She'd been close. I was no marksman.

I tried to only contemplate my fake trip to DC, but my mind wasn't fully onboard. I couldn't stop reliving what had just happened. I loved Alba, so I didn't want to acknowledge that she'd taken Esmeralda's side. However, the facts were clear. She'd lied to me about killing Esmeralda and now she'd tried to force me into captivity. I'd had no choice but to defend myself, but my guilt and grief were overpowering these facts.

I was jostled from my mind when the woman next to me asked, "Are you OK?"

I opened my eyes. I'd been crying and shaking.

I turned to her, and her smile melted a bit of my pain.

She looked like the tiny grandma on *The Golden Girls*, a show my mom had loved. I didn't care for it, but I did like her familiar appearance. I was impressed by how thick her hair was, despite her age. It was gray, but healthy. For the first time in my life, I thought about getting old and wondered how I would age.

I smooshed my tears across my cheeks and forced a smile. "Someone I love died today."

She nodded slowly and grimaced. "I'm so sorry, dear. It's hard to lose someone. Was it someone close?"

More tears came, and she patted my hand.

I jumped at her touch, and she backed off, eyeing the muddy backpack. I empathed fear, so I pinged her: she was now worried I was violent, a junkie, or both.

I looked down, blushing, and said, "I'm sorry I scared you, ma'am. I assure you I'm not dangerous."

She exhaled. "OK, dear. It's OK." She shifted her body a bit towards the aisle.

I took the hint and went back to laying my head against the window.

When the bus took a fifteen-minute rest stop at a station in Philadelphia, most of the passengers got off. Still obsessing over Alba, I decided to wait and get some rest. I leaned back and shut my eyes.

Ten minutes later, I was jarred back to reality by a firm hand on my shoulder. I looked up. It was a security guard with a Greyhound logo on his uniform. He was about my age, overweight, and out of shape.

"Sir?" he asked.

"Um, hello? What happened?" My heart raced. All I could think about was the gun in the bag at my feet.

"Can I see your ticket please?"

"Sure," I said, but I didn't move.

He cleared his throat. "Sir?"

In my haste, I'd shoved the ticket in the bag with the gun. I was not going to open it in front of him. I made strong eye contact, trying to look calm and confident, but his eyes had a sadistically creative look that I recognized from bullies in my youth.

"I'm only going to ask you once more," he said as he put a hand on his hip. I looked at his waist and was relieved to see he only had a nightstick, not a gun.

In every previous scary instance in my life, I'd made decisions based on impulsive fear. I was thus proud of myself for instead consulting Source.

What now?

Grab the backpack and get off. When he tries to arrest you, show him the gun.

Excuse me?

311

There is no time to explain. Do it.

"You know what?" I said aloud. "Screw this. I don't need to put up with this shit." I grabbed the backpack, stood, and pushed my way past him.

He was confused by my lack of deference but didn't stop me. I exited the bus and saw the grandma shaking her head at me as she stood next to another guard.

The first guard yelled, "Hey! Stop right there!"

Obey him, Source said.

I turned and waited for him to catch up to me.

"I asked you for your ticket!" he shouted, pressing a finger into my chest.

I stepped back, unzipped the backpack, and showed him the ticket and gun.

"There's your ticket!" I smiled. I turned and ran to the exit of the Greyhound station. I didn't know where I was, but I didn't need GPS. I had Source.

What now? I asked.

Good job. But next time, don't smile. You're not supposed to be having fun.

OK, OK! So, what's next?

Getting arrested.

I heard sirens and screeching tires behind me, and my stomach sank. I turned around. A police car was racing after me. It cut me off from ahead before another came and parked behind me. The first had two cops in it. One used a bullhorn to scream at me and the other stood in front of his door and trained his gun on me.

More officers surrounded me as I carefully lowered the bag to the street. One handcuffed me while barking orders that made me even more nervous.

As they were reading me my rights and shoving me in the back of a car, I heard my phone ring. I asked Source who was calling.

It's Shirley. She's still in DC, waiting for you.

I felt defeated. *Why did you trick me? Why would you get me arrested?*

Because Esmeralda and the FRH can't kill you in jail.

35
What's Up, Doc?

My family had its issues, but criminality wasn't one of them, so I wasn't sure what to expect when the police took me to the local jail. I was next booked, fingerprinted, and had my mug shot taken. The charges were a bunch of legal words I vaguely understood, with "attempted" in front of all of them.

They asked if I wanted a lawyer. I told them I did, but they didn't let me sit and wait for one. Instead, they cuffed me and led me to a cell with a few men in it.

I pinged the room.

The first guy, Bruno, was in there for attempted assault. He was balding with rolls of fat only on his midsection, and tree trunks for arms. He had gotten drunk at a tavern the night before and tried to jump over the bar and punch the bartender after being refused service at last call.

The guy was still drunk, and angrier than he'd been at the time of his arrest. His main thought pattern was a short circuit of "finding that SOB bartender and killing him." He also had moments of sobriety when he worried about how to hide this from his wife and how to lie to his employer about missing work that morning. Unfortunately for him, he was going to lose his job, and eventually his wife.

Meanwhile, sitting on the cell's lone toilet, fully clothed, was a thin black man named Conrad, who went by Connie. He was in for attempted larceny, but he was innocent. His problem was that he'd been guilty in prior incidents, so he had no credibility. He wasn't going to evade these charges. The good news was he wouldn't serve hard time. This was his 'rock bottom'. His future was bright.

There were two other people, both of whom looked tougher than Connie and Bruno, but they were sleeping, so when I tried to ping them, I only got their dream sequences, which I found terrifying. This reinforced how my 'trick' of pretending to be where I was not had worked on Esmeralda. Mind reading was basic. It reported the mind's current spin, not reality.

Now that I'd assessed my cellmates, I was ready to check in. *What's next, Source?*

The doctor.

Excuse me?

I heard the hiss of the room's pneumatic locking system. A cop I hadn't yet encountered entered with Robin following him.

"Robin!" I shouted.

He didn't return my smile.

"I'm so glad to see you," I said.

He scowled and nodded like I was a stranger.

The cop whispered something to him before opening the cell door to cuff my wrists and shackle my ankles, which made walking difficult. Feeling like an animal, I was led to a chair in a nearby room and ordered to sit. I felt like a bad puppy as I sat and waited while he went outside to chat with Robin.

The holding room was plain and unadorned. I couldn't hear them and got bored waiting, so I finally caved and used remote viewing to spy on them.

"I need to see him alone," Robin said with professional authority.

The cop replied, "That's against protocol."

Robin flashed a badge. "I showed this at the check in. They didn't tell you?"

"FBI?" the cop said. "Jesus. What did that kid do?"

"He's Ardor." Robin paused. "*The* Ardor."

"Wow. We don't get a lotta celebrities here. What'd he do?"

Robin sighed. "Where do I start? Most recently? He murdered his sister."

The cop exhaled a long whistle. "Scumbag. OK. I'll wait outside."

"Sounds good."

The door opened, and they both entered.

The officer shot me a sadistic look. "Excuse me, *Mr. Ardor*, but it's time to settle the bill." He laughed and left.

After the door closed, I smiled and said, "Robin, I thought you were gonna die!"

He shook his head and looked at the floor.

"How'd you get here? I mean, how'd you find me?" I felt dizzy with relief.

He continued to stare at the floor.

"What's going to happen to me? And what was that about the FBI? And why'd you tell them I killed Alba?"

He glanced at me then looked away. "Listen. There's not much time."

I cocked my head and waited, but he didn't say anything. After a long, awkward delay, my euphoria faded and I said, "Seriously, what's up?"

He glared at me.

"What? What's wrong? What'd I do?" I stretched my grin wide, hoping he'd lighten up.

He swallowed so hard his Adam's apple bobbed then he went flush and said, "What's wrong? You're what's wrong, Ardor. You're a disgrace to the FRH and the world." He gritted his teeth and let his voice fall into a low growl. "Look, I don't know how you manipulated me back at the house, but I've learned my lesson and I'm here to put an end to you."

My heart constricted and my mouth went dry.

He nodded. "Yeah. It's over, Ardor. I thought you could work within the system and do what you were told, but you can't. You can't do *anything* right."

"What are you talking about?" I whispered, afraid of my own voice.

"I'm talking about your body count." He enumerated a list with his fingers. "Charles. Josip. Alba,

317

and nearly me. You're nothing but trouble, and I'm pretty sure I know what's next, if—"

"If what?"

He shook his head and glared, but his eyes were on my forehead.

I said, "Robin, you know I didn't kill any of them on purpose — especially Josip! He had a heart attack, I didn't even..." I didn't know what else to say.

Shaking his head, he drew a syringe from his pocket.

I pushed back against my chair, but it was bolted to the floor. "What is that?"

He raised the syringe and calmly walked to me.

"The FRH is lying to you," I shouted, struggling against my restraints.

He grabbed my right arm with force.

"Help." I winced and tried to jump from my seat, but I fell to the floor, more vulnerable than before.

The officer knocked on the door and shouted, "Everything OK?"

"I got this," Robin said in an authoritative voice. He crouched down and clutched my arm again.

I pinged the officer. He wasn't concerned.

"Robin, please don't do this," I begged in my most desperate tone.

He stabbed my arm, but nothing happened.

"Oh I see, it's fake," I said. Then the room and my consciousness faded away.

***

I woke up on a twin bed in a room with white walls. It smelled like rubbing alcohol, and my right arm was killing me. It was heavily bandaged and shackled to the bed. My hands were not cuffed to each other, but I was shackled to several other spots on the bed.

Where am I?

A doctor's office. They have a contract with the jail. You're being treated for a serious virus. You still need to be protected, so this is the best we can do.

Protected? I'm in so much pain. What'd Robin do?

He tried to kill you, but you're lucky.

What? How could you let this happen?

You let this happen. You should never have gone to Croatia. But there's still time.

I slammed my head back into the pillow. The jolt sent tremors of pain from my arm to my brain. *"Ow!"*

As if on cue, the door opened, and Shirley came in.

A heartfelt, cheesy grin spread across my face.

OK. I get it now, I told Source.

She won't let you die from this. But without her, you would've.

She hurried to the bed and tried to hug and kiss me without hurting me. She failed, but it was worth it. I'd missed her more than I'd thought.

"Shirley, I'm so sorry… About the—"

"Ardor, I don't care about anything." She smiled and took my hand. "I'm just so glad you're... well, I mean, I can't believe..."

I felt a sense of ecstasy I'd never felt. So this was love? The sheer sight of her transported me away from my worry. I couldn't think about Alba's death, my son, or the threat of Esmeralda with her around. Even Robin's betrayal was not a blip on my radar. I felt a serene sense of unity and love that nourished me and left me wanting nothing else. Sadly, that feeling vanished a moment later when Robin entered.

He looked bashful. "Ardor?"

I scowled and looked away. "Screw off."

Shirley drew in a sharp breath. "Ardor!"

I pinged her. *Be careful. He's a double agent. Trust only me.*

She shook her head. "Ardor, Robin was tricked. We've cleared it up."

"Tricked?" I narrowed my eyes. "He saw Alba try to kill me!"

"Ardor, I can't remember anything," Robin said with more emotion than usual.

"What are you talking about?" I asked.

"I'm saying that something happened, and all I can remember is Josip dying and then that awful yellow attack. The next thing I remember is waking up with Alba's body next to mine on the floor. I was told you shot her, after trying to kill me, then ran off with my gun. I thought I had to stop you. I was under orders."

"I don't care if you *thought* you had to. I feel like I'm dying. I'm done with you."

"Done?" he repeated. "But Ardor, Shirley set me straight. I'm here to help now."

"Too bad." I looked at Shirley and smiled. I reached out for her hand. She gave it to me, and I squeezed it and held onto it. I looked at Robin. "I'm done with you, the FRH, Esmeralda, and the hunt for my son. I'm done with all of it. I quit." I said this with so much dramatic emotion that I had trouble taking myself seriously.

Shirley let my hand go and gave me a look of pity. "You will do no such thing."

Robin smirked and I wanted to kill him.

"You tried to kill me! This isn't funny."

He nodded and I detected remorse that made it hard to stay angry.

Source piped in, *You're at the end. Don't fall back into bad habits. Finish the mission, Ardor.*

"Fine," I shouted. "I won't quit." I looked at Shirley. "But I want three things."

"Three things?" she asked with raised brows.

"Yeah," I smiled. I held up my index finger. "One. From now on the two of us stay together, at all times." I looked at Robin. "And two? I'm done with you."

"That's impossible." He pulled out his FBI badge. "I'm your custody officer."

I frowned. "Perfect." I shut my eyes and felt like drifting into sleep. I could tell I was on some pretty powerful medication. "Fine. But know this: I don't trust

321

you. Not now, and not ever again." I tried to add a "harrumph," but the drugs were making it hard to speak.

I started to drift off, but Shirley interrupted me.

"And?" she asked.

I opened my eyes. "And?"

She held up three fingers. "You said three things?"

I smiled. "Oh." I giggled.

She looked amused. "Ardor?" She smiled

My heart moved at the sight of her dimples. "I want to marry you," I said.

She gasped and returned my smile.

With the rapture of love and opiates, I fell asleep.

36
Oh Sister, Where Art Thou?

I awoke a few hours later in the same room, attached to the same bed, still reeling from the virus, only now I was also groggy from the meds. The room smelled of rubbing alcohol and disinfectant, and I could hear the soft hum of a fan. Shirley slept in a chair while Robin sat in another, poised like a sentinel, eyes on the door.

Source greeted me, *It's time to get serious. Not much time is left.*

OK, but what about Robin? You said to trust no one except Shirley.

He isn't a problem.

He tried to kill me!

He's been manipulated by Psi energy. A lot of it. Give him a break.

I sighed. *That's easier said than done, but I'll try. So what's next?*

Your health is a serious problem. You need to realign your energy.

Source was right. I felt weak, and it was hard to breathe. I tried to take a deep breath and halfway into it, I broke into a coughing fit.

Robin snapped his head and looked at me with concern. I tried to avoid eye contact, still pissed, but when he gave me a sincere, apologetic look I gave him a weak smile, my version of a white flag.

"Ardor, I'm truly sorry," he said.

I took a small breath and winced. "That's nice to say, but you still gave me this awful virus."

He didn't answer.

I empathed him and was surprised to detect some relief. I guess any dialogue was good for his conscience. He felt bad and hated to see me in pain. I pinged him and he *really* had no memory of what had happened in the house with Alba. He could only remember Josip's death then waking up next to Alba's dead body.

Meanwhile, my heart was beating more irregularly than before I'd slept. I realized that earlier Shirley had been running my energy to heal me, but while she slept, I was on my own and the symptoms were worsening.

Source, I asked, *will this pain go away soon?*

Probably not.

I felt uneasy — something was really off.

Robin whispered, "Are you OK?"

"No. I feel awful," I said. "Like I'm going to die."

He looked down and twisted his hands. "That bad?"

Breathing felt like a task. "I'm sorta scared."

Shirley stirred, yawned and blinked, then adjusted her small body so that she was sitting on both feet, tucked beneath her on the chair. She smiled and started to say, "Good morning," but couldn't finish the words when she saw me.

My heart was now sputtering.

Shirley ran my energy, but it didn't seem to do much. In fact, I felt even more light-headed.

"Why do I feel so shitty?" I looked at Robin. "What did you give me?"

Shirley looked at him. "Yeah, what was it?"

He shrugged. "Standard-issue stuff."

"What was it?" Shirley repeated.

"I don't know. I just followed orders."

I empathed his sense of shame from being duped.

"Who ordered you?" I asked, but before he could answer, I entered into a coughing fit.

Robin bit his lip and glanced at Shirley, who came my bed, took my hand, and squeezed it, but it made me feel even more fatigue, dizziness, and pain. She turned to Robin. "I need to know *exactly* what you gave him!"

"I really don't know. They just said it was supposed to make him lose his Psi powers so I could take him into custody and back to the FRH."

She shook her head. "We need to contact the FRH to find out.." She was trying, but failing, to use an even voice. Her fear was palpable, even for non-empaths.

I strained my voice. "We *cannot* trust the FRH."

Robin said, "Ardor, I'm sorry, but we had to get you out of jail, and there wasn't much time. I thought I was helping. I should've been more careful."

My pain became unbearable, and I yelped.

Shirley jerked her head back with anguish.

"What's wrong?" I asked.

"It's not good," she said. "I've been scanning you since we got here, and you're not getting any better."

"Can I help?" I asked.

"Not unless you can name the virus."

What's wrong with me? I asked Source.

Bad medicine.

My heart seized and convulsed. I'd never experienced anything like this. It was like indigestion in my oxygen supply. The room wobbled then faded to black. I *knew* I was dying and succumbed to paranoia.

"Bad medicine," I exhaled through chattering teeth. I felt sweat all over my face, thick beads slithering down my temples and cheeks. I opened my eyes and Shirley's look of terror worsened my panic.

"What's happening?" Robin asked, approaching the bed.

"He's... he's going... he's..." she broke into sobs.

I took a breath to calm down, but my mind couldn't offer any optimistic thoughts to distract me. Shirley had never failed to heal any ailment, but now it seemed like she was up against something she couldn't defeat.

"Who gave you the virus?" I shouted at Robin.

"What do you mean?" he stammered.

In that moment, I *knew* that Alba had poisoned me, even though it made no sense, since I'd killed her. I sat up a little and said, "Robin, did Alba give you..." but I couldn't finish the sentence. I fell back onto the bed, barely alive, and that was owed to Shirley's powers. She was my life support.

"Alba is dead," Shirley said.

"No. She's not," I said.

"I don't know, but she's alive," I said

A yellow hue filled the room and Robin gasped.

Shirley and I looked at him. His face turned blue, then he passed out and slithered to the floor.

"Ardor," Alba's voice rang inside my head. "So good to be with you again."

37
Finally, An Explanation

Alba's voice was not a ping. It was in my mind. I could *hear* her. This was different than receiving thoughts. "Alba! Where are you?" I asked aloud.

"Here, there, and everywhere." She laughed. "I know you thought you could kill me, but did it not occur to you that Esmeralda could save me?"

Her yellow hue flooded my vision, but the virus' pain seemed to lessen.

"What did you give to me?" I asked aloud.

The pain fully receded, and my muscles relaxed as she said in my mind, "A virus to claim your autonomy."

"Huh?"

"Your mind. I had to get you to let go of your mind, so I could get inside."

Shirley asked, "Who are you talking to?"

"You can't hear her?" I asked.

She shook her head. "Who? You sound crazy."

"C'mon Ardor. She *obviously* can't hear me," Alba said. The yellow hue and my pain increased. "Unless you want me to also get inside her head?" She laughed and the pain receded.

"No! Leave her alone," I pleaded.

Shirley's eyes widened. "Are you hallucinating?"

"No," I said with gritted teeth. "It's Alba. She's alive, and somehow in my head."

Shirley bit her lip and concentrated harder on running my energy.

I said, "How are you doing this? And why?"

"I can do it all, now that I'm on the right team."

The pain returned, and I ground my teeth to prevent myself from passing out.

Shirley yelled, "You must get her to stop!"

"Why, Alba? Why?" I asked.

"Why ask why?" she teased. "Because..."

She trailed off, and I reasoned that while she'd turned to evil, there was nevertheless a part of her that still loved me. Otherwise, I'd already be dead.

I pinged Shirley, *There's still hope.*

"Because what?" I asked to buy time.

I pinged Shirley, *Run my energy while she talks. I think if I distract her enough and you do it slowly, I can regain control and I'll be OK. But be discreet!*

Shirley didn't nod or look at me.

I returned my attention to the disembodied voice of Alba. "So what? You're trying to kill your own brother because you feel sorry for yourself?"

"What a little brother move. Let me guess." She paused and the pain swelled. My chest felt like it would explode. "You're trying to distract me and buy time?"

It was subtle, but the pain lessened each time she spoke. She was on to me, but I wasn't wrong. While Alba communicated, she couldn't fully control my pain. I steeled myself for a crafty sibling battle of attrition.

"Look, Alba. I'm not a good psychic. You know that better than anyone. Why are you punishing me?"

She groaned. "Great. You're trying to appeal to my sense of pity?"

My pain hit a new note of agony.

"Because I have none," she said.

I sensed Shirley losing hope and shot her an encouraging look, but her focus was trained on my energy. I wasn't a healer, so her struggle was too foreign to imagine.

"Pity?" I said with sarcasm. "If you're trying to kill me and help Esmeralda, the last thing I'd expect from you is pity." My body heated and my hands shook. "I'm just wondering how you justify selling your soul to that monster," I shouted. "She murdered our father!"

"That monster?" Her tone matched my anger. She took a few breaths and refocused so she could talk and still hurt me. "Ardor, please! Esmeralda has her faults, but she's not a monster."

"She took my son from me!" I screamed. At the thought of him, I relaxed and felt even more capable of stringing her along while Shirley healed me. "So seriously, before you kill me, explain how the woman who ran off with my son is not a monster!"

"Life isn't so simple, Ardor. It's not always so black and white, or in this case, orange and green. Also, Esmeralda is a winner, and at some point, I grew tired of being with losers. She may have murdered our family, but maybe it's because they were on the wrong team. Did that ever occur to you? Sometimes you think you're with the good guys, but you're not. Have you ever thought about how different we are from everyone else? Normal humans wage wars over the stupidest things. They have no sense of the bigger picture. They worry about money, sex, and booze, while we're tasked with cleaning up their messes time and time again."

She sighed. "Think about it! We have to constantly run their stupid energy and plant seeds of peaceful thoughts, just to keep them from self-annihilation! From Genghis Kahn to Napoleon then Hitler, it's always been our job to stop these psychopaths, and I've had enough."

She took a deep breath, and her voice lost its edge. "When I met Esmeralda and heard her side, it clicked. It's time to get rid of the *real problem*: the morons and the sheep. They're a drain. It's high time we got rid of them and inherited the Earth." She sent a wave of pain into my body. "But we needed a leader, Ardor."

Another wave hit, and it took all my effort to remain conscious. "A leader?" I asked through clenched teeth.

"Yes, a leader. And we — Charles and I — we really thought it could've been you."

"You trusted *Charles Fay*?"

She sighed. "Ardor, I was on your side, our side, all the way until Croatia." She paused and the pain waned. "But when I was asked to spy on Esmeralda and I met Charles, that's when I saw how futile it all is. Helping others, caring about people who don't care about other people. I reviewed my life, and I saw how takers take and win, while givers give and lose."

I was astonished. I'd never thought about any of this. I'd only thought of my personal saga: Esmeralda, fame, my prophecy, and of course my son.

"And Ardor, seriously, if you saw the FRH, from the inside, the way I have, you'd see that it's a shit show. It's a bunch of selfish idiots playing a game of internal public relations with no consistency or plan. They're buffoons."

I couldn't believe this was Alba. How could she have changed so much?

"It was gradual," she said, as if reading my thoughts. "I didn't give up or really do anything until after I met her."

The way she said *her* got to me and both my anger and pain spiked.

Shirley glared at me.

I pinged her. She was thinking, *Don't give in. You need all your strength.*

I tried to curb my anger, but that only made it worse. My vision blurred.

"Tsk, tsk, bro," Alba teased. "It seems as if your plan didn't work after all." She giggled. "But before you die, I do feel like I owe you one more clarification."

The pain receded enough for me to listen.

"I want to explain what really happened." She sighed. "This didn't start with you, me, or Esmeralda. You see, the FRH has always been open to corruption. Charles Fay was not the first, although he may have been the last if things go our way."

"Our?" I sputtered amidst the searing pain.

"OK, mine. Me and what I would call 'the smart side.' Because you're too immature to understand. You and that stupid waif you love."

My anger flew off the charts at this jab at Shirley.

"At any rate, Esmeralda, and her lineage, they come from smart people who don't feel like we should be so charitable to the takers, the moronic, selfish mobs."

I pinged Shirley. *Keep quiet. It's working.*

Alba continued, "So Charles Fay, with his billions of dollars, he charmed and bribed his way into the FRH and helped us take them down from the inside."

With great restraint, I stayed quiet.

"You see, Charles knew what I've now accepted. That those of us who get it, we deserve a greater life. We shouldn't have to curb our abilities, be they Psi or simply intelligence. Nor should we have to waste them trying to stop all these lazy people from killing us off with their pollution and wars. There are two types of humans in this dimension, the powerful and the powerless."

Alba's tone and pacing reached a fever pitch and she forgot to monitor my pain and failed to notice.

"And our family?" she shrieked. "Our ancestors? They were duped! Thanks to some bullshit story about serving mankind and fulfilling some outlandish prophecy in a stupid book. But they were wrong, and I'm brave enough and smart enough to admit it!"

Shirley smiled at me. Alba had slipped for too long, and I felt much better. However, I wanted her to finish, so I feigned a wince to egg her on.

"I'm sorry things are going to end this way," she said. "When I met Esmeralda, believe me, Ardor, I did try to advocate for you. I pleaded your case. I mean, you are my brother, and he is your son. But ultimately, she was right, so I gave in. You could never join our team. You're just like Dad and Grandpa. You're weak. But your son? My nephew?"

I felt relief. I may have killed Charles and tried to kill Alba, but I felt justified. They were evil and truly out to kill me. Both were acts of self-defense. I smiled. I was on the right team, and I knew it.

Alba felt my sense of relief and sent a retaliatory yellow attack, but I was back in control, so I reflected it with my green energy.

"What the hell?" she screamed.

I smiled as she realized her failure. "Too late, sis!"

"How did you...?" Her voice faded. "You might have stopped me now, but it's too late, and you know it. Atticus, he's ours, and he's great!"

"Atticus?" I asked. His name resonated in my heart, and I sensed his existence and energy. Before this moment, I knew facts about him, like that he was seven years old, but with a name, he became real. Alba had made a big mistake.

She laughed. "Yeah, his name is Atticus, and he's adorable," she said. "But you'll never know him. Because we don't need you."

"So why kill me?"

She laughed. "How dumb do you think we are? You're still the second most powerful psychic in the Universe, and quite a threat, if left unchecked."

My heart swelled.

"Ardor, please don't get happy. Your son will overtake you, and Ez and I are quite capable ourselves. I didn't kill you *this* time, but we'll return and succeed."

"I don't think so," I said. I had Shirley and I knew my son's name. No one could stop me now.

"You idiot," she said. "You've always been so naïve. Oh well."

I smiled at Shirley. "Alba, you don't understand as much as you think you do."

"Whatever. Think what you will. It doesn't matter. We'll be back."

"I hope so," I said. "And please bring Esmeralda."

38
Atticus

After Alba's voice exited my mind, I snapped to attention and assessed my situation. Robin lay across from me, slumped against the wall on the floor. I turned my head to alert Shirley, but she was already striding across the room to tend to him.

She must've been exhausted from her furious energy work during my conversation with Alba, but it didn't show. She pressed her fingers on various spots on Robin's seemingly lifeless body, and a few minutes later her posture relaxed.

"He's going to recover," she said with a smile.

"You need to rest," I said. I scanned her. She was now weaker than me, and I was in horrendous shape. I knew that as much as I wanted to get the hell out here, We'd all be better off resting another night.

I asked Source, *Is there a rush to leave?*

You're doing great. You do have to get out of here, but for now, it's more important that you meet Atticus.

Atticus? I can meet him?

Not exactly. But you can locate his energy and interact with him that way.

I was about to ask for instructions when I realized that I'd already done this when Alba had mentioned his name. I had sensed him, and I could do it again.

I grinned and said, "Shirley, maybe you should rest. I'm about to meet my son."

She weakly returned my smile then slogged to her chair and shut her eyes.

Robin stirred, and despite my burning impatience to connect with Atticus, I knew I should help him get oriented.

He blinked several times and his face flushed. "What happened?"

It was unlike him to show fear, but he'd been out cold, and it had been a hell of a few days for the poor guy. He'd nearly died three times.

The tables had truly turned. I felt sorry for him, contrary to my earlier feelings. He really had been trying to help, all along, even in the early days in LA when he worked for Charles Fay.

I pinged him and felt the stress of being at the mercy of Psi experts. Charles Fay and the FRH had manipulated him many times. We had a lot in common.

"Robin," I said, trying to sound cautious. "I'm sorry to rush you, but while I want to get you up to speed, I also have to start my work, my real work." I smiled at the thought of what lay ahead before forcing myself to refocus my attention on Robin. "While you were knocked out, Shirley and I were able to fend off Alba, but it was temporary, and Esmeralda will probably be with her for the next attack."

He pushed himself into a sitting position with surprising speed, given how much of Alba's energy he'd consumed.

"What's next?" He stood. "What are we going to do? Can you give me more details?"

I liked his attitude, but not his lack of regard for just how close to death he'd been. "Robin, you have to rest." I pointed at the chair near him. "You're weak, and you need to regenerate your strength if you're going to help." I felt bad speaking to him like I was his superior, but my role had changed. I had to guide him and Shirley into battle with Alba and Esmeralda, and Source had said it was possible that we would fail.

"OK," he said as he sat. "Tell me what to do, and I'm on it." He smiled. "I'm on Team Ardor."

Shirley cracked her eyes open and gave him a thumbs up. "Team Ardor," she said with a grin, before shutting her eyes again.

I smiled. Their support renewed my courage. "OK," I said. "You two are going to rest, for the whole night, and I'm going to run some mental reconnaissance before I join you. Sound good?"

Robin seemed confident, but when I empathed Shirley, her heart was beating unevenly, and she had butterflies in her stomach. She was certain I could find Atticus, but wasn't sure I would like what I found.

I pinged for more insight. She was right to be concerned. I'd never considered that Atticus might not like me, or that he might have turned out to be someone I didn't like. Sure, he had my genes, and I'd never given up on finding him so I could be his father, but I'd never thought about how his upbringing with Esmeralda may have affected his personality and perspective.

Shirley could sense when I pinged her, but in this case it wasn't unethical, so she made it a point to shrug and smile. Then she thought, *You still have to try, Ardor. No matter what happens, he's your son, and relationships can change. I just want you to consider all possibilities, so you're not surprised.*

I nodded, closed my eyes, and focused on my son. I thought of his name, Atticus, like a mantra, until I was transported to a state where I could picture the world he saw while feeling his energy and emotions. It was intimate and softened my heart. I wanted more, but this was the extent to which I could connect.

What I couldn't do was read his mind, hear, or see the real world he was in. It was more like a dream where you hover near an energy and somehow know things. It was feeling and knowledge based, but it somehow made up for the struggle to get here. I finally could feel my son, and I loved him. He was perfect.

The first thing I knew was that he was content — he felt loved. He didn't fear the things most seven-year-olds did. Even better, he had a strong sense of trust in the Universe and in the patterns and cycles of life. Something I still had yet to learn.

And he was a happy, benevolent soul, wise and mature beyond his years. He was also equipped with a lot more compassion than I had, and he loved his mother, not in spite of her faults, but because he knew no one had loved her, so she needed his love.

He intuitively understood that even when she was in a terrible mood and letting her temper flare, it was because she felt rejected and didn't know how to react.

It was strange to feel his love for Esmeralda, since I'd never loved her, and had even convinced myself that I hated her.

I tried to linger on his love for Esmeralda for a better understanding, but I was at the mercy of his attention and agenda, so I next experienced his feelings for Alba, his aunt. These were more complicated. While he loved her, he had some animosity against her — no, it wasn't quite that. It wasn't negative. It was about trust. He didn't fully trust her.

My heart melted as I felt his feelings of agitation, confusion, and alarm at Alba's betrayal against me. He knew of me, of course, and he didn't think it was OK to betray family, so he was not at peace with her.

I wanted to talk to him, to explain the situation between the FRH, his aunt, his mother, and me. I wanted to somehow convince him to know the truth and love all of us, so he would never experience the frustration of a painful relationship, but I couldn't.

I next discovered that he'd connected with me a few times previously, but I'd never known it! He liked my energy, but he had to be secretive about connecting with me, since Esmeralda had spent enormous time and energy convincing him that I'd left her and never wanted to be a dad. As much as that pissed me off, I also now knew that she had loved him like a true mother. I had to admit she wasn't pure evil.

I felt my energy waning, so I doubled my efforts to stay connected just long enough to learn that they'd been living in a separate wing of Charles Fay's mansion in Alabama ever since Esmeralda had met Alba in Croatia and convinced her to switch sides.

They'd been there the whole time and the FRH had never known, but Alba had. Alba, with her ability to block anyone's pinging, she had been the key to Esmeralda's success.

Satisfaction coursed through me. I had the upper hand now that I knew where they were. I asked Source what to do next, and it told me to wait, but warned me that no matter what, as soon as I told any of this to Shirley and Robin, Alba and Esmeralda would know that I knew where they were.

That's when I felt a nudge from Atticus to leave. The whole time, I'd falsely assumed he couldn't sense me. He was a child, but he knew how to block Psi energy on a level that even Alba couldn't. He was indeed a truly powerful psychic-battery prodigy.

I returned to reality with a smile, but also some fear. My body was covered in a thin coat of sweat, and my breathing was uneven. I didn't know if Atticus was going to tell his mother about my visit, but it didn't matter what I thought, I couldn't do anything about it.

I looked around. Robin was asleep and Shirley was at my side, her hand on mine, smiling with shut eyes.

"Have you been running my energy?" I asked.

She nodded.

"What did you feel?" I asked.

She opened her eyes and smirked. "I don't know what you did or where you went." She took a breath. "But I can tell you that wherever it was, I want to go there." She let go of my hand and stretched like a cat in the sun. "OK. I have to sleep. I'll be useless if I don't."

I patted her hand. "Me too."

I was about to give in to sleep when Source said, *You did a good job, Ardor. Get some rest, then we'll discuss what's next.*

Why discuss the future? I laughed. *I'm psychic. We're going to Alabama.*

Yes. Too bad you didn't behave this way eight years ago.

Better late than never! Anyway, I feel ready. I'm excited.

Good, but the odds are stacked well against you. Don't lose your humility.

I felt my stomach turn and resented my anxiety.

Ardor, you have to learn to stay in the middle, between fear and hubris. Trust the process. Your genuine effort, regardless of results, will be a spiritual success.

Before I'd connected with Atticus, a statement like that would've angered me, but I now *felt* like a father and understood something about life, love, and how big it all was. I got what 'spiritual' meant, and I liked it. I was now breathing fine, with no butterflies. With these thoughts in my mind, I closed my eyes and fell asleep.

39
The Heart Part

I woke up the next day feeling like myself. I opened my eyes and was surprised to see Shirley and Robin fully awake, whispering in the corner. I felt an urge to ping their thoughts, but didn't. I finally understood the hypocrisy of my lifestyle. All this time I'd been at the mercy of Alba and Esmeralda's treacherous use of Psi, so how could I claim to be any better if I did the same?

I took an audible breath and said, "Hi guys."

They looked at me with warm smiles.

"Good. You're up," Robin said. "We were just discussing logistics."

"Logistics?" I asked.

Shirley nodded and Robin said, "Yeah, for how to get into the Fay mansion."

"How did you know?" I asked. I hadn't said *anything* about their hideout.

Shirley smirked. "Someone told us."

"Someone?"

"Atticus!" Robin beamed. "That kid has definitely got his dad's DNA."

Shirley cut in. "When I woke up this morning, I got a ping from your son. It was short and simple, but it said, "Come to Dothan. We're at the Fay mansion.""

I jumped up, but only got so far since I was still cuffed to the bed. "Did he say anything else?" I asked.

"Yeah. He said he'd try his best to stop Mom and Auntie from finding out."

"Really?" I felt so relieved. My son didn't hate me. Then I had a second thought, which disturbed me. I frowned as I thought, *What if this is a trap?*

Shirley shook her head. "I know what you're thinking." She pointed at Robin. "Trust me, it also crossed our minds that this could be a trick. But as a healer, I can assure you, his energy feels clean. Even cleaner than ours. He's a good, innocent kid."

I exhaled with relief, but then realized that this conversation was liable to be picked up by Esmeralda or Alba, so now they probably did know we were coming. It was *very* likely. I looked away and said, "I don't think this is going to work."

"Thoughts aren't a part of our plan," Shirley said.

Robin's face contorted and he looked mad. "Ardor, I've had enough of this."

"Enough of what?" I asked with a sulky tone.

He stood. "I've had enough of the FRH and their spy games. We're always trying to react to how we think the enemy will act, and it's gotten us nowhere." His face became neutral, and I even thought I detected a smile threatening the edges of his mouth. "Believe it or not, it's been seven years that I've been on 'Ardor Assignment', so trust me when I tell you that we should have listened to you a long time ago. You and Josip."

I smiled. "Well, as nice as that is to hear, Josip is dead and I'm in a hospital bed."

He frowned. "And that's exactly what I'm trying to get at. It's time we left the FRH, for 'Team Ardor." He smiled. "I'm on 'Team Ardor', because I think that's the only team that will succeed." His jaw quivered.

Was he on the verge of tears?

Shirley took his hand, and ran his energy.

He continued, "I never knew my father. My mother told me he was a scumbag. But then, when I was forty-two, a random man contacted me. Turns out he was my half-brother. My dad was dying, and he'd apparently been searching for me for many years. He'd taken fake vacations with his new family, every year, to the town he'd last seen me in. My mother was already buried at that point, which is a good thing." He paused and wiped his eyes with the back of his big hairy hand. "I'm glad I never had to face her after finding out that she lied and that…" he paused and looked at the floor.

Shirley stood and moved behind him to rub his temples. Whatever she did, it worked. He still had tears in his eyes, but he didn't cry.

He said, "So trust me when I tell you that if I have to die today, it'll be worth it."

"Die?" I asked.

He narrowed his eyes. "We're finding your son, Ardor. We're finding Atticus, and he's going to know *his* dad *before* he's on his deathbed. I don't have time for the FRH's lies anymore and I don't care about The Great Book. I don't care about orange and green. I believe your heart is what matters. I believe in your goodness. We're ending this. Today."

"This?" Shirley asked, letting go of his temples.

"This civil war. We're ending it. Now."

I empathed bravery, compassion, and paternal love. It was sophisticated, endearing, and kind.

I pointed at my handcuffs. "Can you help me?"

He came over and took all the cuffs off.

I leaped out of bed, but I had to catch the railing as my feet hit the ground to stop myself from falling. It had been a full day since I'd walked, and my legs weren't ready for such a challenge.

***

When I was young, theme parks sold special tickets that let you skip to the front of the lines while regular customers had to wait. Robin's fake FBI badge was the equivalent of that feature, but for everything.

I couldn't believe how many social, governmental, and logistical barriers magically disappeared with an official-looking FBI badge and digital identity. I didn't bother to ask Robin how the FRH had procured it. Instead, I appreciated how it enabled us to seamlessly leave the hospital and skip security at the airport to get to a private jet that flew us directly to the Dothan airport.

The flight was three hours, but we spent the first two in silence. No one was scared, but we all knew that Alba and Esmeralda were a serious threat with no qualms about using lethal force, so I think we were using the time to contemplate our lives.

With an hour to go, Robin cleared his throat and stood. "All right, team," he said without a smile. "It's time to get serious."

I elbowed Shirley, who was staring out the window with a wistful expression. "You all right?" I asked.

She nodded, but I could tell she was lying. She was sad. I wanted to help her, but I couldn't. What could I say or do, anyway? Her sadness was earned. Anything could happen. It was totally possible that the three of us were going to die soon.

"We can succeed," I said with great optimism.

"The Great Book, Ardor. It doesn't say that. I mean, I'm just…" She trailed off.

I felt a jolt of positive energy, but it wasn't from an external source. It was from my heart. It was telling me that none of us had anything to fear and we needed to embrace this experience, and most of all, the experience of trusting our intuition. I relaxed and thought, on my end, I should also trust Atticus. I decided that I would ping him and tell him all about The Great Book and its prophecy, even if it was scary.

I was about to do that when I reflected on how often in my life I'd done something I thought for sure was the right thing to do, only to regret it later. From Croatia to getting in Charles' limo, I'd made a lot of arrogant mistakes in my life.

I pictured Josip and knew what to do.

I asked Source, *Should I tell Atticus about our prophecy?*

There's no need to. He knows.

Then what should I do?

Nothing.

Nothing? Can I go home then?

No. I mean you've done what matters most.

I got on a plane to Dothan?

No, I mean you've already redeemed many of your previous mistakes by finally listening to spirit, or your heart, or whatever you want to call it.

You mean you, Source?

It's all one and the same. Source, your heart, your soul. It's one whole, with no parts. Love is not a product, it's the source of the product. Love creates, hate destroys.

I looked at Shirley and understood. I was so satisfied with loving her and having her love me. There was immense comfort in knowing that this sort of love could exist. Then I recalled my one and only foray into Atticus' mind and how I felt a similar love. This must have been the meaning of life. Loving without fear, boundaries, but also expectations. Love was a kind leader, and I was ready to obey.

Robin interrupted my epiphany. "OK, team," he said. "Here's the deal, I know the Fay compound well, so I know a good way to approach it without—"

"I have a better plan," I said. I unfastened my seat belt and stood. I wasn't normally so passionate, but I felt a burst of energy that was too much to contain.

Shirley asked, "What's your idea?"

"I'm going to tell Atticus we're coming so he can help us," I announced.

Robin looked momentarily confused, but then nodded. "That resonates with me."

Shirley nodded and I empathed her love.

I was shocked. My heartfelt plan was anything but logical, yet it had won approval from my two partners, both of whom were far more logical than me.

I sat down and closed my eyes and thought of Atticus, and just like that, I was in his heart space again. As I felt his energy, I could tell he felt mine. This connection was so natural it surprised me. I was shocked by a new *feeling*. Everything was already OK.

I thought of those early childhood moments with Granny, when I was answering questions, eating popcorn, and playing with toys. That was the last time I'd felt this sense of peace. Like I was allowed to just be myself and not worry. I took this serenity and massaged it into my message for my son.

Hello son. This is your father. I want to let you know that I'm sorry for missing out on so much of your life, but I have finally made a decision to —

The heartfelt connection sputtered. It was like our psychic call was on the verge of dropping, and I lost my sense of harmony. My mind second-guessed my plan and told me I was an idiot.

I was about to give in to my mental spin when my heart told me to stop being logical and the connection with my son would resume. I took two breaths, focusing on the length of the exhales, a trick Josip had taught me, and just like that, I reconnected with Atticus.

Atticus. I love you. You know this, but you've never seen it or felt it in person. I want to come and meet you, but I'm worried that your Aunt Alba or your Mom might not like that. What do you think?

He didn't answer, but my heart didn't lose its magical connection. I didn't understand why he wasn't answering me, but I didn't feel like saying anything else, so I shut up while keeping our connection without adding thoughts or words.

Moments that felt like eons elapsed, precious father-son moments that I'd never felt, but had always hoped for. Finally, just as I was about to ask Source what else to do, I *felt* Atticus agree with my plan, and the connection abruptly ended.

He nodded, right? I'm not making this up? I asked Source with incredulity.

Yes, Ardor. This is what it feels like to fulfill your life purpose.

I smirked. My first compliment from Source!

"What happened?" Shirley asked.

I opened my eyes. Much more time had elapsed than I thought. The plane was already descending, and the G-forces felt dangerous.

"You have to buckle up!" Shirley said.

I yawned and grabbed my seatbelt.

Robin was staring at me with satisfaction. "Did you just connect with Atticus?"

I nodded as I buckled. "I did, and it was better than I thought."

He smiled. "Well, I guess we don't need my plan then." He took out his cell phone and called someone. "Cancel the chopper."

"The chopper?" I asked with a grin. "Do I look like a Navy SEAL?"

His eyes glimmered. "There are two ways to get what you want in life. One is what people hire me for," he pointed at his holstered gun. "Force." He took a deep breath. "The second way is the wiser one." He put his hands in prayer formation. "Spirit."

The plane touched down with a thud and some skids and skips, before slowing to a safe speed, and Shirley sighed with relief. She hated flying.

I stood, and faced my companions. "All right team. Let's do this. Atticus is waiting for us, and I can't wait to finally give that boy a hug!"

40
Solomon Says

We landed at the small airport in Dothan and deplaned without delay. There was little security there, but just in case, Robin had Shirley and I wear cuffs until we passed their onboarding point. I was surprised no one recognized me.

Once we were in the main terminal, Robin got in line for a rental car, and when he got to the front, he didn't use his FBI credentials. After he got the keys, he turned around and led us toward the rental car lot at which point I whispered, "Why end the façade?"

He smirked and checked his watch. "Because I retired as of ten minutes ago."

"Retired?" I asked.

"From the FRH. I should've quit a long time ago."

Shirley patted his shoulder. "Good call."

I gave them both a perplexed look. "I don't follow."

"I'm no psychic," Shirley grinned. "But I'm sure that what happens next will not be good for the FRH and all the other psychic networks."

"What do you mean?" I asked.

She took my hand and gently squeezed. "Growing up, we were told about many prophecies from The Great Book—"

"Good God! Not The Great Book again!"

She rolled her eyes. "Ardor, just because you hate your part in this prophecy doesn't mean that it's false. If Esmeralda wins, it means we died, and if we defeat her, then we've still undermined our organizations' direct orders. Either way, I think we're officially retired."

I stopped walking, lost in mostly negative thoughts.

Robin stopped and cleared his throat. "Ardor, Shirley's right. Like it or not, this is it. We're about to die, or vanquish a few villains, or maybe both. We're not returning to a covert existence in either case."

I pursed my lips and nodded.

There was a long pause as we stood in the terminal.

Shirley squeezed my hand and ran some energy, but I couldn't stop worrying. After seven years of searching for my son, I'd finally found him, but now I had to fulfill my destiny in a battle with his mom and my own sister.

Robin looked at his watch and said, "We need to get going," then hurried towards the exit.

I remained, contemplating life, death, and the prophecy, until Shirley dragged me along.

We got in the car and Robin kept quiet in the driver's seat while Shirley and I sat in the back so she could run my energy to keep me in full health.

I thought about my relationship with Alba. She had her reasons for joining Esmeralda and helping her keep

354

Atticus from me, and she'd tried to kill me in the hospital, but I nevertheless still didn't want her, or anyone else to die, not even Esmeralda. I'd killed Charles in self-defense, but I was no killer, and we weren't headed to Dothan for self-defense. This was an attack. I was in a prophecy bind, and wanted a way out.

Shirley drew me out of my reverie, asking, "Did you guys ever hear of the Judgment of Solomon?"

"What's that...?" I asked.

"It's a biblical story," Robin said.

"Oh. I'm not religious." I fought an urge to roll my eyes, in case Robin was.

"I'm not either," he said, "but I was raised with the Bible, and it has some good moral lessons."

"And this is one of them," Shirley interjected.

"OK. So what is it?" I asked.

"Maybe Robin should tell it. I only know the basic outline," Shirley replied.

He shrugged. "Basically, there was this king in Israel named Solomon, and one day two women approached him, both claiming to be the mother of a baby boy, and they asked him to decide who was lying."

I held up a hand. "Wait. That doesn't make sense. Didn't they know who was the mother? I mean, babies don't just appear."

Shirley laughed. "They each were *saying* they were the real mom. Of course they knew."

I shook my head and hoped I wasn't blushing.

Robin continued, "It's OK, Ardor, I know it's sort of far-fetched. Anyway, King Solomon was smart, so he told them, 'I'll just cut the child in half, and you can each take a half.'

"What?" My face scrunched. "That's psycho! Even Esmeralda wouldn't do that!"

Shirley squeezed my hand. "Listen. You'll get it."

Robin grinned and continued, "So anyway, long story short, one of the women screams, 'No! Don't kill the boy! She can have him, just don't hurt the child!' and Solomon smiles, because she's obviously the mother, so—" He stopped mid-sentence and grimaced as he used both hands to press his temples.

I looked in the rear-view mirror and saw him shut his eyes and I empathed terror and unbearable pain.

"Robin?" Shirley and I shouted in unison as the car veered off the road.

We each tried to reach into the front to grab the wheel, but it was too late. The car swerved and tumbled off the road. The sensation of flipping and rolling was surreal and chaotic as I tried to brace my body so I wouldn't smack into the interior panels, but it was of no use. The doors caved in and when the car finally stopped rolling, I was so weak and disoriented that I couldn't contact Source.

I opened my eyes and one of them was covered with a sticky film. It was blood, but it wasn't mine. With my good eye, I was able to see Robin's body a few feet in front of mine. His head was crushed, and I could see parts of his brain. He was obviously dead.

The sight of his dead body induced a hopelessness inside me that I had to fight hard against. I shook it off enough to call out for Shirley, but it returned even worse when I heard nothing in reply. I was about to try to crawl to search for her when I was enveloped in a painful orange hue.

"Esmeralda?" I called.

My heart throbbed in my temples. My hearing was nearly gone, and what little I had was distorted.

I shut my eyes and concentrated as hard as I could on restoring my Psi powers, but they didn't return.

I spiraled into a state of deep meditation. I was conscious of consciousness, but not really in my body or even aware of my body's location.

Esmeralda's voice spoke in my mind, saying, *Ardor, why bother?*

I'd rather die than —

Alba replied, *We are here to help you with that, but it didn't have to be this way.*

Alba's yellow energy glommed onto Esmeralda's orange and my breath weakened as I felt a drain in my life force.

Esmeralda said, *I don't understand why you couldn't play nice. Why couldn't you have just let fate do its thing and gone on with your life? When I left you in LA, I didn't care if I saw you again, but you had to fly to Croatia and screw everything up. And now I had*

357

to kill poor Robin just to stop you from coming and hurting me and my son!

I was in too much pain to answer, but I had a lot I wanted to say.

Alba said, *And at one point, you almost did it. You gave up for a bit, right after you met that dumb reporter and fell in love. You could've stopped there and had a new family and done it differently, but —*

But you couldn't give up! Esmeralda shrieked.

I felt a new wave of pain, rivaled only by the nasty machine in Charles' mansion and I cringed. This also felt strong enough to kill me. With my consciousness fading, I realized that when Alba had mentioned Shirley and our love, I'd felt a brief respite from their energy. There was some sort of powerful energy in that love, and it was at my disposal. I needed to use it now.

I thought of Shirley and entered into a space of love where I was disconnected from my body, but in that space, Shirley was somehow physically with me. I felt her lovely blue energy of her soothing and healing love.

But it wasn't enough. I was battling two powerful Psi users who had more strength and preparedness than me. I needed even more energy to defeat them and prevent my death. I knew what to do. I stayed connected with Shirley, but also pinged Atticus: *I love you.*

I felt a new energy, with a silver hue. The mix of our energies, blue, green, silver, orange and yellow, was unique and psychedelic. But the silver energy was dominant in a way that no other could match. It was somehow purer. I could sense it.

Time ceased as the five of us were entwined in our mutual energies.

A courageous little voice said, *Please, everyone, this has to stop.*

Atticus! Esmeralda exclaimed.

Get out of here! Alba scolded.

No! Atticus replied.

Silver energy scoured the dimension we inhabited, and I felt our other energies diminish further. This small act was enough to teach us all a lesson: We had powers, but we were not even close to the level that little boy had, and he wanted us to know this.

I couldn't see anything except colors and energy, but as the silver took hold, I felt so much more.

Atticus was sending us emotions. This was a new, unchartered territory for me, and I could sense that Esmeralda and Alba were equally caught up in it.

I felt tears in my soul that came from my deep understanding of what had gone wrong and what had gone right — not just in my life, but with humanity. I understood the beauty of existence. How I could judge things from my limited perspective? I sensed that since all life came from the same source of energy, which was pure love, it wasn't fair to judge. I *knew* this.

It was up to each human to use that energy to create, and what they created could be good or bad. That was the point of free will, to experiment and eventually learn that selfish manifestations were limited and limiting. True peace came from living in love and learning to tolerate others as they learned that same lesson. The key was to accept it all, the good and bad, with no fear or envy. But this was a lesson we had to learn on our own.

I felt a peace take hold of me, but it was interrupted by Esmeralda.

This cannot be true!

Despite her rage, she didn't try to stop Atticus and I wanted to know if this was from fear of his power, or from learning the same lesson I just had.

Atticus sent more love, and Esmeralda's temper waned as she joined me in silent awe.

However, Alba's resentment was strong. I could feel her trying to thwart Atticus' energy with her own.

What is it you are trying to stop? Atticus asked her.

You're a child, she replied. *You don't know what's best for our world.*

But I'm not doing anything bad, Auntie. I'm simply holding love for all of you.

You don't know what you're doing. You don't understand what you are…

I felt Alba's energy wane and pinged her. She was embarrassed to be the only one still fighting. She reflected on how she'd always been the kinder and more patient member of our family, and she stopped fighting.

My mind relaxed as I felt a sense of balance return to the Universe from our psychic ceasefire.

But Atticus didn't want us to stop here. This was no temporary treaty. Now that he'd shown us love, he emoted that he now wanted to show us humanity.

He delivered powerful psychic explosions of humility that showed us how to find a deeper awareness of the significance of all earthly pursuits. We understood how violence begat violence and how much our individual biases affected our perspective.

I was able to see my life with an enlightened perspective and see how I'd told myself the wrong story, over and over again as I grew up. Instead of finding the blessing in every moment of my life, I'd chosen to blame myself and others over and over again, resulting in a cycle of self-pity and blame, instead of being grateful to all of us for helping me experience the natural progression of life, with love.

I revisited the trauma I'd endured: my alcoholic parents, the stress of living with Esmeralda and her tricks, the shock of her disappearance and my ensuing distress from being alienated from Atticus. I'd spent so much of my life in a dizzying, mental spin of "What can I do about this?" and "How to stop or prevent that?" and "Why did this happen to me?" When all along, the only question to ask was, "How can I make this world better for everyone?" This truth took to me like a well-fitted garment. It was refreshing and life-affirming.

I sighed, deeply, and felt Atticus smile.

You get it now? he asked.

I do. I truly do.

Our collective mental space collapsed, and I was sucked back into my body. Tears of joy welled in my tightly shut eyes. I kept them closed, for just a moment, soaking in the bliss of all Atticus had shown me.

I opened them. I was lying against the corner of the crushed car, and I heard sirens and voices. I tried to sit up, but my body sent an overbearing signal of pain that told me to stay still, crumpled in a pile.

"Shirley?" I shouted.

A masculine voice announced, "I hear something over here."

I heard the crunch of gravel.

An excited voice shouted, "I found another one. And he's alive!"

I heard several people trample towards me and I tried to sit again, but the pain was too much, so I closed my eyes and drifted into a semi-conscious state. "Shirley?" I grunted through clenched teeth.

A hand touched my shoulder and a deep voice said, "Try to relax. We found her. She's all right."

I smiled and tried to give a thumbs up, but I couldn't muster the strength. I released my focus and slipped into a trance that reminded me of the space the five of us had just inhabited, only I was alone.

Am I going to die? I asked Source.

Source didn't answer. Instead, I heard Atticus say, *You'll be all right, Dad.*

Atticus? I felt a rush of love.

Yes, It's me. I'm always here, Dad. In this space. We can share it.

We can?

Yes.

This is wonderful. So am I dead?

No. You're alive, but this is a different space that we can go to anytime.

What about in real life? Where can we meet there?

I'm sorry, Dad, but I can't do that. I can't be there. Not yet. Please understand.

I can't take that. I want to know you on Earth.

I have to do it this way. It's best for everyone. For the Universe. This creates peace. Mom can't handle life alone, but you can. She needs me. She needs a balance.

You talk like... are you really seven?

I'm not like this in person, yet, but here, I'm in tune with cosmic consciousness.

So where are we? Is this heaven?

No. This is pure consciousness. Earth is the weird place.

So what now?

Go back.

Back?

Back to the world. Guide the lost people. Help them. Let them know it's OK, all of it. It's all OK. Everything is OK. Everything has always been OK. Let them feel free.

I felt Atticus leave and with that came terror. *Please! Please don't go. Not yet. Please! I never even got to see you, to hold you, to hug you, to be with you. Can't we just… can't we be together?*

Atticus didn't leave. He sent me another packet of Psi energy that helped me relive the emotions I'd felt earlier. I wished everyone in the world could experience this same sense of awe and joy, as I was again able to see how the only way to live was by fearlessly embracing love. And I *knew* this was the only lesson, the only takeaway for anyone, but it felt so fleeting, and I still wanted to see my son in person, so badly.

It's OK, Dad. We can meet, 'here,' anytime we need each other, and when Mom and Auntie are ready, I'll come. I'll really meet you. Me, your real son, the one you want to know. Can you trust me?

I want to.

Then do it. Trust me and trust the Universe. Trust love. Now do you understand?

I wanted to pretend I didn't, to buy more time, but I knew better now. *I get it.*

I knew you would. That's why you're my hero.

I'm your hero? My heart swelled.

Of course.

But you're the one who stopped the war and saved us all! You're the hero.

No, you are, because you did the hardest thing.

I did? What did I do?

Did you ever hear of the Judgment of Solomon?

I chuckled, but before I could reply I was jolted back to consciousness. Shirley stood over me. I was in a hospital, without cuffs. I grinned. "I'm OK, honey."

She looked puzzled.

"What's wrong?" I asked.

"You were just talking in your sleep," she said.

"Oh yeah?" I sat up. "What did I say?"

"It was weird. You laughed then said, "I am the Judgment of Solomon."

I was about to laugh, but I noticed her hands were wrapped in bloodstained bandages and her arms were covered in bruises. And to think that her injuries were from trying to protect me. I felt tears well in my eyes.

Her smile faded. "What's wrong?" she asked.

I took a deep breath then said, "I just realized something serious."

She drew her head back. "What is it?"

I pointed at her left hand and smiled. "I have to put a ring on that finger."

She leaned in to hug me, and whispered in my ear, "I'd love that Ardor. Please do."

THE END

Longman Dictionaries

Express yourself with confidence!

Longman has led the way in ELT dictionaries since 1935. We constantly talk to students and teachers around the world to find out what they need from a learner's dictionary.

Why choose a Longman dictionary?

Easy to understand

Longman invented the Defining Vocabulary – 2000 of the most common words which are used to write the definitions in our dictionaries. So Longman definitions are always clear and easy to understand.

Real, natural English

All Longman dictionaries contain natural examples taken from real-life that help explain the meaning of a word and show you how to use it in context.

Avoid common mistakes

Longman dictionaries are written specially for learners, and we make sure that you get all the help you need to avoid common mistakes. We analyse typical learners' mistakes and include notes on how to avoid them.

Innovative CD-ROMs

Longman are leaders in dictionary CD-ROM innovation. Did you know that a dictionary CD-ROM includes features to help improve your pronunciation, help you practice for exams and improve your writing skills?

For details of all Longman dictionaries, and to choose the one that's right for you, visit our website:

www.longman.com/dictionaries

PENGUIN READERS *recommends*

Three Adventures of Sherlock Holmes
Sir Arthur Conan Doyle

Sherlock Holmes is a great detective. There are few cases that he cannot solve. In these three stories we meet a young woman who is very frightened of a 'speckled band', a family who think that five orange pips are a sign of death, and a banker who believes that his son is a thief. But are things really as they seem?

The Client
John Grisham

Mark Sway is eleven and he knows a terrible secret. He knows where a body is hidden. Some secrets are so dangerous that it's better not to tell. But it's just as dangerous if you don't. So Mark needs help fast . . . because there isn't much time.

1984
George Orwell

Winston Smith lives in a society where the government controls people's lives every second of the day. Alone in his small, one-room apartment, Winston dreams of a better life. Is freedom from this life of suffering possible? There must be something that the Party cannot control – something like love, perhaps?

There are hundreds of Penguin Readers to choose from – world classics, film adaptations, modern-day crime and adventure, short stories, biographies, American classics, non-fiction, plays ...

For a complete list of all Penguin Readers titles, please contact your local Pearson Longman office or visit our website.

www.penguinreaders.com

PENGUIN READERS *recommends*

Teacher Man
Frank McCourt

When Frank McCourt becomes a teacher in New York, he finds
himself standing in front of bored, confused, angry students. Will
he fail as a teacher? Or can he use his miserable Irish childhood
to help his students? This is the true story of one man's surprising,
upsetting, but sometimes very funny experiences in the classroom.

King Solomon's Mines
Sir H. Rider Haggard

Sir Henry Curtis, Captain John Good and Allan Quatermain are
travelling to the mysterious, unmapped heart of Africa. Sir Henry
wants to find his missing brother. Quatermain wants to find King
Solomon's secret treasure. Is Sir Henry's brother still alive? Will
they find King Solomon's treasure? Does the treasure even
exist . . .?

The Time Machine
H. G. Wells

The Time Traveller has built a time machine and has gone into the
future to the year 802,701. He expects to find a better world with
highly intelligent people and great inventions. Instead, he finds
that people have become weak, child-like creatures. They dance
and sing and wear flowers. They seem happy, but why are they so
frightened of the dark? And who or what has taken his time machine?
Will the Time Traveller ever be able to return to the present?

There are hundreds of Penguin Readers to choose from – world classics,
film adaptations, modern-day crime and adventure, short stories,
biographies, American classics, non-fiction, plays ...

For a complete list of all Penguin Readers titles, please contact your local
Pearson Longman office or visit our website.

www.penguinreaders.com

siege (n) a situation when an army surrounds a place and stops food and other things from getting to it

slave (n) someone who is owned by another person

snake (n) a long, thin animal with no legs, which often has a poisonous bite

spear (n) a long stick with a pointed end, which soldiers used in fighting

temple (n) a building where people of some religions go to communicate with their god or gods

tomb (n) the place where a dead body is put

tribe (n) a group of people who have the same language and customs, and live together in the same area

WORD LIST

achieve (v) to succeed in getting the result you want

adopt (v) to make someone else's child legally your daughter or son

ally (n) a country or person that helps another one, especially in war

archer (n) someone who shoots arrows

armour (n) metal or leather clothes worn in the past for fighting

arrow (n) a thin, straight stick with a point at one end, which you can shoot

battle (n) a fight between two armies in one place

chariot (n) a vehicle with two wheels for fighting or races, pulled by a horse

conquer (v) to win control of a country or defeat an enemy by fighting a war

create (v) to make something new exist or happen

defeat (n/v) the losing of a game or fight. If you **defeat** someone, you win.

democracy (n) the form of politics in which ordinary people can vote

elephant (n) a very large grey animal with big ears and a long nose

empire (n) a group of countries that is controlled by one ruler or government

extraordinary (adj) unusually good or special

gymnasium (n) a special place with equipment for doing physical exercise

horn (n) one of two hard, pointed parts growing on the heads of some animals

immortal (adj) living or continuing forever

legend (n) an old story about the actions and adventures of brave people

noble (adj) belonging to the group of people of the highest social position

philosophy (n) the study of ideas about existence, thought and behaviour

retreat (n/v) a move back, away from the fighting, by an army

shield (n) a thing used in the past by soldiers to protect themselves in a battle

Writing

42 Choose an event from Alexander's life. Write a newspaper report about the event.

43 You are one of Alexander's soldiers. Write a letter to your family after Alexander's death. Tell them why you liked or disliked your leader.

44 You are a historian. Write the introduction of a book about one of Alexander's friends or relatives.

45 You are a filmmaker. Describe the first scene of your film about Alexander the Great.

46 You work for the 'Time Travel Talk Show'. Choose a person from this book to be a guest on the show. Write a list of ten questions to ask him/her.

47 You are one of Alexander's friends. Choose an important day in your life and write about it in your diary.

48 You are a Persian. Write a letter to a friend who lives abroad. Tell him/her about Alexander's defeat of Darius and how life in Persia is now, after the defeat.

49 You are teaching army officers how to win battles. What can they learn from Alexander? Write a list.

50 Write Alexander's speech for his wedding to the two Persian princesses and the weddings of ninety of his officers.

51 You are Roxane after Alexander's death. Write a letter to Olympias, telling her about the birth of your son. Describe your relationship with Alexander and your hopes and fears for the future.

Answers for the Activities in this book are available from the Penguin Readers website. A free Activity Worksheet is also available from the website. Activity Worksheets are part of the Penguin Teacher Support Programme, which also includes Progress Tests and Graded Reader Guidelines. For more information, please visit: www.penguinreaders.com.